NICK SMITH was born in Bristol 
15 he won an award at the A
Festival and has since written for
anthologies and newspapers, inc
Scotsman. He has a scriptwrit
from Bournemouth University and ran the
Scottish Film School for five years. He has
produced several award winning films and
television programmes, and developed *Milk
Treading* as a play in the Edinburgh
International Fringe Festival. His previous book, *Scriptwriting:
The Secrets Unleashed*, was published in the USA, where he will
shortly be living and working.

Milk Treading

NICK SMITH

Luath Press Limited

EDINBURGH

www.luath.co.uk

First published 2002
Reprinted 2002
This edition 2003

The paper used in this book is recyclable. It is made from low
chlorine pulps produced in a low energy, low emission manner
from renewable forests.

Printed and bound by
Bookmarque Ltd., Croydon

Typeset in 10.5 point Sabon and Courier by
S. Fairgrieve, Edinburgh, 0131 658 1763

Cover and author photograph by Murdo MacLeod

Thanks to Ros and Sam

I

WHERE THE HELL AM I?

Julius Kyle was cold, even though he was buried beneath two shovelfuls of sand and his fur coat.

Another frosty morning. Julius half-opened an eye to explore the dawn. A trail of ice clinging to the railings, warning him to stay in the sand. He hadn't woken up this early since his schooldays. Years of sloth, lack of discipline and an air of contempt for the world had got him used to a ten a.m. wake-up call. Later in the day, around mid-afternoon if it was warm enough, he would take a nap to sleep off his lunch. Today was the real wake-up call. He had to be at work on time.

He'd been pulled into the office for a word with the editor, Morris. Tardiness would not do. There were deadlines to meet, celebrities impatient to be interviewed, readers hungry for daily scoops. Julius had been indignant, affronted, dismissive – but he'd taken Morris' words to heart. It was time for a few resolutions to be made.

First resolution: Get to work on time. Julius got up, dusted himself down. Damp clumps of grit fell down his back. This wasn't right. The smell, the bright light, the way that the world around him was moving but he was standing still.

What was I drinking last night?

He kicked sand towards the railings, watching it ghost

away in the morning breeze. He was standing on a mound of the stuff, and starting to feel seasick. His nose was moist with tears and snot. That was supposed to be a sign of ill health, right? A wet nose means you're coming down with something nasty. It had always looked too big for his face, out of proportion. A blot on his copybook features.

'Everybody's insecure,' he told himself.

It took him a while to get his bearings. Mast, funnel, cabin, bow, squared-off stern. He was on a sand barge littered with cat droppings, drifting down-river. If he squinted hard enough he could see the ghettos on the South bank. Now he knew why he felt so cold – he had to get home, get ready for work. He couldn't see a crewmember or a captain. Perhaps he'd thrown them all overboard in a drunken rage the night before. Hardly likely, as he was a slight figure with the width of a standard lamp. The only sensation that clung tight to his fuddled brain was a headache that pumped in time to the barge sluice.

Julius cocked his ears as he explored the cabin. No pilot, few controls. A barge programmed to carry its cargo along the river in an untiring circuit. The rudder controls looked easy enough to operate. He overrode the autopilot, fumbling in his haste. Once he had steered the barge towards the right bank he walked to the stern, leaning on a railing to support himself. The barge was accelerating as it headed for the nearest jetty, water ribboning past the bow, and Julius had no intention of falling overboard.

Accelerating?

The owners of the barge wouldn't be happy. Not that they'd be able to vent their rage at him if he stayed on the boat, which was on a collision course with a small moored tanker.

I'm going to be late for work.

There was no time to get to the rudder controls so he leaped for the jetty, his tail catching on the railing as he rolled through the air. The barge struck the tanker with a dull thud, sinking with alarming speed.

Julius picked himself up and headed for home. He didn't stop to count his bruises; he was still in a daze from the night before. And he couldn't afford to lose his job. Visions slipped into his head as he left the riverbank. A sensation of being lifted, carried; someone had dropped him, he'd hit his head. Around him buildings stretched in lean pillars, giving him something to lean against when he felt woozy. He suspected that someone had slung him onto the barge, but he had no idea who'd done it.

It didn't take him long to reach his house where he gave himself a quick wash. His claws scarped on the linoleum as he rushed to the bathroom, brushed his teeth, smoothed down his matted hair. Sleep clung to the lids of his moon-crescent eyes. He didn't consider himself a heavy drinker, but when he got going with his work mate Mick he would often end up stumbling home. Last night was a speedline blur. He needed some milk.

Julius had insisted that his kitchen be fitted with the biggest fridge in the showroom. It took up half the room. Popping open the paw-marked appliance, he scanned the row of milk bottles on the top shelf.

A mixture of fresh, dodgy, and extremely gone off. Resolution two: clear out the fridge tonight.

White wind rattled at the back window shutters. Julius' ears twitched, stretched back a little. Someone'd been in the spare room again, snooping around. Julius popped out the back to check; he could see the telltale signs. A patch of trampled carpet, overturned trash, a shutter left half-open. The trespasser hadn't bothered to latch it properly on his way out. A burglar wouldn't have been so careless – this was more likely to be a nosy neighbour, or a crazy fan.

Nobody likes to have their privacy invaded; it's something you never get used to. But journalists tend to be cynical about most things, and a hack like Julius had done a little invading himself in his time.

The police wouldn't be interested. They were sick of hearing from him. Still, the intrusion came as a surprise. He'd thought all that was over. He locked the shutters, sniffed the air, took one last look round. Nothing. Paranoia followed him back to the kitchen where he chewed on a dry kipper.

He'd tried to consider aesthetics when purchasing the house, choosing a structure and decor that would impress any guest that turned up. Back when he'd had friends. He still kept the place clean; Camilla bought the odd ornament or piece of furniture to fill empty corners. The atrium never lost its grandeur, with a small pool in the centre for visitors to slake their thirst. But the house was so damned draughty. No matter how high Julius turned the heating, or how many blankets he placed on his bed, he was always freezing. Resolution three: invest in a duvet.

The chime of a clock – ormolu, chosen by Camilla to help clutter the hallway – reminded Julius that he had other resolutions to keep.

Throwing a sports jacket on over his fur coat, he bolted out of the house and jumped on a passing tram. It was full to the brim – another reason why he didn't like getting to work on time – a mass of whiskers, tails and anoraks. He stood for the journey, his left paw clutching a strap. His fellow passengers looked half asleep, their inner eyelids closed, stifling yawns and sneezes. As far as modes of transport went, trams seemed like the unhealthiest. All those germs in such an enclosed space. Julius touched his nose; it was dry and warm.

He missed Camilla.

'Hey, pal–' A ginger face pushed its way into his field of vision. 'Are you, uh...' it was a Manx, not the most quick-witted of breeds. '...Y'know, aintcha that dude?'

'No. I'm not.' The tram had arrived outside Bast Tower, and Julius pushed through a dense cloud of yuppies to get off.

Against his better judgement, he turned his head to see the Manx leaning out of the carriage.

'No need to be so rude,' the Manx whined. 'Us cats have got to stick together.'

Yeah, right. Us cats have to stick together.

As the tram pulled away behind him, Julius watched a stream of pinstripe-suited tortoiseshells, Siamese and Persians shuffle into Bast Tower. They were glum, single-minded, staring straight ahead. A few mumbled good morning to each other at the entranceway, but no one was cheerful. Julius didn't feel like being one of the crowd that day. Instead he walked round the side of the grey building, scuffing his hind paws idly along the pavement. Anything to avoid starting the daily grind.

On the right side of the tower was a neon sign that said *The Scratching Post*. His employer, the millstone around his neck. The sign hung above his office window, wide and smog-grey. The window was currently occupied by a gaggle of reporters and photographers, faces bristling with excitement, gesticulating in a flashbulb frenzy. At first Julius thought that he was the centre of this commotion, until he turned to see the cat on the bridge. It was his best friend, Mick.

Eno Bridge stretched across a river that ran past the tower, spanning a fifty-foot drop. It was a simple collection of red brick and steel girders, built to last. The subject of all the excitement was poised on a metal support, ready to jump.

2

A youth from West Weiburg, Oston, has become the latest victim of a gang dispute that has spread from the city slums to its commercial centre.

Public school-educated Henry Twip, from a well-to-do family, was caught off-guard as gang warfare erupted in his wealthy neighbourhood.

Although authorities have named no suspects in the case, members of the Clute and Wildcat gangs were witnessed during the pitched battle. Several toms fought tooth and claw over old feuds, territories and the right to call themselves 'top dogs'.

SCRATCHING POST NEWS REPORT
MICK McCLOUGH

'Listen, Mick. Someone was in my house last night. Was it you?' Julius edged his way along the bridge towards his friend, who didn't take his eyes off the river below. 'Was it some kind of prank?'

Julius was trying to think of everyday conversation, any kind of distraction from Mick's morbid thoughts. An attempt to snapfit him back to his senses.

'I'm not in the mood for pranks, pal.' Mick's voice was cold, disjointed; he cleared his throat. Moved closer to the edge. Julius had reached the steel support by now, moving slowly, his mind racing.

'This is crazy, Mick. Why are you doing this to me? You can't blame me if you've got a bad hangover. Get down from there.' Mick turned to gaze sadly into his friend's eyes. Julius wanted an explanation for Mick's sudden depression but there was no easy answer. Mick was burnt out, tired, he'd been passed over for promotion year after year. He was a hack, nothing more, and until now he'd seemed content with the role. He shared a desk with Julius, and they knew each other very well – which made Mick's actions all the more shocking.

'Know anything about a party on a sand barge? You're gonna make me late for work,' said Julius softly. Mick didn't smile. He was looking down again, hanging tenuously from the support by one paw. Julius reached out, ready to grab his friend and pull him back, but Mick didn't even see him. He seemed oblivious to his surroundings now as he took a step into thin air, allowing his body weight to plunge him off the bridge. Julius snatched at the air, almost falling with him. He used his tail to regain his balance.

Mick's body made few ripples as it hit the water; just a couple of laughter lines which faded in seconds. Some of the photographers had reached the bank by now, yowling and snapping away at nothing. Julius' eyes quested the river, looking for a sign that his friend had survived. The photographers stopped shooting, walking tentatively along the bank, silt sucking at their paws. The horde of cats held their breaths in tormented silence, broken only by the sound of approaching sirens. The paramedics were too late. A bedraggled object had surfaced on the far side of the river;

the sodden black body of a dead cat. The current moved its limbs in a parody of puppetry. Julius left his vantagepoint and made for his office, heart empty, feeling nothing but a chill ache.

There was a paw print on his desk – Mick's desk – where some roving reporter had gained a ringside perch to catch the action on the bridge.

Julius wasn't amused. He scowled as a cleaner began to clear Mick's notes and belongings into a box. Only following orders.

Not much to show for a lifelong career at the *Post* – a dictaphone manged with newsprint, a stack of ten notebooks filled with spermlike squiggles, a photograph of Mick's lady, playing with a piece of string coy-as-you-please, a spike holding sheaves of faxes; a rolodex. They all went into the grocery box that was stashed under the desk.

That'll be me in a few years, thought Julius. *Dead, retired or* (if he was really unlucky) *moved North.* He closed the window, refusing to meet the eyes of his colleagues. No one clapped him on the back in consolation, told him how sorry they were. There was an air of excitement in the office, subdued yet tangible, and a couple of reporters quibbled over who would cover Mick's life story.

The office was open plan, so when the editor wanted you, you knew it. All he had to do was flex a claw in your direction and you'd be summoned. A thrill of annoyance tickled Julius' belly as his boss beckoned him over. He watched the editor's tail, waiting for a twitch to signal that Morris was in a bad mood. Instead, it drooped lazily towards the floor.

Morris was a big tom. His stomach barely squeezed

between the arms of his swivel chair, fat and greased fur ooz-ing through the gaps. He seemed to spend most of his time dozing, eyes closed, but if one of his staff put a step wrong he'd bawl them out in a second. His word was law, although he was never described as fierce. Any warrior traits etched on his face were obscured by the *pince-nez* he always wore. The faded strip lights above his desk gave him a sick yellow halo.

'You knew him best.' Morris shifted behind his desk, folds of flesh like the rollers on a mangle.

'I ain't doing the obit. I don't want anything to do with this. I... I'm too close to it.'

'You want the rest of the day off?' asked Morris impa-tiently. Julius shook his head.

'I was only gonna ask if you knew why he did it. Somethin' musta provoked him. Mick had a reason for everything he did. Roy's coverin' the story – front-page material. He might wanna talk to you later. In the meantime, I want you to pick up where Mick left off. The Wildcats.'

Until recently, gang members had always been dismissed as boisterous kittens. There wasn't much for an unemployed youth to do in the city of Bast, short of hanging around with friends, roaming the streets. But the youths had become more disaffected, less tolerant, as the city increased in prosperity. They'd recently taken to attacking cats who were from a dif-ferent street, wearing different clothes or – most irrational of all – a different breed.

'There was no such violence when I was young,' said Morris with a smile. Good news stories were the only things that made him happy. He licked his red slug lips, his mind on the blind date he had set after work.

'Mick was planning an interview, wasn't he?' asked Julius, pulling a notebook from his jacket.

'Just keep plugging at it. Something's gonna break. I can smell it.'

Morris closed his eyes, and Julius left him to his doze. *One of your best employees has just topped himself and you're thinking of headlines. A born journalist.* That was why Morris was editor and Julius was a humble newshound.

Julius scrabbled under Mick's desk and pulled out the rolodex. It was half-empty and the cards it held were grubby, well perused. None of them seemed to relate to the gang story until Julius came across a card marked 'Area Disputes'. Julius took the name underneath to be that of an informer:

KING MARTI

Everything fine and good, until he saw Marti's address. The hairs on the back of his head stood on end.

3 MIRO STREET
THE DOGHOUSE

3

Vast tracts of tundra dominoed with villages separate the major cities. Goats roam there and newcomers are never made to feel particularly welcome.

Open to invading rivals at all times, until 100 years ago Bast was always in a state of emergency with a heavy reserve army. Yet its culture and sophistication belie its hostile past. The earliest art originates from this cool forest area; mighty trees and lakes add beauty to its environs. Although Bast is not the largest city, it has the densest population. It's easy to leave the built-up urban centre for a while, and breathe the cleaner air of the green belt. The River Hune splits Bast (a derivation of Bubastis, meaning 'House of Bastet') into two regions, and the inhabitants of each bank differ in their character and back-ground. They look down on each other, but any feuds are short-lived.

The accent in the city is on art, leisure and shrewd commerce. The richer urban areas are refined and clean, while the poorer streets South

of the river are less appealing. One of the
Southern districts has earned itself the nick-
name 'The Doghouse'.

SEE THE WORLD ON A MOUSE A DAY
Ed. MITCH MAHOIN

If you were old, small, rich or scared easy, the Doghouse wasn't
a safe place to be. The housing estate stretched for twenty
blocks by twelve. Bad enough at night, it was scarcely safe
in daylight either. In more well-to-do areas of the city, cats
exercised tolerance in all its civilised forms. You crossed a
neighbour's territory to get from A to B, they put up with it.
You stepped on someone's paw, stopped to sniff their fence,
that was okay – so long as it didn't happen again.

The Doghouse – sprawling, seedy, rundown but ugly
from inception – was a little more hostile. So much as
breathe in the wrong direction and there'd be trouble. Big,
life-or-death trouble. Patches of land were marked out by
scents and lines in the dirt; maybe the odd picket fence or
two. However, if you stumbled into the wrong territory,
were caught unawares, or if a young male made a play for
your piece of land, there were two choices. Lie down with
your belly in the air, yield and give up your property (live to
fight another day); or raise your hackles and defend yourself,
look out he's about to pounce, mind those claws, those teeth,
don't get petrified in the green headlamp eyes of your attacker,
defend what's rightfully yours –

The residents of the Doghouse knew the gig. Stick to your
own home, your own street, or the designated paths that bordered territories. Strangers were less than welcome and Julius

knew it. A sense of dread lingered at the back of his brain as he entered the district. No tramlines ran through the area; all public transport skirted it intentionally. Miro Street was a short walk from the last stop, but a shower of treacled rain made the journey more difficult. His fur, grey with a patch of black around the right eye and ear, was drenched. Miro Street was too quiet and empty for his liking.

The deluge had sent everyone scurrying for cover. He was glad when he found the right address. King Marti's house was prefabricated, red-tiled, ramshackle but dry. Julius stepped up to the front entrance with caution; he didn't want to be mistaken for the member of a gang, or a cop. He never had time to knock.

Julius was thrown against the front wall, the air knocked from his lungs. A claw was hooked under his chin, ready to slit his throat if he moved. He looked down, blinking raindrops from his eyes. His assailant was pint-sized, a pale white kitten who could barely reach Julius' neck. Little more than a cub – with lengthy, stiletto sharp claws.

Leaping upwards, Julius wrenched away from the cub's claws and swatted him square in the face. The kitten sprawled onto his back, clutching his nose, more angry than hurt.

'You better be who I think you are, pal. Round the side. Now.' The cub headed for the back of the house.

'Can't we go inside?' The cub didn't reply, still nursing his face. Julius started after him. 'I do have an appointment, you know.'

The back of the house was more sheltered and secluded. The cub seemed more at ease, more confident. 'You gotta be quick round here,' he explained in a lazy drawl, lounging next to a fence. 'I had to make sure. What's the idea meetin' at my house, anyway?'

'I don't know the Doghouse all that well, Mr Marti.'

'Call me King. I do.'

'All I had was your address, and when I called –'

'I wasn't all that helpful.' King offered to shake paws. 'No hard feelings. It's a pleasure to meet you. I've always wanted to – I mean, I'm a big fan of yours. Read all your books. Got them down the thrift store. The Living Dustbin, The Smell of Fur, Wonder Cat on the Dole... Anyway. It's an honour.'

A thrift store?

'I've heard a bit about you, too. Mick told me some stuff –'

'Yeah, sure I was helpin' him. I wouldn't say that too loud, I don't brag to my friends about it or nothin' like that, but I was helpin' him. I was his number one source, his main scoop supply. All those exclusives and headlines, and shock horror probes? They all came from me! If not for King, your rag'd be blank, y'know? Nothin' to say, nothin' to smell. I had his number. That's heavy, what happened. Major. You a good friend of his, something like that?'

'We shared a desk. Chased the same tarts. Liked the same movies.'

The sky cleared. A weak sun peered from behind cloud curtains.

'Perfect couple.'

'He was a good writer. A good cat. No one seems to miss him.'

'Hey, I miss him. I was cryin' like a puppy when I heard. Didn't know what I'd do for cash – sorry Mr Kyle, I ain't serious. We all got our own ways of grieving, ain't we. You,

you get on with your stories. Bury your nose in a notebook. Me, I make jokes. Go figure.'

'Where did Mick leave off?'

'He was gonna meet Samson, the boss of the Wildcat gang. Nothing to do with me. Samson makes or breaks the gang. Starts wars and finishes 'em. Mick had some serious dirt on that cat, or so he told me. One heck of a hack.'

Julius was tempted to argue with King's description of Mick. He would want to be remembered for more. Instead he got on with his job.

'Do you think I could..?'

'No way, pal. Deal's off. Even Samson is entitled to get cold feet when someone takes a long jump off a short bridge. I don't wanna get involved; might blow my cover.'

'That would be a shame.' King held out a paw again, this time for something more material than friendship. Julius pulled out his wallet, found a couple of bills, then hesitated.

'You got anything in return for this?'

'Huh?'

'Information. You're a grass aren't you? How about some news?'

'Keep it down, Mr Kyle. I don't want trouble.' King sidled up closer to Julius and his money. 'I don't know how much Mick told you, but I've always been an outsider round here. Never quite accepted. Most of the cats in this neighbourhood are purebred ginger toms. Siamese like me don't get into a gang very often. I'm being blooded. Gonna be a Wildcat – in name, at least.'

'That's great.' Julius tried to sound pleased. 'That'll give you greater access –'

'To what's going down, what the boss is planning, you got it. Of course you know what this'll mean.' King took Julius' money hungrily. 'A raise. Top level info. All yours at a price.'

Tarquin had overslept again. A heavy evening meal combined with an exhausting week's work at the office had sent him into a granite sleep.

He needed sixteen hours a day and if he didn't get them he became grouchy. Most folks found him grouchy anyway, sleep or no sleep. But he was always ready to tell them where they could stick their comments.

Tarquin hated walking to work, but a little exercise was preferable to the daily horrors of public transport. He could stand the taunts, the pushing and shoving, the ill-mannered stares. But the sheer *lower class*ness of his fellow passengers put him off. Better to stroll the couple of blocks to work, and brave the inclement weather.

Leaving his plush one-storey house, Tarquin walked along the concrete canyon that led to the City Chambers, his coat tails flapping in his wake. Scimitar skyscrapers towered on either side like giant breezeblocks sheltering Bast, forming claws on the skyline, scooped gutters draining rainwater towards the city's green belt. Cats had always harboured an inexplicable desire to climb, build upwards, head for the heavens. The skyscrapers killed more birds than cats did, scudding the clouds in architectural hubris.

Halfway to work Tarquin accidentally brushed against a passer-by, a squat yob with a torn ear. Tarquin apologised, but this only made matters worse.

'Watch where you're going, Sinner.' Tarquin was sure

that he was about to be struck, but before he could raise his hackles the yob had disappeared into a crowd of shoppers. Tarquin was used to receiving abuse. He was asking for it. He was stuck-up, well spoken, reedy, and an Abyssinian. A rare caste in the city of Bast, Abyssinians had been mistreated by other breeds since their integration. Most had taken low-level jobs deep in the bowels of the metropolis; Tarquin was the exception. Private secretary, advisor, confidant to Otto, the Mayor of Bast.

He spent the rest of the journey with his head bowed, body stooped, trying to look as small as possible. Within minutes the Chambers loomed before him – a great green orb.

His office. His ball and chain. It was a monument to strength and functionality. Every civilian agreed that the best view of the city was to be had from its windows – because that was the only place where you couldn't see the Chambers.

Two leopards with sturdy pikes guarded the entrance, standing eternally to attention. Tarquin squeezed past them – they always made him feel short. That was the Mayor's intention: all citizens were supposed to feel lowly here, in this place, at the heart of Bast, in the presence of its ruler. Tarquin often wondered whether the guards were there to defend Otto, or keep him in the building. The most hated creature in the city, and the most feared – no one volunteered for Mayor.

A thick-pile red carpet lined the hallway and steps that led to the Mayor's office. Tarquin liked the way his pads were cushioned by the shag. It was a luxurious comfort after the soil and gravel of street paving. Heavy pawprints marked the slight stairwell, and Tarquin followed them to find Otto slumped in his chair, stifling a yawn.

'How's your mum?' asked Tarquin. 'Haven't seen her on telly lately. She hasn't – er – lost her marbles again, has she?'

'Her sanity is perfectly intact, Tarquin.' The Mayor sounded pompous. 'We visited her only last night.'

'This is the royal We?'

'No. The cubs and we. I mean I. Thought it would be good PR if I let them tail along with me for a weekend. Little beggars. Don't know why the public're so fond of 'em.' Otto scratched his lion face idly.

Tarquin often found himself mesmerised by the Mayor's huge nose and razor teeth.

'They're the future, sir. And they're cute. Your two children are walking bundles of hope and optimism.'

'If you say so. I take it you have an explanation for –'

'I know, I'm sorry sir, deepest apologies, it won't happen again...' Tarquin was playing for time, his mind racing to find an excuse for being late. Otto had been known to chew off the heads of lackeys who displeased him. At least, the assistant had heard some disquieting stories. 'The accounts, sir. I have to tell you, you've been spending far too much. The budget isn't as large as it used to be.'

Wrong excuse. Otto let out a low roar. He enjoyed the informal relationship he held with his secretary, but the subject of budgets always made him lose his temper.

'I know how much I've spent. I have a lifestyle to uphold. An image to project. Can't disappoint the populace.' Otto examined his manicured talons in the light of a desklamp.

'But you can spend their money. Clothes. Furniture. Toys for the kids.'

'Enough!' Otto raised his voice. 'Do you know how long my family has sat in this office, watched over this city?'

'Countless generations, sir. And I feel very privileged to be in your presence.' Tarquin wrung his paws. 'You do a much better job than your mother used to, by the way.'

'Leave my mother out of this! Crazy bitch bunged the post over to me years ago, and she still won't keep her mouth shut. I'm aware of our... budgetary difficulties. I've decided to cut Church expenditure. It's not as if they need the money. I spent this morning looking at the figures – could have done with some help – attendance has been falling steadily for the past decade. I visited the cathedral the other day. Nothing but old ladies there, and they were on the way out. If you know what I mean. The Church gets plenty of contributions from fat cats on their deathbeds. Y'know what they got at the back of the cathedral? Envelopes. For small change. There's multiple choice stamped on them. 'Please Father, say a prayer for my aunt/uncle/other, who has died/fallen ill/gone doolally.' They're the best entrepreneurs on the block. Why should the state fund them?'

Otto was out of his seat, wagging a broad talon at his secretary. 'Bastet is dead. Sooner those priests get that idea in their thick heads, the better.' Tarquin, who worshipped Bastet every Sunday morning out of habit, nodded and stayed silent. Otto was convinced that he was right; nothing would change his mind. The Church coffers would have to be plundered, and to hell with the consequences.

'You were a great writer. At least *I* think so.' Julius was still cornered in King's back yard. It was obvious he'd get no more concrete information that day. But once his informant started talking, it was hard to get a word in edgeways. 'I learnt all my big words readin' your books. Tiger Straight, he was my hero. My role model. I wanted to look like him and act like him. He was so cool! Sharp suits, black shades. Just one note on his saxophone and the bad guys'd be blown off the page!'

'So you're a fan then, are you?' Julius wondered if King was old enough to appreciate sarcasm.

'One of a legion!' King lit a cigarette. 'A whole generation's grown up on your reprints.'

'It's pretty naive stuff. Adolescent hokum.'

'No way, J. You should write another book. Give the public what they want.'

'I don't think so. It wouldn't be the same. You can't recapture the past. I'm sure if demand was that great, the publishers would be queuing up outside my house.' Julius' attempts at modesty were interrupted by the arrival of King's sister, statuesque and porcelain-white. She had curved pink strokes shaved into her fur at patterned intervals, rippling as she moved.

'What're you boys doing round here? King?' Her brother stubbed out his cigarette, eyes lowered.

'Moira, my big sis, this is – a friend of mine. From way back.'

'No shit.' Moira sidled up to Julius, looking him up and down. 'What's your name?'

'Julius.' He was backed up against a wall, her face so close to his own that he could smell her sweet breath.

'That's a new one on me. We don't get many Juliuses to the pound in these parts. Always nice to see a new face, though.' Her eyes were huge, with amber sparks around the cornea. Her wrists were long, slender, paws grasping thin air as she spoke. Julius watched the lines shaved in her fur as they glided around her neck, ruffled by the dank wind. He cleared his throat.

'I can't stay.' It was his chance to make an exit. 'I've got to be getting back.'

'Back where?' Moira asked too many questions. 'My brother's such a bad liar. It's always obvious when he's telling stories.' She moved to block Julius' escape. 'Do you tell stories?'

'Not if I can avoid it. It was nice meeting you. Seeya round, King.'

Julius pushed gently past her and left the back yard. The threat of further rain was keeping most residents indoors, but a couple of Wildcats with brightly dyed head fur and chains around their jackets stood under a solitary tree. A radio at their feet blared the latest rap hit from ghetto group Suspicious Package:

Pick a fight with me my friend
Your bones will never mend
I'll rip you limb from limb
Turn you over then start again.

In between watching for a break in the clouds, they turned their heads in unison to follow Julius down the street. He could tell by their black headscarves that they were gang members. For a moment he felt a twinge of concern for King, but then self-preservation got the better of him and he hurried out of the Doghouse.

4

'I DIDN'T EXPECT YOU to turn up.' Camilla had been sitting in the restaurant for forty minutes. She'd ordered a saucer of milk, but nothing more.

'I didn't know if you'd be here either. Always off gallivanting.' Julius peeled off his jacket, hung it on the back of his chair. It dripped quietly to itself, limp as seaweed. 'I got waylaid – a story south of the river.' The two cats rubbed their foreheads together tenderly.

'That's fine, whatever.' Her fur had been styled in flamboyant, full-bodied ridges. Mascara highlighted her lime green eyes. 'Can we order now?' The Grand Canary's spectral waiters were gone one second and flitting between tables the next. Those not quick enough to catch their attention as they slipped by would go hungry. Julius' stomach was too empty for him to let that happen. He reached out for the Maitre D'.

One of the waiters came to the rescue. He'd obviously spent some time developing not-looking-a-customer-in-the-eye into an art form. Julius was passed a tall yellow menu, the waiter remaining a leg's length away from the diners at all times. Camilla grabbed the menu as quickly as etiquette would allow and sniffed it appreciatively, reading it with her nose. She licked at one section, a brief taste test that helped her to make up her mind.

'The Special, please.' Julius rolled his eyes. Trust his girl-friend to go for the nouvelle cuisine.

'I'll take the rare rabbit.' The waiter didn't acknowledge Julius' smile. Instead he snatched away the menu and pointed at a buffet table near the cash register.

'Help yourselves to the smorgasbord.'

Camilla was at the buffet before her partner. Over her shoulder, he saw something moving among the salad and dressing. The food was alive. The table was laden with small rats, mice and insects, trapped in tubs and bread rolls. The Grand Canary was a swanky place, but the smorgasbord was a free-for-all, cats grabbing their food with paws or teeth before it could escape. Some took plates back to their seats, their teeth chattering and grinding, trying not to dribble on the doilies.

Julius forewent any niceties and stuffed a rat in his mouth, head first. He joined Camilla at her table; in a daintier mood, she split her mouse open and pulled the intestines and gall bladder to one side of her plate. Julius chewed hard, crunching bones between his teeth, and pulling out the skin when he was finished. He covered it discreetly with his napkin.

Sitting at the next table was the recognisably balding fig-ure of Swampie McMahon, the famous wrestler. This was the place to be seen, or for those less fortunate, to watch the celebrities. McMahon was staring at a glass wall on one side of the restaurant, the only thing saving a tankful of fish and seafood from instant death in the mouths of diners. His emerald eyes followed the mobile feast from one end of the wall to the other; when he finally caught the attention of a waiter, he pointed to a fat cod and waited for it to be deliv-ered to his table.

Camilla made small talk, her ears pointing forwards in total relaxation. Julius watched her closely, but his mind was on King's sister. He wasn't exactly sure why.

Camilla's too young for you, and Moira's just my age. Camilla's fat – scratch that, big boned – but Moira's skinny as a chicken. My girl's pretty, Moira's plain.

'This is delicious,' Camilla was saying. She proffered a wriggling beetle, but Julius shook his head.

Camilla is sexy, rich, from a good background. Moira's full of herself, poor gutter trash, but she's interested.

An insect leg trailed from Camilla's lips. 'Do you love me?' Julius asked, but she didn't seem to hear him. She wasn't looking at him at all. Instead she was looking at Swampie. Fair enough, he was a famous cat, he'd given a lot of money to charity, and he was a well-renowned sex icon. She was fluttering her eyelashes at him, damn it! Swampie was returning her look! Julius called over to him, a fixed smile on his face. His bristling fur betrayed his true feelings.

What did she see in him? He had no hair on the top of his head; it looked like he had a cowpat between his ears. His eyes were brown and runny. At second glance, Julius decided that Swampie was quite ugly.

'Hiya! Howarya, Mr Kyle? Sorry to hear about your friend.' Swampie was all whiskers and grins. *No wonder, with my girlfriend in the bag.*

'Why don't you go home with him?' Julius hissed at his mate.

'Don't know what you're talking about, darling. Mr McMahon was kind enough to make conversation with me while I was waiting on you.' Camilla found Julius' fits of jealousy quite endearing. They hinted at a few cracks in his unshakeable exterior.

'I'll bet he was.' To Swampie: 'hope you're keeping well. Enjoy your meal.' End of conversation. Julius had made his position quite clear. He hated himself for being so hypocritical; one minute dreaming of another girl, then acting overprotective with Camilla. He was glad when the main course arrived – saved by the *belle du jour*.

Camilla picked at her food, her brow furrowed. The Special consisted of two strips of crabmeat framed with herringbones.

'You've got a couple of white hairs there.' Camilla smoothed down a piece of fur behind Julius' ear.

'They're blonde.' He moved her paw away.

'What was it like?' asked Camilla, wondering which part of her meal she should eat.

'What?' Julius' rabbit couldn't have been fresher; it tried to hop off his plate as soon as it was served. Julius held it firm with both paws and killed it quickly with his teeth on its throat. He savoured the taste of warm blood on his tongue.

'South of the river. The Doghouse.'

'I wouldn't call it that down there. Don't think the natives would like it.'

'They restless?'

'Antsy. I don't know. I really didn't find all that much out. Just showing my face.'

'I'm surprised you set paw in the place. I would've thought that the residents would have you for breakfast.'

'What are you saying?' Julius asked, drawing closer to

Camilla. She raised an eyebrow; he knew she was kidding. Their paws touched under the table.

'I think it was quite brave.'

'You know me darling. I don't do brave.'

'Well, I do. At least my editor seems to think so. He's sending me on foreign assignment,' Camilla announced proudly. 'Seems you're right about the gallivanting.'

'Isn't that going to be a little dangerous?' Camilla listened intently to Julius' tone. Was it concern or jealousy that she could detect in his voice? 'Where's he sending you?'

'Can't say, honey. Not just yet anyway. All I know is it's big. Big and juicy.'

Swampie had finished his fish and was rolling out of the restaurant. Camilla didn't return the celebrity's wave, to Julius' relief. She'd just been playing, as usual. Stirring trouble. He hoped. The couple ordered a pint between them, shuffled their seats close together, and drank to the memory of a dead friend.

DUSK IN THE DOGHOUSE: the main street outside King's house was littered with vomit and black bin liners. The windows of derelict huts were boarded up and scent had been graffitied across the wood panels by brave youngsters. The copiously sprayed scents conveyed threats and gang slogans. The domiciles that hadn't fallen into disrepair sported some insipidly expensive decorations; bettering your neighbours was worth the slog of a life lived on credit. Blankets on the makeshift pavement displayed cheap sunglasses, clockwork mice and dancing puppets – useless objects sold by slack-muzzled hawkers who insisted that they were the most valuable objects in the world. A butcher's shop held a fly-ridden hog carcass in its window; the neighbouring newsstand and tobacconists were filthy with sand and mud. At the end of the street was a tall tree that formed the meeting place for the Wildcats. Notches in the trunk – arcane scratches, childish glyphs – held codes that only fully fledged members could read.

King felt awkward, and when he was pressured (which was most of the time, he never had learned how to relax) he talked real fast. So the two gaudily hued Wildcats that'd agreed to meet him were assailed by a string of breathless words, falling higgledy-piggledy over each other.

'Gladyoucould makeitfellas howsithangin you'relookin-cool whatyougotplanned?' the Wildcats looked down at the newcomer, their jaws set, faces moody, body language anti-social. The bigger gang member, Warren, wore baggy jeans and a jacket. His left ear was tattered and he kept his fore-limbs folded. His companion, Sal, was jittery, shifting from one hind paw to the other, shaking as if he was cold, his arms clamped stiff to his sides. He brushed a tuft of hair repeatedly behind his left ear and had a beatific smile on his face. He didn't say much.

King stared at Warren's heavy brow, wondering why the Wildcats had decided to tolerate him. Or had they? Warren started to move off, turned back as if in afterthought.

'Don't bother, son. If you ain't the kind of cat who knows what's going on, then you may as well stay in your tray. Know what I mean? You been eating too much of that litter, boy. It's started comin' out your ears. Pat your head and wet sand comes out, know what I'm sayin'?' King opened his mouth to reply, but Warren didn't give him the chance.

'Now next time you think you got somethin' to say, don't think and don't say. Savvy? Damn, these kittens gotta problem these days.' Warren had started walking. King fol-lowed. 'So, King Marti. You been walkin' on the wrong side of the street again, aintcha?'

'Yeah,' ventured Sal, 'where the big boys play.'

'Always in the wrong place with the wrong angle.'

'I don't know what you mean.'

'What I mean is – You're still in your nappy! You still got your mommy lickin' your fur!' King started to lose his tem-per as Sal continued the taunts.

'Hey, you learnt to walk yet?' snickered Sal. 'Does your neck hurt from bein' carried round in your momma's teeth all the time?'

'Still suckin' on them titties, huh? When you get through with your litter box training, come back and see us, okay?' King grabbed Warren by the jacket and tried to push him off balance.

'Back off!' The kitten's voice sounded awfully high. The big cat didn't budge.

'That's it! That's what we wanna see out of a potential Wildcat.' Warren adjusted his black bandanna. 'Some fire. Now let's put some of that potential into action.' He led the way through the Doghouse, leaving King to cool down gradually. The young cat wished his friends were with him, but they were geeks, not gang material by a long haul. As Warren had put it, *your friends ain't invited to this party*. His initiation. What form would it take?

He wondered what the Wildcats would consider cool. His best bet was to keep quiet, pretty much monosyllabic like them. He tried, but couldn't keep it going for long.

'What do the hieroglyphs on the tree mean?'

'They mean, 'Don't ask what these hieroglyphs mean, on pain of death.' ' Warren gave a smirk. 'There was a guy round here today, looked just like Julius Kyle. Damn, his stuff was cool.' King was surprised that the Wildcats could read more than a sentence. Usually their response to anything that made them think was to hit it.

'You read his stuff?'

'Yeah, sure, when I was little. Last of the great storytellers. Wonder what happened to him?'

'Drugs,' Sal smiled, 'or a accident. Or both.' Sal stopped

behind Warren, who was looking down at a street sign grey with dust. Beaverbank Place. The border. A cobbled street marked the end of Wildcat territory.

'What d'you want me to do?'

'Play a game of cat and mouse – and you ain't the cat. Here.' Warren gave King a bandanna, Wildcat colours. 'We want you to take a trip down there –' pointing to the Beaverbank, 'that's Clute territory. You remove the bandanna, or turn and run, I never want to see your face again.'

King didn't give himself a chance to think. His heart was already pounding as he made for the dark street. *I'm just a kitten*, he told himself. *What in Bastet's name am I doing here?*

This is where you become a tom, this is where you grow up, the day your balls drop, the day you run the gauntlet. He could tell he was in the wrong territory from the broken windows, graffiti, lack of light. His nose wrinkled at a bad smell in the air, like rancid meat. The Wildcats were long lost in the shadows behind him. He was halfway down the Beaverbank, no sign of the enemy, only distant footsteps –

Keep walking, it'll be cool, this is stupid, I'm asking for trouble, maybe I should take the bandanna off...

Too late. Enter the bad guy, Tufano, leader of the Clutes. Surrounded by cronies with greased back fur, shiny buckles and a confident stride. Tufano was lanky and shabby-looking, but he emanated power with eyes black as coals, soaking up the moonlight. Searching the darkness, heading straight for King. Tufano's face was carved from a rock, swivelling on a caber torso. King ducked into an entranceway, curling up in a tight-crouched ball. He wrapped a paw over his mouth to silence his breathing until the Clutes had passed.

I could have grown up tonight. Instead I ran and hid. I'm nothing.

The Wildcats were waiting at the other end of the Beaverbank – they'd skirted round the Clute territory. Not as dumb as they let on. Maybe they didn't fancy a rumble that night. King was almost pleased to see them, but Warren didn't have much to say.

'You can keep the bandanna.' The Wildcats turned their backs on him, and started for their meeting place. King dogged their footsteps, one of the gang now. He should have been pleased; instead he felt numb. He was beginning to understand what it felt to be one of the gang.

Julius sipped a glass of water, a dozen 'phone conversations echoing around him. He liked the office. There was a healthy discipline in writing from nine to five, talking to colleagues, getting your head down, looking forward to a regular salary at the end of the week. And he needed that paycheque.

He'd squandered so much, back in the days of caviar and fame. So many people had wanted to read his books, interview him, flatter him. They'd actually cared what he thought, what his opinions were. For once he hadn't had to chase around for offers of work; the world had come to his front step and waited patiently. He'd captured the zeitgeist of the era, he'd told the people how they felt. Burn out had been inevitable.

It had come one Friday morning, in bed, an hour before breakfast. He had been under contract to create another right cat, right time best seller when suddenly he'd realised... he couldn't. There were no stories left inside him. A career right in time for middle age.

Now it was all Julius could do to keep the house and pay

his restaurant bills. Ten years ago, after teeth-clenched visits from the tax cat and his bank manager (*look, sorry Jules, the bone china crustaceans have got to go*) respectively, he'd come out of retirement. He couldn't write any more, so he became a journalist.

Beneath his desk the floor rumbled steadily. In the basement lurked the printing presses, cranking out the early edition, hundreds of tiny nozzles spraying scents onto the newspapers; sensational aromas to accompany the text. By the time the scents dried, the papers would be bundled up and ready to ship out for the public to smell.

An office junior rushed past Julius' station, stopping to take a breath:

'Mr Kyle – the queen's got something for you.' The cub vanished. Julius rested his chin in his paws. *Oh no. Do I have to speak to her?*

The queen was a grey-haired mainstay you avoided at all costs. Assistant news editors are always notoriously grim, but this one was serious to the point of morbidity. And female, which made her even more difficult for him to talk to.

He peered over his terminal to look at her, making sure not to catch her eye. It was the way she constantly pursed her lips in a wince, that was what put him off. Her whiskers bowed down as if there were heavy weights on each end. In the ten years he'd worked for the *Post*, he'd never seen her smile. Still, he had to talk to her. Retrieve information. No sense putting it off.

Julius climbed stiffly from his seat and moved across the office slowly, careful not to alert the queen to his presence any sooner than necessary.

When he arrived behind her, he found that his voice wouldn't work. He opened his mouth but no words came out. He licked his lips, tried to moisten his throat, but before he could say anything the queen jumped.

'Julius! You scared me, lurking around like that.' Angry.

'Sorry. Just wondered if – if, uh, you had something for me. On the gang disputes.'

'Word's coming in about a nasty little *contre-temps* on Miro Street. There's a Number Seven leaving in four minutes.' The queen gave him a chit and he rushed out of the office. He barely caught the tram, which never seemed to stop – it just slowed down enough for passengers to hop on or off. It looked like a row of egg boxes, packed tight with farm fresh class 'A's.

He spent the long journey going through his notes. Sparks flew from the cables above him, and the tram hurtled round corners, jarring his arm as he wrote. Pedestrians had to be quick-witted to avoid death or injury by tramwheel.

On his walk through the Doghouse, Julius sensed that something was badly wrong. He got to Miro Street as quick as he could, but he'd already missed the action. He could only pick up the pieces: a few Wildcats had been attacked in their meeting place. No bystanders had stepped in to save them. The roots of the tree were sated with blood, three bodies were strewn across the street, police had cordoned the area off with tape and were taking pictures for the record. A middle-aged female was crying, cradling a brotherless cub.

Julius knelt down beside a small, white form that lay face down near the tree. There was a lump in the reporter's throat – he wasn't quite sure why. He turned the corpse onto its back and was relieved to see that it wasn't King Marti. So much death. Had scenes like this driven Mick to suicide?

King wasn't home, but his sister sat at the kitchen table eating tuna. Her eyes were red with the trace of tears. Her fur was slicker and smoother than Camilla's refined coiffure.

'No, I haven't seen him and I know you're a journalist and yes, I would like your help.' Julius nodded, sat down and waited for Moira to finish her fish.

6

Who is that gorgeous creature? Hello? Haven't I seen you some-place before? In a fashion show perhaps? A beauty pageant? My goddess, if you've never entered one you should. Bound to win. Your eyes are hypnotic, darling. Simply mesmerising.

Bridget Canders could hardly bear to wrench herself away from the mirror. She didn't know how she ever got anything done. She turned for another glance at her reflection, approving of the smooth downy fur, the glittering eyes and tapered ears. She'd never seen a more beautiful cat.

Like the Church, Bridget was supported and sponsored by her many admirers. The organisation she had set up in her youth had earned her a substantial following, because of the ideals that the organisation aspired to and her heavily manufactured public image. Bridget didn't mind, as long as she retained respect and money kept flooding in.

She sat in a nest of soft velvet cushions, chewing on a chocolate-coated pilchard. She practised a lithe pose, check-ing herself in a full-length mirror, blinking in slow motion. Everything was prepared. The chambermaids had been dis-missed. The windows were blocked with wooden shutters. Sweetmeats had been placed with precision on the table beside her. Bridget wanted everything to be perfect for her boyfriend when he arrived.

The hunk in question probably wouldn't appreciate all her efforts, considering his background and bearing. But at least he was a tom who used his brain. She had fooled around with so many dullards and bores in her time.

She'd met him at a reception thrown by her son. She hadn't been invited, but crashing parties was her speciality and she couldn't resist the promise of a good shindig. And it had been an affair well worth crashing – she'd seen her beau alone, looking lost, canapé crumbs on his chin. Smitten. That was the word. She'd waltzed over to him, drawn by the bright spark in his eyes, shared some small talk to check that he was capable of stringing two words together in a sentence. In the time-honoured tradition of a bitch on the prowl, she'd locked eyes with him, blinked, then looked away. It hadn't taken him long to get the message. She hadn't been able to drag the tom off to bed with her son in earshot. She bided her time. Everyone knew where Bridget lived; she'd waited for her prey to come to her.

It had been the supreme victory for Bridget. Taking her son's personal assistant under her wing, stealing him, coveting him, spending as much quality time as possible with him. She didn't know how long the love affair would last. Tarquin seemed more worried about Otto finding out than she was. She found the whole idea quite amusing.

Tarquin was right on time for a change, bustling into the room, dressed in ochre finery, sniffing Bridget's head affectionately. She smiled up at him, offering him a sweetmeat. He wasn't that bulky or strong, but he was young and intelligent and their affair was juicily illicit. If her son, the all-powerful, omniscient city Mayor, ever found out that his best friend was sleeping with his least favourite female, there would be hell to pay. Bridget found that more attractive than any physical trait.

'What do I have to do to get it through the Mayor's thick skull that without me things would grind to a halt?' Tarquin sat down in a heap on a red-draped couch.

'He lets you get away with murder, my darling, and you know it.'

'Oh, he throws me the odd bone.' He flashed a smile at Bridget and her heart leaped. 'But I do all the work and he takes all the credit.'

'This sounds like a familiar conversation,' said Bridget in mock boredom. 'Why don't you hold it with Otto instead of me for a change?' Tarquin said nothing. 'Come over here. I don't see enough of you as it is.' The tom joined her for a tender embrace. They looked into each other's eyes, Tarquin's shining with youth, Bridget's jaundiced and watery.

'I'm sorry,' Tarquin said without a second's thought. She always had him apologising for nothing. 'How's the MMA today?'

'Same old same old. Hundreds of cats all over the city, ready and willing to maintain the Monitoring of Morality in Advertising.'

'You get a real kick out of being a busybody, don't you?'

Bridget stiffened. For a moment, Tarquin thought he'd pushed things too far.

'It keeps me in the news,' she warmed just as suddenly, clinging tighter to him. 'And best of all, it needles my son. Can't see the harm in that.'

Tarquin's eyes wandered around the room as Bridget

started to groom him, licking his fur, smoothing and tugging at it with her teeth. The walls were lined with gold-framed mirrors, crystal statuettes, reflective surfaces. He knew who Bridget's favourite person was.

'Hank said I should drop it. Dared to suggest that I was getting too – busy for all this campaigning. The cheek of the fellow.'

'Don't let him get to you.' Tarquin stroked her pelt with gentle pads.

'Darling, he hasn't got to me since our anniversary. And that was only because I'd been on the milk all evening. To be honest with you –'

'And you always are, I hope?'

'I always am, you hope – I can hardly remember what it looked like.'

'Probably shrivelled up since then.'

'Yes. Probably.'

'It's always at the back of my mind.' Tarquin furrowed his brow. 'I don't want him to find out.'

'So, what if he did? He's a very old lion. What's he going to do? Have a heart attack all over you?'

'You love him really, don't you?'

'Of course I do. He's my husband.'

7

THEY FOUND KING IN a bar on the river's edge, soused up with sour milk. He'd been drinking there since noon, and his stomach felt queasy. His father had always warned him not to mix dairy products, but King had never been a model son.

It was the last drinking hole they'd tried, full of the rougher elements of the Doghouse, and Julius felt more out of place than usual. He wanted to grab King and get out as quickly as possible, but to his consternation Moira propped up the bar and ordered a couple of pints.

Julius' eyesight was about average for a cat. He found it hard to pick out particular details, relying more on his other senses – the tension that Moira radiated, her soft pawfalls, her stilted breathing. But he could swear that she'd been looking at him in a special way. Just every now and again, when she thought he wasn't watching. She found him attractive, he was sure of it. He made her whiskers twitch.

'King,' Julius grabbed the white kitten by the arm, gripping it tight, 'I'm extremely pleased to see you.'

'Here you go.' Moira passed Julius his stein. He looked at the foaming head and set it down carefully on King's table. 'Still in one piece, baby brother?'

'Only just.' The kitten had missed the rumble under the

tree, but caught the aftermath. He'd known some of the youths involved since nursery school. The blood, the frenzy, the casual waste had all hit him in a molotov cocktail of guilt. *It should have been me. It could have been me.*

Julius, Mr Kyle, the big reporter was expecting a scoop. King did his best.

'I'm gonna see him.'

'What do you mean, you're gonna see him?' Julius pulled his chair up closer.

'I'm in. Accepted. Part of the family. The boss wants to meet me.'

'That doesn't sound so good to me,' Moira butted in.

'He bestows his blessing on all his new people,' King explained. 'It's traditional.'

'Like a priest or something?'

'Like a father.'

A voice barked from the shadows. 'You've already got a father.'

'Have I, Pa?' King asked tartly. Moira pulled another chair up to the table and Pa sat down, his legs akimbo. He had a huge nose and a grizzled brown hide. Most of his face rested perpetually in shadow, tucked under a coiled hood and cowl. Giving Julius' suit the once-over he quaked, 'A bit overdressed for these parts, aren't you?'

Julius slid his stein across the table towards Pa and watched as it was quaffed in one rude slurp. There was something different, something strange about King's dad.

'Pa's a bit of a hero in these parts,' Moira explained, her lips pursed. 'People look up to him, relatively speaking. Give him a wide berth, at least.' Pa howled for more milk stout.

'Hate the stuff,' he said, hastily snatching a fresh pint. 'There ain't much else to drink round here, though. Lessen you like river.' Pa shook his head as King opened his mouth to speak. 'Don't bother, son. I know what you're going to say. What am I doing here, showing my ear-of-corn face, don't I have any shame? (I bust up this joint in a drunken frenzy a couple of weeks back.) A little fatherly advice, King. Steer away from the Wildcats. You're going to get your tail cut off, it don't just happen to farm mice you know. Stay at home with your books, that's where you're best at.'

'I don't have to listen to you –.' Moira touched King lightly on the arm and he stopped mid-sentence. 'I haven't joined them or nothing, Pa. I'm just putting a couple of deals together is all.' Julius caught a glimpse of the newcomer's amber eyes, round and unfeline. They held a hint of innocence, none of the cunning of a cat. Julius tried to change the subject.

'I've got a question for you. Why name him King?'

'What did you say?'

'Why did you call your son 'King'?' Julius turned to the kitten. 'If you're the king, then that makes your dad –'

'Deposed,' said Pa, finishing his drink and pulling himself upright. The light struck him properly for the first time and Julius saw coarse black hairs jutting from his jowls. The reporter realised that he had been sitting near a dog. His flesh crawled for an instant. King, Moira and the other occupants of the bar seemed happy to have a dog in their company. Sitting so close – Julius' claws instinctively sprang from their pads. But he did nothing.

'I got to go,' said the dog, dragging his hind paws through the dirt. 'Places to go, itches to scratch.' Julius' eyes widened as Pa looked at him. 'Puss off back where you came from, bass breath.' The dog shambled off. Julius wasn't all that affronted; he expected such behaviour from dogs.

'What was he doing here – don't you realise..?'

'We do,' Moira replied gently, 'but Pa doesn't. He thinks he's one of us.'

'He really thinks he's your father?'

'We humour him,' said King, 'so he doesn't chew our ears off.'

'Nice bloke,' said Julius between gritted teeth. King shook his head slowly.

'I don't think so.'

8

JULIUS WAS STILL SMARTING from his encounter with Pa as he sat in the Bast Train Station diner, waiting for a fish platter. It would be cold by the time it arrived, and he would not have time to eat it. But he'd ordered it anyway, in a bid to fool his gurgling belly.

With a pencil stub he was scribbling some notes for his article. Thanks to his years as a journalist, Julius had the ability to write a thousand words on any subject, no matter how mundane or ill researched. But he found it difficult to describe the carnage he had seen that day. What was his angle? A sensational scoop? A moralising, judgmental overview of the gang fighting? Or something more personal?

Julius decided that wasn't his style at all. He turned the napkin over and started to doodle, a threadbare sketch from some lazy corner of his subconscious.

The manager of the diner wandered over, slapping a fish platter in front of Julius. The reporter covered the doodle with a paw, embarrassed.

'That'll be a fiver, mate.' The manager looked harassed, hadn't found the time to wash his fur for at least an hour.

'Hang on a second –' There she was. Strolling past the window. He was going to miss her. Julius left the diner in a flash, stumbling along the platform to catch up with

Camilla. The manager looked down at the napkin. Julius had drawn a tall cat in a trenchcoat and sunglasses, playing a saxophone. As notes flowed out they changed into moths and butterflies.

Julius' ears were assailed by noise, squawking cats, huffing gears and hydraulic jacks, carriage windows slamming shut, bags thrown onto passing carts.

There was Camilla's train, narrow and streamlined, pistons straining to depart, coiled round the platform like an iron sidewinder. A third of the carriages were carrying sand to the northern border; four buffet cars would serve the needs of the hungry passengers. Julius looked for porters; surely Camilla would have a mountain of baggage with her. But porters were rare in Bast – few cats could endure such a servile profession. The odd derelict cat hung around looking for alms in return for the minimum of fetching and carrying. By the time they'd foraged, played and eaten there wasn't much time for part-time shift work.

Julius looked through carriage windows, heart beating fast. Tails wagged out of the portals, cats clung onto the roof claws out, seated amongst piles of baggage. A steam mist obscured Julius' vision. He couldn't hear the announcements from the tannoy overhead. Everyone was talking at once.

He spotted a pair of downy ears swivelling, graceful radar antennae that lowered behind a curtain as Camilla took her seat in carriage AA3. He pushed past a fat cat with baggage to match, clambered aboard, and squeezed his way down the aisle towards his girlfriend.

'What are you doing here?'

Julius looked bemused, as if the question was the last thing he expected from his girlfriend. He'd finally caught up with her on the northbound train out of the city. She'd already placed her bags on the overhead rack and taken her seat.

'What does it look like?' He passed Camilla a small box, about the size of his paw, wrapped in shiny paper. She opened it to find a tiny gold bell on the end of a ribbon. It was beautiful.

'And what am I supposed to do with this?'

'In case you get bored. On your trip.' A stationmaster was calling cats aboard outside. Julius wasn't in any hurry. 'I'm trying to say goodbye here.'

'You never were good at verbal communication were you, Julius? Prefer to write things down. Poems.' The train whistle blew one last time. 'Love notes. Court summons.'

'You think I'm old fashioned?' Julius stood up, half-indignant, half-worried that he'd be stuck on the train.

'Romance is old fashioned. Don't beat yourself up about it.' Steam drifted past the window and the brakes clunked beneath them. 'You're going to end up coming with me. And you don't have a ticket.'

'Yeah. I'd better go.'

'Thanks for the present.' Camilla smiled for the first time that afternoon.

'Don't mention it.'

'Too late.'

As the train lurched forward to begin its journey, Julius jumped onto the platform, tugging his forelock at the stationmaster. The official shook his head, folded up a patterned flag and headed into his office for a long tea break.

9

THE WILDCATS OFTEN MET at the cemetery. It was overgrown, quiet and secluded, easy to guard. Best of all the crypts, built in memory of the city's forefathers, consisted of boxed compartments; the empty ones made perfect sleeping areas. There was nothing more safe and satisfying to a Wildcat than a squared-off nook to nap in.

King had been summoned to the cemetery with a note sprayed on the communal tree, and he'd dropped everything to get to the rendezvous before nightfall. As he passed through a pair of bleached bone gates he expected an ambush at any moment. Instead, he became the focal point of twenty pairs of slitted green eyes.

Samson, the feared leader of the Wildcats, would be waiting in the central crypt, a conical affair with a spiralling peak. It was too dark to see anything inside, but King could hear shallow sighs, a powerful breeze tickling the walls.

As he stumbled past a row of sarcophagi set in the wall, a paw reached out and took a swipe at him. King spun round – someone lit a torch and he saw a dozen cats climb from their dry stone perches. The breeze he had heard came from these yawning creatures. Their hair was spiked or sprayed blue, their clothes sagging and torn, with pins through their whiskers or ears. Warren punched him playfully in the shoulder; and Sal sniggered behind him.

'Here's the new cub, boss.' A face emerged from the gloom. King's eyes were fast becoming accustomed to the crypt, picking out details as surely as his nose selected the tell tale scents of aggressive males. Samson didn't look so threatening; King had heard many stories of the gang lord's lack of compassion and unsociable eating habits. His face was a mass of soft fur; in fact Samson looked quite cuddly.

'Pleased to meet you.' Samson's spine was twisted into a sharp arch, his vertebrae brittle with age and angry combat. He was flanked by Warren and Sal.

'Is it my imagination, or did this little pip just squeak?' snarled Warren, edging closer.

'Squeak when you're spoken to, runt.'

Samson glowered at Warren, who shut up in an instant. King realised how Samson had gained his fearsome reputation as soon as the big cat opened his mouth and showed a row of barbed wire teeth.

'You're the King, right? You got delusions of grandeur?'

'It's my name,' the kitten blinked.

'I've been hearing bad things about you,' Samson continued, sounding deadly serious. 'Some say you're a cop lover.'

'That ain't true.'

'Others say you hang round with the wrong crowd. I know how easy it is to get an undeserved rep. Look at me. When I started out, I wasn't so big. Happened to bump off a mouse. Things got exaggerated. Before I know it, one consonantal shift leads to another and I've polished off a tram load of mooses. I'm respected. Since then, of course, I've had to live up to that reputation. It ain't easy, this responsibility. But you wouldn't know about that, would you? If your dad wasn't who he is (or what he is), I wouldn't waste time on you. But you got a good pedigree. So you're a Wildcat now. How's it feel?'

'Gives me a sense of power. I think maybe it'll get me some respect for once in my life.'

The Wildcats looked at each other. This was the wrong thing to say. They made it a rule never to think in their leader's presence.

'I like you, King. You're all right for a new kit.'

'Are you going to swear me in or something?' King asked with an innocent face. Sal rolled his eyes and squatted down with his friends in a corner of the crypt. A lemon-faced tom removed a small paper-wrapped package from his jacket, giving it to Samson with great reverence. Samson knelt down with the other Wildcats, and bade King do the same.

Sal brought a bowl from behind one of the crypt's makeshift sculptures. Samson emptied the contents of the paper bag onto his hefty right paw and crumbled them into the bowl. He inhaled deeply, then passed the bowl to King kneeling next to him. He hesitated for a moment.

'Go on, take the nip.'

Usually he didn't touch the stuff. Too easy to drop your guard once you were under its influence. But he didn't want to offend Samson or seem like a sap. As the cats breathed in the fumes they loosened up, and Samson became more open towards King.

'Leading this gang of brutes ain't a job anyone would ask for, bucko.' King wished he had a tape recorder. 'Most of the time they don't want a boss. It's only some kinda crowd instinct that keeps 'em under my pads. They could turn at any moment – any one of 'em could stab me in the back (or the front, come to think of it – traitors are none too particular as a rule) or turn in their colours and leave.'

'Join the Clutes?' The bowl had been passed round the cats, back to King who took a few grains of catnip and sucked them into his mouth. He could feel the world moving beneath his feet, but he seemed to be suspended in a bubble of happy stasis. He could take on the world.

'Run with the enemy? Heck no! That's something a Wildcat would never do. Pride in our colours, that's another thing that keeps us together. Desertion's one thing, but joining the enemy's never been an option. Not so long as there've been gangs in the Doghouse. You got a lot to learn, King.'

'Who's gonna teach me?'

'I am.' Samson gave a rare, toothsome smile. 'Go join yer buddies. This afternoon, you can come walkabout with me. Okay?'

King followed Samson out of the crypt. He couldn't feel his hind paws. Before he could catch up to the leader, Samson had disappeared through the tall white gates. The nip was taking effect on the Wildcats and with their leader gone there was nothing to restrain them. Some of the younger gang members were coughing up hairballs, defecating on gravestones, puking or breaking wind. The older cats made sexist jokes, scrawled graffiti across the crypt, before running out of energy – rolling on the chill ground, their heads spinning on nip. The drug made them feel hot, so they muddied themselves to cool down, enjoying the sensation of moist grave dirt on their bellies.

Warren spun King round, a stupid grin on his face.

'You can come walkabout with me,' Warren mimicked, making his friends laugh. They'd followed him out of the crypt, eager to see the fight that was due to develop.

'I don't want any bad business, fellas.' The kitten tried to back away but Warren held him firm.

'You think you can come in here and replace me, little one?' King broke free from his rival's grip and adopted a threatening stance – back arched, fur raised in an attempt to make himself look bigger, mouth open in a jagged hiss.

The Wildcats closed in. Sal blocked off any escape through the gates, but King had no intention of bolting.

'The King is dead.' Warren attacked.

THE BISHOP STRETCHED HIS limbs across the plush carpet that furnished his stately office. He was reclining beside his granite desk, dragged from the northern plains by willing followers of the goddess Bastet. The cylindrical office had a view unparalleled throughout the city, placed as it was at the summit of the Great Temple, overlooking the centre of Bast.

The Bishop had been joined by his cohort, Father Boris, and a favoured old priest called Kafel. All three bore the prized velvet plumage of purple fur that denoted their righteousness.

'Do the books not say that a chief cannot become a true leader until his people grow to love him?' Boris offered, quoting from his favourite holy rite.

'No one loves this cat.' The Bishop got up, smoothing down his gold-leafed robes with demure precision.

'That's what I mean.'

'Not even his own parents.' The Bishop paced towards Kafel, who lounged in a corner.

'I believe that his mother resents him.' Boris folded his arms, recalling a slice of juicy gossip he'd heard during confession.

'What's going on here? Is this Mayor such a demon that we cannot speak his name?'

'The walls have ears, Brother Kafel.'

'I don't care.' Kafel bounced around the room singing, 'Otto, Otto, Otto, Otto...' The Bishop made hushing noises at him.

'Such a fine voice,' Boris smirked.

'Like an angel. If only his morals were as pure.' The Bishop shrugged. Kafel was a priest, after all. Matters of the soul were more his field; socially moral considerations rarely entered his mind.

'We need that money, Kafel. We've grown used to these earthly comforts...'

'In other words, we got a good scam going and it'd be a shame to give up the holy ghost now?'

'We must appeal to the Mayor,' Father Boris suggested.

'He is not a pious lion,' the Bishop pointed out.

'He's a politician.'

'Then we must be politicians too.' The Bishop washed his head with the back of a paw. 'Meet with the Mayor. Sound him out. Appeal to his better nature, if he has such a thing. And Kafel –'

'Yes, Bishop?'

'Discover his weaknesses. With my blessing.' Kafel left the office hurriedly, the repercussions of his mission echoing through his mind as surely as the sound of his pawsteps. They bounced off the walls as he descended a dizzying spiral staircase. He didn't particularly like the Church or his brethren, but he enjoyed the power he assumed when he donned a priestly robe. If he completed this particular mission with aplomb, he would be one step nearer to bishophood.

King wasn't sure how he'd ended up flat on his back on an

overgrown grave, and for a moment he tried to convince himself that he should stay there. Warren was standing above him, twice the size, jaws slavering, crazed with the success of his first blow. There was no time for him to rest.

With one flick of his tail he was up, snarling at Warren, claws jutting forward to form offensive weapons. The muscles in King's hind legs packed up like springs and he leaped forward with a spin. Instead of raking at his opponent, he used stabbing motions, catching his claws in Warren's chest. Surprise froze the bully for a moment, colder than frost before he stepped back, folding a forelimb to staunch the wounds. King opened his jaws to go for Warren's throat, but he never got close enough for the kill.

Snatched bodily away from his opponent, he was lifted away by the other Wildcats. A sizeable crowd had gathered during the brief skirmish. They were going to tear him to bits.

Instead a giggling cheer erupted from the crowd, and he was congratulated on his bravado. Now King was really one of the gang. He saw the twisted tail of Warren as the loser loped back into the crypt; let him lick his wounds. King would have to watch his back, but as a resident of the Doghouse he was used to that.

By the time the gang had eaten, drunk and swapped stories of empty-headed daring, the sun was beginning to set. King wondered whether Samson would be true to his word, and take him on a tour round Wildcat territory.

'You won't be a fully fledged member of our gang until tomorrow,' Sal mewed in King's ear.

'Why not? What's happening then?'

A scrawny cat not much older than King leaped up, fist

raised. 'There's gonna be a rumble!' His friends yelled their approval.

'A rumble? With the Clutes?' His head swung from side to side, eyes rounded.

'No, with the MMA,' Sal replied sarcastically. 'Of course with the Clutes!'

'Where?'

Before the scrawny cat could answer, a heavy shadow fell over King. It belonged to Samson, who had returned with more food for his troops.

'You ready for the walkabout?' he asked, not caring whether King answered. The newcomer would go with Samson. There would be no argument.

The central area of the Doghouse was a maze of narrow streets, with folk lying in sun patched porches or milling about seeking lunch. A typewriter clattered as some housewife wrote an elaborate diary in her front garden. Cats squatted on the makeshift pavements, scarred or crippled from constant territorial spats. One small wretch, used to being mugged or abused, barely put up resistance as he was picked on by two stronger toms. They started teasing by batting him with their rolled-up paws, then set in with their teeth and hind claws. The small cat squealed, trying to turn and expose his belly in surrender. He wasn't given the chance.

It took Samson a matter of seconds to reach the fight. King was amazed that an animal of such bulk could move so fast. Samson sank his teeth into one bully's neck, snatching him off the victim and swinging him from side to side, a bestial yell emitted between mouthfuls of fur. King was about to help but his new boss seemed to be handling things neatly. Jaws still clamped round one tom's neck, he grasped the other in a huge right fist and tugged him away, expelling him into the gutter.

While Samson disposed of the yobs, King helped the shaking victim upright.

'Why did they do it?' asked King, wide eyed.

'I was on the wrong part of the street.' The small cat disappeared, too shame-faced to wait and thank his saviour. Without batting an eyelid, Samson motioned King to follow him as he continued his stroll down the street.

Fishmonger stalls were lined up at intervals along the way, enjoying constant trade from ever-hungry patrons. Samson passed them all by until he reached a hardware shop.

'First stop,' he said in low rumbling tones. He halted at the shop window, instantly recognised by the family inside.

Samson slipped the shopkeeper an envelope, putting a smile on the old cat's face. 'For the kits,' the gang leader explained, and King's respect for him increased.

'Come and see how the new cub's getting on,' said the shopkeeper, and before Samson could decline his wife had brought out a tiny kitten wrapped in swaddling. Its fluffed face was puckered in hunger, beady eyes questing from side to side. Samson looked embarrassed as he sniffed its forehead.

'Lovely.' Samson passed the bundle to its mother, and making their apologies, he and King left as quickly as politeness would allow.

'Have you ever met Tufano?' King looked up at Samson.

'Sure, lotsa times – for sit downs, pacts, throwing down gauntlets, declarations of war...' the boss rubbed his hoary chin.

'He doesn't look like a big talker.'

'Don't let appearances deceive you.' He faced a torrent of well wishers – tough toms shook paws with the leader, ugly queens screamed declarations of love and kittens begged for his autograph. Samson stopped to acknowledge every one of them, and King decided that this was the secret of his success. He was willing to give the time of day to his people.

'Tufano's chatty when you get to know him. Talks about his music. He loves hip-hop. Wanted to be a rap star when he was a kitten.'

'I heard he managed Suspicious Package for a while.'

'Maybe he did. He's fat enough. You've gotta be a fat cat if you're a record producer. Ain't that right? Yeah, that's right.' A local official in a heavy green suit slipped a bundle of notes into Samson's paw, hardly pausing as he vanished in the other direction. The gang leader pocketed the cash without counting it.

'So Tufano's your friend then?'

'No. My mortal enemy. The yang to my personal and professional yin.' Samson allowed himself a wry smile. 'Not my friend.'

'Could you ever have made friends with him, Samson?'

'Only to get close enough to kill him.'

'So that's why you're meeting with him?'

'No. I wouldn't get my paws dirty like that. Not when there's a third party more than willing to do the job.'

'Third party?'

'Secret.' Samson put a purpled pad to his lips. 'They got their own reasons. I don't ask questions.'

In a cluttered square stood an old totem pole, vestige of some pagan religion from before the birth of the Bastet cult.

Locals used it as a stropping post, dragging their claws down the wood in leisurely strokes to clean their barbs, rid their claws of old sheaths, shedding their skins like a snake. It also served as an opportunity to mark the territory with their scent. Samson clamped a paw around the pole, his pads almost covering its girth.

'Is this where we're headed?' King declined to join his boss. Samson said nothing, content to scratch at the pole, but took the time to point at a grain silo at the far side of the square.

There was no grain in the whitewashed silo. Samson opened a shutter on one side of the silo and led his charge inside. They were struck by the stench of rotting flesh. The silo contained something very dead.

'This is a little secret I can let you in on. Nice to widen your mind now and again, isn't it?' They stepped deep inside the silo, the dark interior soaking up all light from the torch that Samson provided. 'Take a look round.' On a bed of down, King saw a mound of bird carcasses, necks torn, the blood drained from their tiny bodies. 'My tributes.'

Samson closed the shutter behind him. King wasn't sure how his boss had kept this carnage a secret, deep in the heart of the Doghouse. A combination of fear and apathy had kept curious cats at bay. He understood why Samson was respected by the local yokels.

'Where's the rumble?' King started to sift through the corpses, his nostrils twitching at the harsh smell. All the birds had been carefully killed so that as much of their bodies had been preserved as possible. Trophies laid at the feet of the Doghouse Don.

'Itching for a fight? You'll be told where to go. Down on the river bank somewhere.'

'I'll be there.'

'I don't know what started all this,' Samson admitted, 'but I want to see an end to it.'

There was something beyond the mound of dead birds, lying in the darkest recesses of the silo.

'Surely killing the Clute leader will make things worse?'

'Don't know. Gotta do something.'

King had reached the back of the silo, something damp underfoot. As Samson opened the shutter to leave, the kitten found himself standing amongst the blanched eyes of a hundred lifeless cats and dogs, with rival gangs or rival scruples. The Don nudged one of the bodies into a deep vat full of greasy fur, long rubbery tails and beady eyes. It was feeding time for his tame rats.

'They're crafty little beggars,' the proud owner explained, 'they'd escape from their pit given half the chance. That's why I have to keep this place clammed up tight.'

'They're your secret weapon?'

'No. There are worse creatures visiting this city.' The rats had already finished the dead cat, leaving dirty white bones for their babies. 'Now you know, little one,' said Samson with a wink, 'why it's important to tow the line with me.' King stumbled back into daylight, his boss' forelimb wrapped round his shoulder. He felt cold.

II

If you were my world
It would never spin on its axis
If you were my dream
I'd remember nothing on waking
If you were my one true love
I'd be lying to myself
If we fit like paw in glove
Those mitts wouldn't fit in court.

If you were my all
My realm of experience would be tiny
If you were my better half
It would be the one without the wit
If you were my muse
I wouldn't write a line
If you were my boss
I'd have to resign.

If we were an item
The bulletin board would be bare
If we tied the knot
It would unravel like a conjuror's string
If you were the brains
You'd still have to supply the brawn
If this was a game
You'd break the rules like I break balls.

If we were close
I'd have bad breath, you'd shut my mouth
If we had a kid
He'd end up lonely, miss us both
Two of a kind
The kind most cats can do without
Both in two minds
That's what a couple's all about.

LOVE STUNG
MIMI MIMU

Julius' house was a two-tone tomb of a building, with its frosted glass windows and four walls. The walls had been an important selling point when he'd bought the house, reasoning that it would be difficult to work there with a continuous draught blowing through. Four-walled houses were considered quirky, unnecessary, and expensive. Three sufficed for the average home owner, undemanding and often out on the prowl.

The interior was as comfortable as any bachelor's home. The place needed redecorating – paper peeled itself from the dining room walls – and furniture was sparse and functional. A low-level table for serving food; a cushioned chair for relaxing. In the study was a drawing board, a coalscuttle, piles of books and tapes.

A poster of Julius' favourite singer, the sultry caterwauler Mimi Mimu, hid a damp patch in the living room. A pair of red velvet curtains were fat with a fresh draught. Julius watched them rustle as he pulled his own fur out with his teeth, frustrated and listless. He slapped a pile of notes down on his coffee table, streaked with furniture polish.

He had no story and little to go on; he couldn't tell the readers of the *Post* anything that they didn't know already from Mick's pieces on the Wildcats. King was the key – through him Julius would be able to meet Samson, get inside the leader's head. He felt he didn't really understand the situation in the Doghouse, or the motivation behind the mayhem that occurred there. An excuse to get to know Moira better, perhaps. Julius cursed his deceit. Camilla, his love, would be home soon and he would feel better. Less lonely.

He'd seen her for the first time when she was on heat, surrounded by a group of slavering toms. In civilised society, wealth and position carried more clout than physical strength. He hadn't had to fight for her. But he enjoyed fighting. The fireplace glowed amber, lining the hearth with its ambiguous signal. Potted plants crisped towards the night stand, hungry for sun. He pulled out a filofax chunked with details of old friends who never called, added the names of King and Moira. He coded her as 'M', in case Camilla chanced to see it.

I've got to give Morris a story or I'm out of the game. He'll think I can't cut it any more. Julius stepped over to a black bookcase which gave a camp performance, leaning slightly to the left, ready to collapse at any moment. He picked up a fresh notepad and squatted with it on his wood-tiled floor.

He began to write about the deprivation he'd seen on the other side of the river, of the paranoia that lurked in every street. Neighbours would defend their homes with tooth and law, and cubs foolhardy enough to leave themselves open to attack could lose their lives under a tree on a public road. He wrote about how he had felt when he'd come across the products of the latest skirmish, the unhappy thrill he'd experienced seeing a white cat face down in its own grue.

The floor was varnished with crumbs, soups and spilled coffee. The leftovers from Sunday lunch had created a grain all their own. He threw his notebook on top of the radiator that idled in one corner, staring out of the window, sulking. It refused to work and would only talk to electricians.

Julius switched on his wireless, hoping for some soothing tunes. Instead he got Suspicious Package shouting full-blast at him in their vociferous monotone.

```
TV spinning lies
Bringing up kids with cartoon apron strings
Their spines warp under its wings
No need for inkwells, slate or chalks
When they've got a duck that talks
```

He couldn't go to bed, didn't like to sleep alone. But as the moon began to sink and bronze in preparation for another dawn, he curled up on the tiles, nose tucked under tail; his lids shuttered closed involuntarily. He dreamed of the river, and of shattered glass ships.

12

WARREN AND SAL BUST into King's place without a knock. He was fast asleep when they woke him, riled him, dragged him into the street with the rind still in his eyes. He rubbed his peepers clean and blinked at the early morning sun, barely risen above the prefabricated rooftops of Miro Street. The orb blinked back, nudged by greying clouds, a pawn in the game of the gods.

'Up and at 'em, sleepy head,' squealed Sal, snatching King by one arm while Warren clung to the other. 'The battle commences an' all that.'

King had tried to forget all about the rumble. He had expected to be left behind, miss out on the excitement, and he certainly didn't want to be fighting for his life so early in the morning. That seemed uncivilised to him.

Throughout the three cats' trip to the river bank, Warren said nothing and Sal said too much – nattering on about the gang members he didn't like, the ones he did like but steered well clear of for fear of losing an appendage, and the ones to watch out for during the fight.

'You'll learn a trick or two, new boy. Stick with the warriors, you can't go far wrong, that's what I says.' Sal was okay in King's book, but the company he kept left a lot to be desired. Warren held a permanent snarl on his face for King's benefit – or in practice for the skirmish to come. He could understand why Sal hung around with the larger cat, though; without the constant protection, the snivelling tabby would become a minute's worth of mincemeat.

A secluded part of the bank formed the battlefield for the day; apart from a few patches of grass and discarded trash, there was no sign of life. Few locals would come this close to the water and it had never formed part of a police cat's beat. Perfect for a little death and disorder, the barren earth was valuable only as a battleground.

A rumble singles down to one thing – which gang puts the frighteners on its rival first. Who looks the biggest, the deadliest, the most ferocious. Chances are, one gang'll back down, call for a truce or turn tail and run. Whatever option they take, they're done for. As soon as the Clutes saw a weakness in the Wildcat ranks – a slight hesitation, a step backwards, an unfamiliarity with the turf – they attacked, in a sea of erect whiskers and thrashing tails.

King looked from side to side. Warren screamed and raged as he threw himself into a throng of mottled bodies. Sal tagged along as if lost without his friend. King's group seemed to be dispersing around him; some had already bolted. He adjusted his black bandanna and faced the onslaught: Twenty berserk tomcats bounding towards him, teeth bared, claws unsheathed. Wildcats milled around, feeling exposed; King coiled up his hind legs, defending his moon white abdomen.

There was a flash of red and a Clute pulled its claw from King's face. The kitten squealed, falling backward, driving his hindpaws into the Clute's thigh. The Clute was thrust over King's head and landed with a neck-shattering crunch. King grappled with a second Clute, spitting in the enemy's eyes, emitting a cautionary growl. The Wildcats were already routed and King was forced back into the undergrowth. He drew a claw across the Clute's lips, gashing open the face and felling another opponent. There were too many of them; King's fellow gang members were being punched and kicked, rolling on the ground, some exposing their bellies in submission.

Torn ear, blind running – no thought for personal safety, piling into the furry throng. There's screaming, high-pitched, tortured enough to freeze your veins. Hair and whiskers fly through the air in a lawnmower flurry; a tail's wrapped around someone's neck, an emerald eye is plucked from its socket and gets ruined underfoot. King's frozen. He remembers cowering in the Beaverbank, his perceived failure; he doesn't want to live his life in fear, like his father. You mussed up, but you're still alive. He comes to his senses in time to fend off an attacker.

There's a cracking sound like a wounded branch inside his body. A warm sensation spreads across the left side of his chest. The Clute is jamming his elbow into the broken rib, applying as much pressure as he can muster. But in his sadism he's left his throat vulnerable to a pair of razor sharp teeth. King goes for the kill, rips at the Clute's jugular, then staggers away clutching his side. The warmth has become a hot ache. He feels suddenly fatigued. He stumbles into the trees, looking for something to lean against. There's no peace.

13

'HEY, DO YOU THINK Mick was scared of heights? I heard he didn't know how to swim. That was a pretty dodgy backstroke he was doing. They say cats and water don't mix.' Roy had the whole office on his side. His fellow journalists were curled up on their cushions, paws resting on typewriters, listening to him attentively. Their fur was unkempt – they were always under duress and had scant time for grooming. They made a captive audience for the resident clown. He'd always been irreverent; he found that sort of humour suited his cynical colleagues. 'He was looking a bit down in the mouth that day. Needed jollying up. Obviously didn't get cheered up enough –' Roy's colleagues had stopped laughing. He heard a cat approach and swallowed hard. He was in big trouble.

Roy turned to see Julius standing behind him, forelimbs folded. His tail twitched viciously from side to side. As was always the case when he was in a sticky situation, Roy tried to talk his way out.

'Healthy office humour, old chum. No hard feelings, eh?' *Not like Mick must have had when he hit the water*, Roy thought to himself, unable to resist a dry chuckle. Julius slung his transcribed article onto the news desk, then walked over to the notice board with a scowl. None of the bulletins on the board were pertinent to him, except the clipping pinned in the centre. His best friend's obituary.

Mick McClough, winner of two bronze journalism awards, committed suicide this week.

He joined the *Post* as a young cub, bearing great responsibility at a very early age. His first duties included sourcing archive information for reporters, and interviewing people in the streets to beef up back page articles. It took him years to earn his reporter's wings but once he gained them, he used his new role to make readers more aware of the plight of discontented cats everywhere. His stories covered such topics as discrimination between different breeds, sexism in the workplace, and the violence of the ghettos – subjects that some fellow reporters took pains to avoid.

Mick turned down the post of deputy editor three times, preferring instead to remain at his news desk. He asked for no praise, but has received much since his untimely death.

The reasons behind Mick's abrupt suicide remain a mystery. He will be missed.

ROY FURY

Julius lifted a shaking paw to rip the clipping from its yellow beaded hook, but was interrupted by a despairing cry from Morris.

'Where's the story?' the editor clutched Julius' Wildcat article in his fist. 'I hire you boys 'cos you know how to write. Allegedly. I don't wanna be wasting my time editing all day. I got better things to do with my time.' *Like making bigoted pleas to readers in overblown articles about teenaged milk abuse and the inherent dangers of poor litter tray hygiene.*

'If you don't like it,' Julius lowered his voice as he approached, 'spike it.' Morris screwed up the story and slung it in his waste paper basket. Julius controlled his temper and turned to the reason why he'd come into work that day. 'Have you heard from Camilla?'

'I haven't spoken to her since she left.'

'But where did she leave *to?*' Julius leaned his forepaws on Morris' desk and tilted his face close to the editor's.

'North.'

'North? Is that all you're gonna tell me? My girlfriend's out there, sleeping with who knows whom who knows where, and you get all monosyllabic with me. You trying to mess with my blood pressure, Morris? 'Cos you're succeeding in spades.'

Roy and his colleagues were entranced. Only Julius would dare stand up to the office monster.

'I'm surprised you're even here to ask me such questions, Julius. How did you build up the energy to get out of bed this morning?'

'How did you build up the strength?' There was an audible intake of breath around the room. 'Inquisitiveness got me up this morning. Curiosity. Unanswered questions. I am an investigative journalist.'

'Oh, are you now?' Morris' mock tone changed sharply. 'How dare you give me grief? I've chewed up and spat out more has been hacks like you than you've had hot scoops.

Now go and earn your crust. Go on, I'm glad to see the back of you. No skiving neither.'

Julius left the editor's desk, fuming. Morris called after him: 'If you can't keep a leash on your girlfriend, don't expect us to help!'

Julius' colleagues laughed, more to release the tension in the room than to spite the reporter. But their giggles rang in Julius' ears long after he'd left the building.

'Copy!' Morris shouted, blowing off steam. He sent one of the cub reporters to prod an elderly cat awake. Some of the older or cockier cats would take naps when they needed them, so Morris had issued his copy boys with pointed sticks. The wheezing hack blinked his eyes awake in a slow motion daze.

'You missed a treat there.' said Roy. 'Won't be seeing Julius around here for a while. I know him. Whenever he's told off, he goes and sulks for a while.' Roy's mouth clamped shut as Morris shouted across the office:

'I think you've mewled enough for one day, my lad. Get back to your millstone.'

'Sure, sure.' Roy winked at the old cat and loped back to his desk. He grabbed a cake from the food trolley which sharked constantly around the office. He had another obituary to prepare.

14

I'm no preacher. I spin my discs and take no risks, though I do like to put a modicum of thought-provoking comment into my spiel. So here goes.

A wise Siamese once said: 'A cat is like a lick of flame. Tend to it, and it will bring you light and warmth; abuse it, and it could cause you serious injury.'

So be good to your neighbours tonight, to the tabby commuters on their way home from work, the ginger toms givin' it laldy down the pub, the alley cats scavenging trash, beggin' for loose fish.

Ain't we all cats, deep down? Don't we all got fur and whiskers? When we're hungry do we not mew? When we're stepped on, do we not we spit? When we fall, don't we land on all fours – most of the time?

CENTRAL CHANNEL RADIO BROADCAST
DJ SCRATCH

This was no fun any more. The cats' blood was up, they had become increasingly frenzied and a small group refused to stop fighting. Caught in the middle, King had grown tired. Paws outstretched, claws half-sheathed, inner eyelids sealed to cut off the horror – his limbs were sore with exertion. A shallow swamp of blood lapped against shredded tunics, a tide influenced by the quake of passing traffic. Useless leather armour plates were used as shields or petty bludgeons. King saw teeth locked ownerless in a Wildcat's shoulder. He felt defenceless, sick and lonely. He wanted to retire to lick his wounds but the cats that fought around him formed a tight net of writhing fur. *This is stupid.* One of the Clutes rushed towards him, brandishing a makeshift spear that had once been a scaffolding pipe. King tried to back up – there was no room to retreat. Weak and resolved to death, he allowed himself to fall backwards onto his haunches. His attacker brought the spear up to ram into his gullet; for the first and only time in his life, King closed his eyes and prayed to Bastet.

All that exercise, all that fasting, those months wasted weight-watching. Still Moira's stomach sagged, jellying from side to side when she walked. She looked a state. Fur unkempt, eyes bloodshot, whiskers crinkled. She'd read countless magazines full of the most up-to-date grooming tips but she still couldn't look like a respectable lady. She seemed destined always to look like she'd just got out of her basket, ungroomed and unsightly.

The lads she courted didn't agree, said she was tops. The sillier ones told her she was skinny as a chicken. They only had one thing on their minds, and that one thing always led to another. She'd made up her mind at an early age: she was plain.

She had a tendency to let herself go, especially during the winter. It was too cold to go outside and so gloomy that she ate to cheer herself up. Brightly coloured fondants and ice cream helped to balance out the greyness; her body suffered as a result. So much inactivity, so little healthy food that she had become a blob. Not obese, but blobby all the same.

A book lay half-opened on the floor, hardly sniffed. Pulp nonsense, of course, but the author was obviously in touch with his female side. When she'd finished feeling sorry for herself, Moira picked up the book and ran her nose along the pages, breathing in the yarn.

No good. She needed to know what had happened to her brother. He'd got into scrapes before, come home wounded and tearful. Sworn he'd never do it again. King seemed to have a knack for attracting violence, and Moira had heard about the rumble on the riverbank that afternoon. The gang fights were escalating in their frequency, more and more cats lost in the bloody shuffle. She tried to convince herself that he wouldn't be foolish enough to get roped into something so senseless.

Moira had raised her younger brother, named him, protected him, washed him. With the minimum of help from Pa, she'd taught him how to hunt and fight, ready for the day when she'd become fertile. These days, it was his duty to provide for her while she courted suitors by the cartload.

I wish. I'm going to end up an old maid. The youngest old maid in the Doghouse.

Her brother could look after himself, she'd made sure of that. When he was very small, she and Pa had thrown him in the river to sink or swim. He had survived, paddled back to the shore, hadn't spoken to her for days. He'd accepted her food readily enough, though. He'd always been endearing – her feelings towards him were almost maternal – and enjoyed the company of plenty of friends. Okay, his strange father put the more narrow-minded neighbours off from visiting the house, but King had made friends with the underdogs, non-achievers and lame-duck slackers that filled the area. Although the rest of the family – grandparents, uncles, cousins and bastard aunts – were dotted around the furthest corners of the community, they still came to see King at regular intervals, stroking his fur, making cooing noises as if he was still a newborn cub. He hated that.

Moira didn't give a flying forkhandle. The only cat she cared about was herself; she'd become hard, unsentimental. No sense getting attached to a sibling when they might pop their clogs on any given day. She'd begun to mourn the day King was born. With that responsibility out of the way, Moira could concentrate on achieving her own happiness – once she was content, she could afford the luxury of worrying about others.

Was Julius someone who could bring her that contentment? If the book was anything to go by, it was a possibility. Trust your senses, Moira. He was certainly a looker – not as attractive as herself, of course, but still… she wondered when she'd see him again. Pretty soon, she hoped.

Poring over the book again, she inhaled its musty scents. She hadn't taken the trouble to sniff at a book for such a long time. Quite relaxing. Perhaps it had some secrets to reveal:

Offspring are a mystery, a misery and a miracle. They bring fulfilment and tragedy. They age you and rejuvenate you all at once.

Tiger had never sought fatherhood; it had found

him. In his crimefighting days he would act as
an idol for cats everywhere, a good (if violent)
example to them all. When they saw him hogging
headlines or accepting awards, they knew what a
good guy was. The closest Straight had got to
cubs was a school talk or a treetop rescue. Now
he was more likely to be found changing a nappy
than making the world a better place.

He'd been amazed when his wife had given birth.
It had been the most otherworldly, disgusting
sight of his life. She'd asked for some privacy,
but Tiger had stuck with her till the last cub
had emerged. He hated to see his wife go through
such discomfort, with a half-hour's wait between
each birth.

Moira's book was interrupted by the arrival of the author in
her hallway. He mewled to her, and she jumped up to greet
him.

'Julius?' she smiled warmly.

'We're going to get your brother.'

'You know where he is?' Moira was already dragging her
scarf from a coathook.

'The Wildcats have been attacked. On the riverbank.' The
writer's eyes shone like bright round buttons. 'Cops are on their
way.'

'What about King?' They rushed out of the house.

'I think he might be in trouble again.'

The spear stopped within an inch of King's left eye. The
young cat had forgotten to breathe, opened his mouth for a
gulp of stenched air. Samson wrapped his paws round the haft
of the spear and drove the hilt into the Clute's soft stomach.

The Clute fell to its knees, facing King, flapped like a suffocating guppy. Wrapping both paws together, Samson slammed his fists against the Clute's temple, snapping the head back at an unnatural angle.

'We're going,' said Samson, offering a paw to his protégé. King didn't flinch. 'We're moving out.'

Questing for wounded, Samson dragged King through a horde of brawling cats, swatting any offenders who dared approach him. Most of the Clutes gave him a wide berth. The Wildcats used the swathe their leader cut as a diversion that allowed them to beat back the Clutes. The rumble was almost done.

Nursing his scattered ribs, King allowed himself to be taken away from the riverbank to a large warehouse on the outskirts of the Doghouse. Blood swimming before his eyes, he saw an imposing structure with Wildcat colours pinned to the walls; he could smell scent-messages warning any passers-by that this was the gang's HQ.

Samson deposited him near the entrance. 'You'll be safe here,' he said gently. The cub mewled softly, his strength already returning. He stood up, leaning against a wall, trying to find the wherewithal to thank his leader.

'Why were – the fighting. What caused it?'

'For fun, I suppose.' Samson shrugged. 'A bit of a giggle. See ya later, King.' Samson could see the young cat hadn't quite got the message. He changed his tone, added a little more menace. 'See ya later, King.'

Samson entered the warehouse, slamming a dull metal shutter down in King's face. It clamped shut with an iron lung wheeze. King could hear muffled voices in the room beyond, so he gathered his strength and stumbled round the building looking for another way in.

Before she'd left to seek her fortune in the North, King's mother hadn't given much advice. She'd abandoned him to fend for himself after a matter of months – didn't believe in moggycoddling her young. She was part of the old school that favoured leaving cubs to survive on their own four paws at the earliest possible stage.

She had offered her sons and daughters one piece of advice. 'Don't get curious,' she'd said in her sour, matronly tone. He remembered her warmth, the smell of her nipples and those three particular words. That was all he missed.

Out of a litter of six, only he and Moira had survived. Two had died shortly after birth, discarded by mum as weaklings and rejects; students in a Bast back alley had kicked another to death; the fourth had got herself killed in a Clute initiation ceremony.

The slate walls held one small window – more of an aperture really – on the east side of the building, letting some light into the Wildcat headquarters. King stacked a couple of crates up to make a crude ladder. If he stood on the tips of his pads, he could keek through.

He had little for Julius. He'd promised the reporter a fat story with plenty of gossip, ghetto adventures to amuse the hoi-polloi across the river. He felt he knew Samson well now, and was beginning to gain his trust. But as for the big cat's plans – little to report.

He looked up to Julius, cherished his support. King wanted to impress him. So he peered deep into the warehouse, catching the shadows of four occupants. Three had large ears and thick whiskers. The fourth was obviously Samson:

'You're lying.' The big cat sat back on a dusty cushion, sounding weary.

'We'll do it. But you know what we want.' One of the big ears, this one was hoarse, voice as deep as a pit in a chasm.

'It'll cost ya,' ventured a second big ears in a languorous growl.

'He's got to be taught a lesson.' The first big ears again. 'Getting too big for his size eights.'

King wished he'd stacked the crates beneath him in a more sturdy fashion. Desperate to get a closer look at the guests within, he began to teeter.

'We'll do more than teach him a lesson,' a third big ears piped up. 'We're talking about a masterclass here.'

King tottered, trying to see more. But Samson's guests remained in shadow.

'Don't overstep the mark,' the big cat was saying, trying to assert some authority.

'We'll overstep whatever we want.'

'You want him dead as much as we do,' the deeper voice giggled. 'With the Clutes leaderless they'll be running round in a blind panic.'

'Little minnows swallowed up by bigger fish...' the third guest chuckled.

'Before you know it everyone'll wanna be a Wildcat.'

'Eating out of your paw.'

The guests turned, the noon light striking them at last. What King saw made him sick with surprise. He allowed himself to fall and ran towards the riverbank, but he'd been heard. Not daring to look back, he picked up the sound of the shutter snapping open and the noise of pursuit. They were running faster than him. All three of them, come to snatch him before he could tell anyone what he had seen.

King pushed his punished body to its limits, hurrying past derelict huts and cracked walls. Concrete twisted like a kaleidoscope past the corner of his eye. He could hear a sand barge chugging up ahead. If he could make it to the river – snarling cutting at the air behind him – if he could make it that far, catch the barge captain's attention...

Blood coughed from his gullet as he was knocked onto his stomach. His ribs felt strange, as if they were laced at the wrong angle. His face was slammed into the dirt; damp dirt. He was almost at the bank. Water rushed by in front of him. He tried to pull himself away from whoever was pinning him down but instead he was dragged from side to side like a puppet. With a strength and ferocity he had never felt before, his attackers were tearing him apart.

Where was Julius?

King crawled forward. He could taste the saline filth of river water on his lips. A paw split his stomach like a can opener and began to rip out his guts. Then nothing but the fading clump of his assailants as they scattered.

They've left me for dead. King rolled into the river, allowing the current to carry him away from the nightmare. He didn't get far, snared by a fallen branch a hundred metres downstream. He was fished out by Julius and Moira half an hour later, the water around him turning to rust.

'You little idiot,' said Julius, shaking his head slowly. He took a scrunched length of black cloth from the youngster's outstretched paw.

'Gonna be a war,' said King, breath escaping from his

punctured lungs. Julius hunched down close to hear the kitten speak. 'It was horrible... they were horrible... they're going to finish Tufano.'

Julius held him as he fought for breath, unable to suck in another gasp. He died with a flutter of whiskers and a lash of his tail, Julius nuzzling him tenderly. Another friend gone. He wailed, not for King, not for Mick, but for himself. What'd he done to deserve a life of misery? He couldn't deal with the pain. He turned to Moira, his heart growing cold with grief.

'What do we do now?' he asked, his voice breaking.

'We throw a party.'

15

THE CITY CREATED A heat trap, the surrounding skyscrapers acting like huge breeze blocks protecting the citizens from the gales beyond. Conditioning fans the size of a ship's propellers blew cool air across the streets, lest the cats fall asleep in a sunpatch halfway to work. When the fans failed or the summer was at its height, the cats' fur matted with sweat and they spent more time washing themselves than working at their desks. Some blamed the city builders for poor planning; others were happy to be sheltered from the harsh winds outside Bast. The city was older than history; no one knew who'd built it. But although it had been built to last, a large proportion of the municipal budget was spent on repairs.

The heat didn't bother Kafel, low high priest of the city's favourite religion, who had donned an ornate flowing robe befitting his order. He moved in a stately fashion through the Council entranceway; as the gown touched the floor and his hind paws could not be seen he appeared to glide past the leopard guards. They bowed their heads in deference to the priest, but never took their eyes off him.

Kafel dodged potted plants, leather-padded chairs and a marble bust of Otto's mother, hovering up to the Mayor's desk. He clutched at his luggage like a jealous mother protecting her young. The leather bag seemed to squirm in the flickering squint of the firelight. Otto bade his guest sit down by the amber flames.

'How far have you come, monsignor?'

'From the East. A long journey. Tiring. No, I need no refreshment. It would be wasted on an old carcass such as mine.' For the first time Otto realised how old the Brother looked. The light picked out his parchment skin, his craggy ink-line features. Above all the eyes, staring inexorably into his own, spoke of great age and a practised world-weariness.

'We have more in common than you imagine, Mr Mayor. We both worship something far more material than a temple goddess. But the city relies on religion as much as money. People need something to believe in. We provide them with reassurance and yourself with a peaceful populace. If they didn't have Bastet to pray to every evening, they might start thinking for themselves. That would never do, would it?'

'No. No, I suppose not.' Otto tried on his best kindly grin. 'I try to have as little contact with the Church as possible,' he admitted, 'and what I have seen of it hasn't impressed me.' His smile disappeared. 'Woolly thinking. Minds as old and decayed as the religion you prize. Now I can't speak for yourself, your gracefulness; I mean, we've only just met. I'm talking about some of your Brothers who – you must admit – don't get out as much as they should.'

Kafel nodded, and Otto was pleased. Perhaps the priest could be reasonable.

'They're steeped in tradition, which is fine, but we have to look to the future. That's one of my jobs, considering the destiny of this city. Making the right decisions so that it'll keep running long after I've gone. Your religion is dying, it's on its last legs.'

'The people still care for Bastet, Mr Mayor.'

'Not like they used to. Not for much longer. Everything dies, Brother Kafel. In a few decades your temples will be monuments to an outmoded belief and a whole heap of wasted cash. I need those public funds. I'm going to get them.'

Kafel shifted his position on his fireside cushion with a rustle of holy cloth. His tail twitched. He had to convince the Mayor that there were more important things in life than moolah.

'This is not the first time I have visited this office.'

'I'm sorry, your gloriousness. I don't think I recall...'

'Your mother was in residence at the time.'

'Kindly keep my mother out of this,' Otto snarled, 'please.'

'I was merely going to say that she was as adamant as yourself. This was a long time ago, there was a recession I seem to remember; she (in her municipal wisdom) was taxing her citizens to the hilt. They didn't like it. Once I had explained to her that we were the cornerstone of their faith in existence, that the poor offered us the most generous contributions, that we taught our flock that suffering would bring them closer to their goddess, she stopped trying to close us down – she got a sweetener, of course.'

'She never told me.' Otto clamped his mouth shut. He wasn't used to speaking first and thinking afterwards.

'It would have been bad for her image, of course. The people would have been inconsolable if the temples were closed down. Playgrounds, hospitals, research clinics – their closure is met by apathy and little more. Ever see a temple closed down? No way. It would not be allowed, Mr Mayor.

Still, your mother was short of cash so we helped her set up a small account.'

'How much?' Otto stoked the fire, trying not to sound too interested.

'An allowance from us, most secret.' Kafel spoke slowly, an inscrutable ancient explaining something to a cub. 'Nothing underhand about it; simply a regular payment in gratitude for her sterling work for us. Protection money, if you will.' It was Kafel's turn to smile. Otto walked to the marble bust of his mother and turned her so that she faced the wall.

'So this morality crap –'

'PR for us. In a very indirect fashion, of course. Carrying on the work she did for us while she held your illustrious office.'

'She doesn't hold it any more. What's to stop me getting an allowance like this?'

'Your mother.'

'I can't believe we're talking about this! I won't be at your beck and call. I'm not interested in any dirty deals you may have spun in the past. This is the here and now. There is no place for a Church in this city.' Otto threw a scroll at the priest. It bore a plan of the city, dotted with jaundice marks. 'The yellow areas denote potential construction sites, your brightness. The population's growing. Commerce is replacing leisure activity in Bast. We need more houses, more office blocks. You can never have too many office blocks. Some of your temples are getting in the way.'

'I don't think you know who you're threatening, Mayor.' Kafel stood up, crushing the scroll between his hairy paws.

'Oh, you're going to put a hex on me, are you? You're a broken down old wizard. Your curses won't work on me.'

'We do not call on our goddess lightly.' Kafel left the scroll burning on the fire, and walked over to the Mayor. 'You've noticed how the city's getting hotter? More violent, blacker, uglier? We cursed this city once. Church attendance was low. The foundations of our temples soft. There was infighting amongst the brothers. Oh yes, we're cats as well. Quite capable of pettiness and arrogance. Especially self-love. We felt that the city wanted rid of us so the Bishop cursed its name, called upon Bastet to bring it down in a hail of ugly heat. Now our congregation has returned, our temples have been repaired and we wish we'd never made that prayer.'

Samson wasn't the only cat who liked to walk amongst his people. Otto was as likely to be the recipient of abuse as a well-meant tribute. But he did enjoy keeping in touch with the little people, fostering a reputation for keeping a keen eye on their concerns. He made more promises than he broke, was vague without being aloof and disingenuous without seeming sly. He could dissemble with the best politicians in the city, but when he roared his public listened. They had little choice.

Otto passed clothes shops and department stores, avoiding the temptation to stop and admire his reflection in the windows. Through one store display he saw cautious cats ascending a steep escalator, swaying from side to side, their tails indicating uncertainty, their footing unsure. He couldn't smell the advertisements within, but some of the shoppers wandered from aisle to aisle with their chins tilted up and their nostrils flared, sighing in the aromas. The streets were flanked by gaudy, moving video screens. They pitched the latest craze, multicoloured string with high-tensile dangling action. The citizens were so beset by ads that it was tough to get their attention; the string campaign used the hard sell angle, all high-pitched sounds and tingling bells. The cats put up with it. They liked to be kept up-to-date with the latest technology.

The Mayor entered the central mall, looking for a bench to rest on. Once seated he was surrounded by flashing screens, sent to target individual shoppers on remote robot arms. Gimmicks promoted food in all its glorious, fattening forms. Surely you've gone long enough without a bit? Come on, treat yourself! You deserve a little fish. It'll be lunchtime in a couple of hours. Isn't your stomach feeling a little hollow there? Food! Food! Yeah, that's exactly what you need right now to boost you, fire you up, stoke your belly. Cure your apathy. Keep you going till tea.

These days the cats who ran the fash mags pushed food therapy – if you are what you eat then shove a load in and make yourself a bigger, better person. A tin of meat 'n' jelly could comfort you, bring good cheer, pep you up, release repressions and fill you if not fulfil you.

Food therapy was the key. Stick it down your throat, smother it on your fur, lick it off your partner's paws – be decadent, delicious, tasty, edible, sauce up your sex life, eat the most expensive can of salmon in the supermarket before you're at the checkout. How could it hurt? By the time heart disease, diabetes, high blood pressure, gall stones or infections ravaged your innards you'd be ready for retirement anyway. Your kids could roll you around. Give your aching pads a rest. Feed you with a rubber spoon till the day you died, with a salutary rumble and belch.

City cats get bored oh-so-quickly. Routine, grey surroundings, the adoption of a cool nonchalance meant that they were desperate for entertainment and distraction to keep them busy. Food gave them something to do with their mouths; still they were desperate to amuse their other senses as well. For such a lazy race of creatures, they indulged in a heap of sport and recreation, from hunting and fishing to chasing fake rodents on a treadmill at the local gym. A range of possible pursuits had built up over centuries of civilisation, all vying for the cats' cash with neon billboards and needling jingles. Joe Public wanted the newest things, no one else has done that, sounds scary or silly but it's new, I've never heard of it before and that's the main thing. The city was never safe, its people seldom secure so when it came to taking risks – testing your own mettle, proving your worth above others, rediscovering the agility of youth, enjoying the feeling of your blood pumping through hungered, sweaty arteries – cats would do anything for kicks.

Meeting minimum resistance on this particular walkabout, Otto soon returned to his gloomy (air-conditioned) office and a dour expression on the face of his favourite aide, Tarquin.

'What's the matter with you now?' asked the Mayor, hoping Tarquin had done his homework this time. 'Looks like you've seen a goat.' To Otto, a goat was the most appalling creature imaginable – for some reason they had always given him the willies.

'No sir. I've seen a rough estimate of the fatalities

incurred during the hostilities this afternoon.' Tarquin twiddled his carefully manicured claws, tail drooping in deference to his boss.

'Hostilities?'

'Two gangs. Eighty to a hundred youths and agitates. The ground on that blessed battlefield is red.' Tarquin lowered his head, breathless. 'There was nothing we could do.'

'Good riddance.' Otto turned away. He pressed a paw to his right breast, checked his heart was still beating. Maybe I should act like it.

Like every other cat in the city, Otto was desperate for entertainment.

'Inform the guards. I'm going out again.'

16

NIGHT SEEPED INTO THE city, tainting it black. In the Doghouse porch lights still burned, flickering with uncertain electricity. Instead of seeking the tranquillity of sleep, half the population of the district gathered together in the streets. It would be a long time before they could doze peacefully again.

Charcoal lights led Wildcats, relatives, friends and hangers-on down Miro Street in a cold procession. Bookish kittens stumbled awkwardly alongside alleyway warriors in their ragged bandannas. Too many of their brethren, no matter how new, were dead and it was their duty to mourn. There had been so much loss in recent days; they were numb with the misery. The Wildcats would never get used to death.

The females wore black trousseaux, constricting their necks, itching at their throats and bunching their fur up to give them mock double chins. The younger females had wrapped maroon ribbons round their tails, displaying them erect and giving the procession a flamboyant swish.

Julius found Moira close to the procession's head. She was crying. He wrapped a limb around her, giving her a tender smile. She didn't acknowledge his presence.

Moira's legs ached. She hadn't rested since her brother's death, pacing round the house, volleying calls from curious neighbours. They didn't care about her. There was no one left. Pa couldn't even turn up to the funeral – his appearance would cause too much of a stir – and even if he'd had the opportunity, she doubted whether he'd have chosen to attend. Pa had seen plenty of death in the slum where he lived, lost so many siblings and friends that another body on hell's heap meant next to nothing. Pa cared about his heritage, his community, his bowel movements and that was all. Moira wrapped a paw round Julius' scrawny elbow.

Julius looked solemn, troubled. He couldn't help observing the mourners around him, their lowly postures and downcast eyes, examining them with a reporter's rude scrutiny. He expected to see anger in their faces, hatred for the gang that had stolen the lives of their sons and daughters. Instead he saw a reluctant acceptance of what had happened.

The procession shambled to a halt outside the Fat Tavern, where a pyre had been erected in the middle of the street. Superstitious locals had taken pains to detour past the pyre that day, and in the tavern all revelry had stopped. Its occupants, drinking to regret, stepped outside to watch.

The bodies of the Wildcats were wheeled towards the pyre on makeshift wooden towers, high above the procession – to bring them closer to Bastet, and also to keep any festering infections out of harm's reach.

The towers were tilted and the bodies slid gracefully into the fire. Julius noted that King landed on all four feet.

Males and females alike began to wail. The dead cats rapidly burned to black, their fur crisping, bones curling. Flesh popped and crackled, uglified by the fire. Old and young hunched together, gazing into the flames, enjoying the warmth despite their mourning.

Moira hunched her shoulders, ears cocked. At first she thought she heard a breeze. Murmurs spread amongst the congregated cats, breeding whispers, giving birth to muttering. Heads turned in a wave of fluttering ribbon. They'd seen someone in the distance that they never thought they'd see in this part of town at this time. Someone they didn't want to be there, out of place, out of friends. He'd brought an entourage of guards, advisors, PR men – five or six in all.

Julius craned his neck as well, recognising the new arrival as a public figure who'd fallen under his hack's axe a few times in the past. Julius had enjoyed the hatchet jobs. It was easier to criticise than to be impartial, and risk being mistaken as a pawn in Mayor Otto's political game.

Otto began to greet the menage, expressing his deep regret, shaking paws with withered widows, cracking gags about the weather. The locals were too dumb to complain, too meekin to get ugly. They'd had enough woe for one day.

Yet Otto saw they weren't beaten, the fight hadn't been yanked out of them. This was a reverie in the midst of battle, a breather before the next hunt began. Their chests heaved and fell, ice breath steaming from their nostrils. He could hear nose-breathing from a hundred widowers and orphans. It disturbed him.

Now and again he received a curtsey, smiled thank you, mumbled response to his greetings. It took him a while to reach the head of the group, guards in tow – the Mayor was close to his voters but not *too* close – and arched his eyebrows at Moira.

'Lost some good friends today, my dear?'

'What would you know about it.' Moira tried to match the lion's haughty gaze.

'My brother and I used to go hunting together,' said the Mayor. 'A family event. I was very small, we didn't stray far from home, I could only catch mice and insects. There was an accident, he stumbled down a steep bank – broke his legs. He was writhing his head from side to side, agony, I held him still. Called for my mother. She found us, in the dark. Brother in a bed of upturned tree roots. She didn't wish him farewell or try to help. She placed the tip of her claw against his eye. I thought she was going to kiss him. She thrust down hard, punctured his brain. Put him out of her misery.'

Julius watched the Mayor, admiring his considerable presence. They stared at each other for an instant, two opponents at the weighing up. *He wouldn't know me*, thought Julius. *I'm a face in a crowd, another yabbering reporter desperate for a soundbite when you stand on your office steps. You've won another rigged election. You'd sooner kiss a goat than grant me an interview.*

Otto turned back to Moira, the moment passed. Julius was well-dressed for a local; perhaps the Mayor dismissed him as a nip dealer or a misplaced tourist.

'What are you doing to stop all this killing?' Moira asked, edging closer to Otto. He couldn't answer, couldn't match her stare. 'Get out of here. This is our part of town. You don't own this.'

No, thought Otto. *I own you. All of you.* He was a diplomat, tried not to speak without mentally validating his words in triplicate first. So he said nothing and left, drawing his entourage along with a sweep of his winter cloak. Moira gazed at his retreating form, a numb frost forming in her mind.

'I have to go,' said Moira, slipping away into the throng. They moved as close to the fire as they could get, huddled against the cold.

Sparks flew from the pyre. Some alighted on the congregation's fur but they didn't notice, or didn't care.

It was usually a tradition to wait for the flames to die. But the pyre had been so heftily stoked and fuelled that the embers would not fade until dawn. So the mourners left in dribs and drabs, heading slowly back towards Miro Street, picking their way carefully through lanes littered with loosed ribbons and dead torches.

Moira waited on her porch to welcome in a group of the mourners, offering meat titbits on a salver, flashing a coy smile to the ones she knew. The cats had grieved enough and life went on; their bellies were empty and needed some serious filling.

Cats don't like to be shoved together in a confined space, especially when a couple of the girls present are on heat. Hey, they can't help it, all right? The drive to go and play Mating Martha, strut around waiting to be courted had been overridden by King's sudden death.

They couldn't help but give out a few scents and signals. A whole room full of cats struggling with their heavy-breathing hormones! They chattered intermittent sentences, scared of silence, not sure what to say. What topic of conversation is appropriate to start an afterglow rolling?

Pa knew.

He rolled into the house, swaying with age and liquor, took one look about him, scanning for his surrogate daughter. He acknowledged her presence (ignored Julius) with a wily blink, collapsed on his haunches next to her.

'Where's the canapés?' Now the guests had something to talk about. The newcomer smelt funny, bore himself in a peculiar fashion; his nose was large enough to sniff the next city. They looked to their hostess for her response, took her lead – she accepted his presence with a demure smile.

He never was one to keep things under his hat. Spoke his mind, enjoyed sharing his opinion with anyone in earshot. His grandfather had been an orator, that's where he'd got it from; by the time he was three, he'd learned to project his voice and make people listen, using nothing more than a considered tone of voice and a tongue of quicksilver.

'What are you all looking pallid for? You didn't know him like I knew him. Didn't look after him. It's too late to care for him now.'

A roomful of cats gave him a unanimous look of disdain. Public displays of self-loathing were uncommon in this part of town. A roomful of cats! Pa fought the urge to bark and chase them. There was something about them that always got to him – their skinny asp tails, wriggling whiskers, their high-pitched mewly conversations that set his eardrums ablaze – he put it down to instinct, an ancestral foible.

Back in the Pride Age, when animals had roamed the globe with heedless barbarism, it had been quite natural for dogs to chase cats. Probably eat them for supper. Pa smacked his lips. As he recalled, his orating grandfather had been quite a cat-chaser. Strung a row of tails on his rotary dryer when friends came over for a barbecue. Grandfather's garden parties had been famous for their good cheer, loud music and the unique taste of the burgers.

'I wasn't invited to the funeral. Don't mean I can't gate-crash the afterglow.'

'You know you're welcome here anytime,' said Moira,

trying to calm him down. 'Hard to get hold of. Welcome all the same. You remember Julius Kyle? The writer.'

'Someone's gotta do it,' Julius mumbled. Pa hadn't finished with Moira.

'You know how to reach me.' To Julius: 'She never sent me so much as an invite chit. 'So sorry your son's died, come an' join in the celebrations''

'He's not your son.' Moira bowed her head, sorry she'd spoken.

'No that's right. I don't have no kin. Jus' a barrowful of wishful dreams. I'm there for you, girl. Let me know if you're desperate. You, my friend –' The dog returned his attention to Julius. '– have caused enough trouble for one weekend. Stick to your own kind.'

'I could say the same to you.'

'That you could. Take a leaf out of my tree. I don't think anyone here would advise it.'

Julius was also beginning to accept Pa, though he was more interested in Moira. She was alluring in her mourning dress. Eyes of polished emerald, rich and large. A long, tapering face of downy white fur. Best of all, she was interested in him.

'Where's the eats?' asked Pa, ungracious in his grief. He was hypnotised by a tail looping back and forth, hungry to sink his teeth into it. He wiped drool from his maw with the back of his paw.

His eyebrows rose in stereo as a quintet of black platters were brought into the room; he was disappointed to find that they each held several thimble-sized cups of water, one per guest. The platters were followed by a pair of water pipes, for those who wished to smoke.

Julius placed his cup before him, light glinting off the silver rim. He hadn't mentioned Camilla, told Moira that he hadn't been on a date for ages.

'I'd hardly call this a date. I thought I could smell a female on you.'

'Must be all the smoke.' Julius bit his tongue. 'Plays strange games with your sinuses.'

A neighbouring guest shifted closer to Julius, nodding a silent greeting.

'Don't often see a celebrity at these sorts of things,' said the guest, a tabby with a bald patch.

'I'm old news,' Julius replied with a well-worn sigh, 'I haven't been interviewed in years. The stuff they write about me is lazy conjecture, padding to fill in the gaps on a slow month.'

'Still, nice to see your name,' said Moira, trying to be helpful. 'Someone remembers you.'

'They're mourning my passing is what they're doing. They know I haven't got it in me any more.'

'Have you checked recently?' she smiled, her eyes glittering. 'Maybe you could check for me.'

Pa looked at the cats squatting round the corners of the kitchen. Several green bundles wrapped in plastic had been placed in the middle of the room. The plastic was dewed with condensation. The cats' eyes widened as they looked for the juiciest package.

Moira unwrapped the closest bundle with reverent slowness. The foot-long blades of grass within had been kept moist with a little water. She took a blade and tore its tip, rolling it up and placing it in her mouth. The other cats followed suit, chewing the grass slowly with their back teeth.

Julius retained some grass in the side of his mouth and gradually added more, building up a bolus and washing down the juice with water. He offered some of the grass to Pa, who refused with a vigorous sake of his shaggy head.

'A dog chewing that? I don't think so, do you? For one thing, it would give me a funny tummy. Those kind of runs I can do without. It tastes weird. I like things that taste good. Meat things. Junk things. For another thing, I'd look like a hamster, all bulging cheeks and green juice... it's not for me.'

Pa, still grumbling to himself, sat down between Julius and Moira. The dog's fur stank of sweat, but the guests were too respectful to say anything.

Julius dampened his blades of grass with a drop of water from his silver cup and added more to the ball in his mouth. The healthy plant contained vitamins that thickened the blood, strengthening the chewer's metabolism. It also acted as a relaxant, heightening whatever state of mind was held before the chewing began. It had been a while since the reporter had dropped folic acid, and he observed the effects with interest. He could almost feel the world turning beneath him.

He suffered a waking dream in which his city destroyed itself. Families feuded, houses burned, intolerance erupted. Friends died. He had to sequester himself. It seemed the obvious, safe thing to do.

Pa spat in disgust, picking himself up in a shower of filthy hairs. He looked at his daughter, leaning against Julius.

'This is a social occasion for you, isn't it?' said Pa, wrapping his coat tight round him. 'I can't blame you for enjoying yourselves. I wouldn't want to spoil it for you.'

'It's not like that at all!' said Moira, getting angry.

'Some of you don't see each other very often, some of you have travelled a long way to be here. So have fun, and sod my son. Sod 'im!' Pa raised his cup for a toast. 'Here's to forgetting he ever existed.' Pa stormed from the hall and, without a word to Julius, Moira scooted after him. Julius gazed down at the floor for a moment, dazed, wondering what he should do. He looked around the hall and realised that he knew no one, got up, and followed Pa and Moira outside.

The happy family was long gone. Julius looked at the position of the sun in the sky, obscured by amber chemical clouds. It was time for his appointment with Boston.

The city was as busy as ever, yuppies and housewives oblivious to the war fought in the Doghouse. Julius found the teeming life reassuring as he pushed his way to the Lauriston Building, hopping onto one of the elevators that scaled its exterior. His tail wrapped itself round his leg, tucked in a hip pocket to avoid getting caught between the elevator and the wall.

He could see half the city, lumps of granite hugging each other in a corporate scrum, domiciles looking up at them like infant siblings.

On the top floor, Boston was waiting for him. Arms out-stretched in welcome, a toothsome smile on his chops. Julius played the game and shared a hug with his long lost pub-lishing editor.

'Hey J, what d'you say? It's been too long, baby, too long. You may not believe this but I've been keeping tabs on you. That's right. Watching you from anear. I've got one question and one alone to ask you – what are you doing with your life? Slaving away on some dead-end rag when you should have come to me soonest.'

Boston's office walls were adorned with durable, shiny book covers, painted with bright colours of orange and canary. There were plentiful pictures of scantily clad females – males are easy marks as far as publishing is concerned.

'I tried to call you, Boston. You were always in a meeting.'

'Meeting shmeeting! That's just a secretarial ploy to give me a rest every now and again. You've got to see through their foolish wiles, baby; publishing is a business of deceit and treachery. Maybe there's a book in it somewhere for you. I thought you could come in, sling some of your ideas at me, I'll be a brick wall for you to bounce your balls off.'

The fur on the editor's head was splayed – he was one of those unorthodox, creative types. A snappy dresser, he'd made his fortune publishing books on pyramids and healing balms – particularly popular from the scratch and sniff point of view. Boston had quickly moved on to cookbooks, using tantalising aromas to grab his customers.

'I've been planning something about –'

'Tiger, right? That Straight cat has cult appeal, J. That's the key, that's the hook. You gotta write us a sequel.'

'Just how much creative control will I have over this novel, Boston?'

'Creative what?' Boston froze for a moment, leafing through a mental dictionary. 'You're the writer! Without you, we'd have blank pages to sell and nothing but. Listen, don't see me as your editor. Think of me as a confidant, someone you can express your creative angst to. Here's an idea. Straight's never been underwater, has he? I can see it now – oxygen tanks, snorkels, submarines, females in rubber wetsuits. An underwater action adventure. What do you say?'

'Bye.' Julius turned his back on the publisher.

'No, no, wait, wait. I really want some new product from you, my friend. What about that book – what's it called – by that author, kind of a horror romance, you know the one...'

'Give me a clue.'

'I just did! It was in the best-seller list for, ooh, ages. Now she knows how to write. You should write it like that.'

'Like what?'

'Like kinky, speedy, wise and a little bit weird. Actually, no. Doesn't sound quite like you.'

'And what is "like me"?' Julius asked with a sigh. Boston tried to choose his words with care.

'Hmmm, action-led/plot driven. Yeah. Intensely moral. Appealing to kids, but with a dark and meaningful subtext for the adults. A new born-to-run franchise with every novel.'

'Unlucky, Boston. I don't have the energy these days. Nobody would read a book by Julius Kyle, and I'm not writing anything that won't get read.' Making his apologies, he bade the editor farewell and headed home for his morning nap.

17

WES DIDN'T TAKE TOO kindly to hanging on his boss' heels, waiting on his word. Servility was for Abyssinians, leopards and lemurs. Every now and then Tufano would turn to him, offer a chummy word, give him respect and Wes stuck around. Being Tufano's right paw gave him status in the gang.

He had made some good friends and the ladies would coo like lusty doves as he passed by. Wes had no leadership qualities; he wasn't much of a team player. He could follow orders, though he preferred to translate them as requests – carrying them out because he felt like it, not because he had to. Some said Tufano carried him, made allowances for his mistakes. They were long term friends. Wes knew that Tufano didn't make allowances for anyone, no matter how close a playmate they were. The Clute leader would slice your neck open if you messed up, made him or his gang look bad. Wes preferred to see himself as the main cog in the Clute juggernaut, knowing his place, ensuring that his tasks were performed smoothly, keeping a close eye on the boss who steered this ugly gangland monster truck.

Wes didn't ask many questions as a rule. It wasn't that he didn't have the intellectual capacity. He had accepted his place in the war-torn scheme of things, and saw no reason to rock his environment. So long as he got the opportunity to look tough, splinter some bones and father plenty of children, he was content.

He knew why Tufano had come to the factory, dragging Wes and Missy along with him. The boss had received a message from some unknown source, scribbled in bad grammarese as a kind of dare, setting up a rendezvous late at night at the abandoned yarn works. He also knew that Tufano had to enter the potentially health-threatening situation; a reputation of honour and dumb bravery depended on it. Wes didn't ask why Tufano insisted that his two henchcats waited outside for him. Wes didn't agree with the plan. As was his way, he said nothing and mooched instead, looking at Missy.

She was a girl of few words as well; more than a claw-catching bodyguard, she was an aide de camp, veteran of long intergang campaigns, her beauty forever submerged under a sea of scar tissue. Wisdom still shone up from the depths, flickering in her eyes. She didn't have much time for Wes. Peered into the factory. Kicked a loose stone. Tufano could handle himself, didn't need a nursemaid. He was her hero.

She'd looked up to him for years, watching him fight his way to the top of the Doghouse heap, starting small – training to kill using kittens and rodents as practice dummies – always on the offensive, picking fights with anyone unlucky enough to have an R in their name. Once he'd established that he was an unconscionable mother, he'd started using his smarts and using people.

Did they mind being used to make bacon for this boy? Not at all. Clutes queued for the chance to work for him; like Wes, they sought protection and a higher status in their trash community. Perhaps they wanted salvation, or at least someone to believe in. A hero.

Missy had been hauled from a cold hearth life, a nothing – a sassy, don't-mess-with-me nothing, but she hadn't been headed anywhere all the same – exploited. Used as everything apart from a living shield in the heat of battle. She wouldn't have minded. She was willing to go further. As Tufano'd figured, if you want followers who are prepared to sacrifice their lives for you, pick characters with nothing to exist for. They won't be missed anyhow.

Thousands of cats had given up their lives for Tufano over the years, ready made gang cause attached. Missy had lost good friends and seen ugly rivals die slow and painful, for the sake of the simple, childish need to prove who was the biggest, strongest boss on the block. Some days it was Tufano. Up until recently, Samson had often enjoyed the upper paw. Most of the time, Tufano was so busy orchestrating gang politics (nurturing the sycophants, knocking back troublemakers) that he didn't seem to care which gang was winning the great Doghouse popularity contest. No one else would ever know, and the papers only wrote about the Clutes so they could demonise and damn all cats under the age of adolescence. They didn't understand. The gangs were trying to keep ancient traditions alive, so that future generations would know what it meant to be a cat. Living on instinct, hunting with your bare teeth, defending your territory and conquering all enemies. None of this stay at home, watch TV, eat from a can business. This upholding of traditions business was only a small part of the Clute remit. They lived each day as it came.

Missy wouldn't be pushed around by any old tom. He had to be a demigod, a forthright buccaneer. A veteran of life and love, like the boss.

The last guy who'd pushed her round had tried to be charming, proposing marriage to her while they ran from the cops down a sewer pipe. They'd caught sight of Charlie pissing against a wall, marking his territory and trying to impress her. A minor offence you might think, but the cops had seen the kids' gang colours and were determined to catch them before they did anything worse. The pursuit included a trudge through soiled sand, past gritted walls in the tunnels that ran under the smellier parts of the city. Used litter was deposited in the sewers, flushed towards wasteland beyond the city. A perfect place to hide. Not a perfect place to make a pass at Missy – a fact that had escaped Charlie's attention. He'd grabbed her by the waist, tried to rub his head against hers. It had been too dark for him to see her tail lashing.

The cops had found him eventually, although Missy was long gone and there wasn't enough of Charlie left to arrest. Another casualty in the battle of the sexist. A victim of the harsh conditions found in the slum Missy had been raised in.

Tufano could hardly see his paws in front of him as he reached into the darkness, using his whiskers and shoulders to follow a labyrinth corridor into the belly of the factory. He felt the nausea of fear welling in his belly. He hadn't been able to express his misgivings to Missy and Wes – that sort of bag had never been part of his upbringing. He liked to be in control. He needed to be in control, covering his front back and sides, one heavy leap ahead. Not tonight.

This was probably routine, another challenge from a jumped-up cub that would try to take a bite out of Tufano's hide and choke mid-munch. That didn't mean Tufano wasn't wary. He'd been getting slower recently, his gut widening, tufts of fur turning grey. Worst of all, the muscles in his left hindleg had been getting steadily weaker, wasting from some old wound. Within a year he would be lame – limping kings were no mainstay in the Doghouse.

Tufano's eyes adjusted to the dark, helped by two grimy skylights inviting moonlight into the building. He made out looms, piles of grit and dust, heard clanking metal far in the distance. The old factory had spun tons of hairballs into fine garments. It had long since had its day.

Cobwebs netted the walls and Tufano could smell graffiti on the factory floor. Something about equal rights for dogs. A disgruntled employee had smeared something nasty on the walls. Yarn stretched like tripwires across the factory floor at shin height. He stepped gingerly over them.

That left leg was definitely slower these days. He stopped as he heard voices. They seemed to be coming from a vault at the far end of the factory floor.

'In here!' deep, grunted, from the back of the throat. The voice echoed round the metal corridors. He entered the dark vault.

'Over here!' He hoped the cats waiting outside were okay.

'Gotcha, sweetheart!' He turned, ran for the exit, tripped a yarn wire. The vault slammed shut.

Tufano licked his lips, dazed. He'd landed hard, knocking his head on the concrete floor. The voices had gone, replaced by scrabbling sounds. Tip tapping on the grey stone. Brown needle eyes of light pricked the gloom, bright crescents in hovering pairs, getting larger. He could smell something oily, filthy. Charnel breath, shallow panting. Weaving tails patting at the walls. The lights surrounded him, staring him down. He began to pick himself up, hoisting himself by his elbows. Felt a nip on his left haunch, razor teeth treating him like corn on the cob. More teeth joined in, ripping at his clothes, drawing blood, fur, flesh, semen. He could hear them drool and gobble, jaws engulfing him before he could react. He despised them. He didn't fear them. But there were too many of them – within seconds he was unconscious.

The aching fence groaned pitifully. A yellowed branch wagged its twigs in the bracing winter breeze. Frost nipped at Julius' heels as he sidled through the dark, edging his way down the garden. A tufted figure was stooped in a corner, hunched against a wheelie bin. Rummaging through Julius' rubbish!

Julius realised that the intruder was engrossed, so he abandoned any attempt at stealth. He pounced on the intruder, and found himself wrestling with a sausaged bin liner. Rotten meat, old milk cartons and screwed paper burst out on top of him, sticking to his fur. He released a mew of consternation.

Torchlight flickered inside the house. At first he felt embarrassed, then angry. There was a trespasser after all. He paced carefully into the house, nostrils flared, brow creased. In the front room, someone was hunched over his desk, reaching into a drawer. In his paw was a letter and King's bandanna. A spy! Julius ran across the room, dragging the figure out of its camouflage shadow, found himself muzzle to muzzle with Pa.

Exchanging a glare, they picked themselves up. Pa breathed fast through his bristled nose and Julius struggled to prevent himself from following through on his attack. Bemusement held him in check. The old codger had been trespassing on Julius' territory – typical of a mongrel dog.

Pa passed the letter back to Julius who snatched it against his hip, smoothed out the creases and placed it in his coat pocket.

'I never trusted you, you thieving son of a bitch.'

'I wasn't doing nothing, J.' Pa shrugged his shoulders, empty palms upwards. 'You know me. I wouldn't mess with you.'

'But you'd mess with my trash. What's gotten into you?'

'What do you think?' Pa felt something behind him, got ready to bite at it the realised that it was his own tail.

'How many times have you been here?'

'I never come here, J. This ain't my area, wrong side of the river. I'm out of place here.'

'You're out of place everywhere, Pa. Why're you bothering me?' Pa looked up at Julius, his puppy dog eyes glittering in the torchlight.

'I got no one else to bother. Dogs and cats don't mix, I don't need to tell you that. That's why there's a ruddy great stinkin' river separating us. Your lot polluted the water, not us. You'd rather put up with that stench than coexist with us. It ain't as simple as that. We swim. A lot.

'I don't know what happened wit' King and Moira, they never had a dad as far as I know. Their ma was a liberal, tried to help the sick puppies round my way. I was trying to keep pups off the street… She had to go back, took the kids. Very intelligent lady – didn't deserve to live where she lived. Died after she left us, probably of some doggy disease. Wasted away to a nothing. I try and help out still, I'm tolerated. The dogs never agreed with our relationship. I'm not included any more.'

'You could move up North.'

'This is my home. The only world I know. I felt responsible for King and Moira. They relied on me sometimes, other times they would pretend not to know me.'

'This was given to me.' Julius took the bandanna from Pa. 'You can't steal it. It's not yours.'

'Five.'

Julius didn't understand.

'This is the fifth time I've been here. For him.'

'Only a dog would come sneaking round here…'

'I was collecting stuff for King. I didn't mind rooting through your trash. He asked me for stuff.'

'What do you mean by stuff? The only things you'll find in my bin are empty tins. Chicken bones. Old manuscripts.'

'He was a bigger fan than he let on, was my boy. He wanted to be Tiger Straight. Got a bit mixed up, I think.'

Julius shook his head. Impossible. He was a has-been. He'd grown used to obscurity, working for the gutter press. Nevertheless somebody had cared.

'Take it.' He gave the black bandanna to the dog, who held it to his grizzled face, lovingly breathing in its scent. Julius looked away, an interloper in his own home.

'I'd better go,' Pa grumbled, hiding the cloth inside his

jacket. 'I know a river needs to be swum.' Bast needed some-one like him: a cultural ambassador between slums with no culture.

Julius did not move for long moments after the hound had left. He'd had enough of the Doghouse and its sordid secrets. Enough of Morris, feeding on copy like a pig stuck in a trough. He went to his study and dragged out some faded notepads. He had a book to write.

Missy's impatience had been outrun by worry. She looked at Wes, who was amusing himself by swiping at a butterfly. She stayed alert, ready for trouble and worse. She could smell death. It had always been a gift, registering a unique odour when someone was about to die. Some cats had the stench about them for weeks before they copped it. The notion that her boss might be the victim of a mortal attack never crossed her mind. He was too strong, too quick-witted. She checked the joint anyway.

She followed Tufano's scent – it was masked by conflicting whiffs, must, urine, a dirty sweaty smell. Wes stayed close behind her, eyes probing the walls, guarding her flank. The darkness was unremitting, hiding fearful glimmers that toyed with their imaginations. Even the bravest Clute had fears to harbour, unless he was an imbecile and rash with it. Missy knew the nature of fear, and as her boss did not respond to her constant mews, her greatest fear became solid – to lose Tufano meant losing her world.

Dust clung to her fur, camouflaging her shoulders and arms in mottled grey. Streaks laddered her wrists as she brushed her way through the aged corridors and into the vault. By the time she found Tufano he'd been stripped clean. Most of the yarn had been removed. Just one length remained, tied to the vault entrance.

Missy choked back a sob. Wes looked at her with renewed respect – she did have emotions after all. He bent down, examining the yarn. 'Rats are getting too clever these days, ain't they?'

'Quiet, Wes.' Missy looked down at Tufano's bleached bones. It was hard to connect them to the idolised image of her buccaneer.

18

BRIDGET WAS BORED. She groomed herself, rudding the back of her paw over her head, allowing her mouth to stretch into a king size yawn.

'There seem to be two kinds of feline in my life, often connected with gender. There is the kind that knows everything has a place, understands the basics of aesthetics and domestic protocol; then there's the earthier sort of animal who moves your ornaments around with aplomb, doesn't put anything back where it should be, knocks things over and makes a mess.'

A spotlight pooled her chin, flaring red on the left side of her face. Dust danced a ceroc jive in the steady beam. Her nose was dry and cracked as a desert mesa and skin puddled round her neck beneath grey strands of fur.

'Mentally, boys are just as bad. Make no mistake (and I shall not make any apologies to the males in the audience); their brains are festering litter trays. Filth. Dirt buried under scant layers of social conscience. Only a few well-worn scruples stand between moral order and the contamination of their female kin. We can catch their disease, girls. If the toms of this city don't clean up their minds and pull up their socks, we all face a terrible decline. Society will fall apart, our streets will be filled with topless bars and loose dancers who are prepared to lap more than milk.

'That's why I'm here. To show you the light; clean living, healthy attitudes to our fellow citizens and plenty of red meat. That is the answer.'

'Very good,' Tarquin applauded. 'Not sure about the social conscience bit.' Bridget glowered at him. He crossed his legs awkwardly. 'I mean, you don't want to lose them. Plain speaking always worked best for you, wouldn't you say?'

'I value your judgement as a top spin doctor, Tarquin,' Bridget replied in slow, patient tones. 'However, you may have noticed that I don't take criticism very well. I would be grateful if you tempered your opinions with – with –'

'Silence?' Tarquin butted in. Bridget's eyes met his and that was a sufficient answer. He shut up as the lofty female continued her speech.

'Before you know it, they'll be strutting around, marking their territory with urine and inseminating anything with fur and long eyelashes. Violence – children are picking up on daddy's uncontrolled urge to hunt and maim. Discounted as instinct but we know better. It's sheer irresponsibility, especially coming from the fathers.'

The conference hall seated 400. Bridget looked small standing at the front, peering down at her notes on a podium. She didn't use a microphone; she hardly needed to raise her voice for her audience of one.

Tarquin had begun to notice Bridget's blemishes, the folds of fat on her limbs, white hairs, watery eyes and blotches on the tongue. Bridget had become near-sighted; whilst wooing Tarquin she'd probably mistaken him for a handsome Sergeant Major type rather than the rugged worm he was.

Tarquin hadn't been interested in bedding her for political

reasons, to improve his career prospects or climb another couple of rungs on the ladder to civic excess. The relationship was too secret to help in that department. He'd known how powerful Bridget was before they'd got together. She had plenty of important contacts, enjoyed many financial bonuses thanks to her long stretch as Mayoress. What he hadn't been aware of, hadn't taken long to sink in, was her determination to hang onto her power. It overrode family ties, her personal life. Scotch that, it was her personal life – every public audience and TV appearance affected her personally.

Her status may have been noble but it was also fragile. One wrong word, one slip of her velvet mask in front of the proles and she would be yesterday's news. Then she'd find out who her allies were. The class she frequented was dominated by well bred fly-by-nights, fickletons, cats who'd always back the winning side no matter how many coats they were required to turn.

Bridget was spiteful, unscrupulous and desperate to maintain her reign until her death. Or beyond. Some forgotten scandal had dethroned her, allowed her son to take charge when he reached the age of dissent; she'd done everything she could to erase all memories of the incident from the public consciousness.

'Why do you put up with me?' Tarquin wondered.

'I'm not happy with my son. He's got a mind of his own. I was hoping for a direct copy, a new improved version of myself to do Bridget's bidding. Instead he's gone his own way. He's too selfish.'

'You don't think I've got a mind of my own?'

'You'll do as the fatherer of a new breed of little Bridgets, Tarquin. I'm pregnant.'

19

BROTHER KAFEL WAS SICK of the Bishop's repetitive questioning. It had taken him days to arrange an appointment, and now he had an interrogation to endure. He needed the bathroom.

'Has the Mayor come round to our way of thinking?'

'All I'm saying is I told him a few home truths. Opened his eyes a little wider. It may take time to win him over completely.'

The Bishop sighed, impatient with the lackey. 'I'm not interested in winning this particular game. We don't have time. Otto could pass his money-grubbing statute any time now, whisk our cash away before we knew it. Once a statute is passed –'

'There's no unpassing it. I know.'

The Bishop pulled on a bell cord and a hatch in the ceiling opened. A plate of sweetmeats was winched carefully downwards, spinning at the end of a length of string, until it reached his desk. Kafel had never seen the Bishop up and about in his life.

'These are rather good,' said the Bishop with his mouth full. He didn't offer Kafel a treat. These were property of his holy Fatherness, and no one expected the head of the church to fetch his own snacks.

'I have something to show you, my lad.' He opened a drawer and picked out a furry object, grey in the middle, pink at either end. Kafel looked at it with suspicion. The Bishop twisted at it, forcing it to utter a sharp clicking sound. Clearing an area on his desk, he placed the object on the edge and set it free to scurry along the surface. More clicking. It made Kafel jump, snatching the article and holding it close to his face.

'Not for eating, Brother. Place it back on the desk.'

Kafel did as he was bid, still curious. The something looked like a mouse – beady eyes, baby paws, coning snout – yet it was artificial. A stainless steel key stuck out of its left flank, spinning as the creature scurried.

'It's a new invention,' the Bishop explained. 'Just the sort of unseemly creation we're here to protect the public from. They think they can play Bastet, rule nature. This must be nipped in its clockwork bud.' Kafel began batting the toy with his paws, chasing it across the desk. The Bishop stifled his glee with a pious frown. 'The citizens who are being asked to buy this junk – they need direction. Faith. If they lose their sense of belief, we lose our existence. A world without faith would be a most unhappy one.'

'What do you suggest, father?' Kafel took a deep breath.

'We've always been in the line of defence, my dear brother. It's about time we started offending.' The Bishop slammed his paw down on the mouse then released it, allowing it to scuttle behind a desk tidy.

```
The rendezvous point was a narrow lane on the
outskirts of the city, where only the rats and
lowlives bred. Tiger was on his guard as he
approached. He knew not all the rats around here
```

were little guys with twitchy noses and pink feet. Some of them were wide cats willing to do anything for a fast buck, as long as it wasn't anything pleasant. A lantern died overhead, forcing him to move on to the next lamp post. He'd be a sitting target if anyone decided to take a pot shot at him, but he didn't want to miss Bug.

She'd promised information and Bug was a lady who always delivered. While he waited, Tiger unbuttoned his coat and blew a few baleful notes from his tarnished sax, the sounds rising into the starless sky like angels looking for their boss.

THE KITTY KILLER CULT
JULIUS KYLE

Sniff this: Different! Unusual! New improved author, brought back from the gutter press brink to thrill you, amaze you and present the best read of the year. Words flow from his dazzling pads like spit from a whistle. Read them on the tram, crossing the road, aloud to your friends or to your Sunday lunch. Alternately take an early night and let your spouse read it to you as you drift off – guaranteed sound dreams and a renewed moral perspective when you wake up in the a.m. Wherever, however you read it you'll receive satisfaction or your book tokens back.

The words look pretty on the page too. A perfect companion for kittens of all ages. Handy for the beach, the train station or those quiet moments at home when the TV's on the fritz and you've got nothing more constructive to do than look at a book. Suitable for coffee tables, coffee bars and barnyard animals.

This was too easy. The sentences were pouring too fast, too thickly from Julius' brain to his typewriter. At this rate he'd be finished within the month, ages before his deadline. Perhaps he was being too wordy, overwriting, belabouring the points he made. It hadn't been this easy in the good old days – he'd malted over every stinking syllable, wasting years of his lives for the sake of trash literature and a slow, slow buck. To the public, the critics, his painstaking work had shown, shone through, brought him glory and weighty awards and wet snaily kisses from old ladies who wanted to bed Tiger Straight but settled for his creator.

Now Julius hated those books, remembered only how much time he'd wasted sitting in a dark room sparring with his writer's block, his fur growing grey in the sunless study. Missing out on weddings, births, relationships, the death of friends and all to eke one more paragraph from his muddled subconscious. Tiger Straight had stolen half his life away. Julius wasn't ready to forgive him. And what did other people care? As far as the rest of the world was concerned, Julius could have spent his life stitching nets in a fishing village. His sacrifice meant nothing.

This book would be different. It would make the readers think and feel, raise awkward questions about loyalty, bigotry and acceptance. It would be a proper book, a real labour of literature. Who knows, if Julius plodded on, tried a couple more stories in the same vein, he might be remembered by future generations of writers as a cat to look up to; not one whose books could only be tracked down in a thrift store.

A thrift store!

He had poured every iota of experience, anger, sagacity, his own personal bitter mistakes into the tale that was taking shape. That was why it grew so stout. It was all inside him already, waiting to leap out, grab the readers by the scruff of the neck and shout *I know what you're thinking! I know what you care about, how you feel. That's how great I am. Your superior.*

Empathy had always been one of Julius' strong points. He'd put that into the book as well. He'd considered dressing up as Tiger Straight, popping down the high street to catch a shoplifter, foiling raids on the fishmonger's. Get inside his protagonist's head and promote the book at the same time. He didn't need to. He knew how readers expected his hero to react to any situation, and as for promotion – the book would sell itself. If it took one year or twenty, it would go down in history as – Bastet help us in this buy-it-if-it's-new consumer hell – something more than a product or franchise. Something that mattered. And watch out for the sequel.

'It is time,' the Bishop bowed his head forward, mitre teetering on his brow, 'for communion. Please join me in prayer.'

The congregation closed their eyes, green night-lights blinking off in pious succession. They placed their forepaws together, balanced carefully on their cushioned pews, tails tucked in neat loops against their haunches.

'Great Bastet,' the Bishop also closed his eyes, stooping over the lectern. 'Let us commune with you in good faith, as you watch over us each day of our petty existence.'

The Bishop relaxed his breathing, regulating it to a steady rhythm, mouth closed, chest lifting and falling in a shallow motion. A deep, soothing, whirring sound emitted from far within his being, the sound of utter contentment.

The congregation joined him, their breaths cooling until they reached the same tempo as their Father. They reached a meditative state, a thousand cats purring in unison.

Standing at the back of the Bast Municipal Church, Otto could hear the prayer and it made his flesh creep. The church-goers were searching for enlightenment; all they would find was mind control.

Empty your minds and your pockets, give your souls unto me.

He looked up at the vaulted ceiling, carved like the inverted ribcage of a whale. Otto didn't believe in the afterlife or a nine-headed goddess. He believed in mistrust, political swindling, creative accountancy. What he couldn't believe was the blind faith of the Bishop's followers, cats with nothing to lose, not enough money to feed their cubs, giving everything away to this sorry cause. He understood how the Bishop could take money without conscience, just as he understood there was no all-knowing deity above. Bastet would never have allowed such injustice.

Once the meditation was over, a cluster of four acolytes brought a bowl to their master. It contained milk blessed by the Bishop, slopping at the sides as if trying to escape.

The acolytes placed the mother's milk in six gold saucers, one for each holy teat. They were passed between the priests who sipped and looked beatific. They'd been trained, long hard years of sipping and lacing feminine robes around their waists. Beatific School was tough, there were plenty of casualties, let downs, realising priestly life wasn't for them and their calling had been a wrong number.

Some of the younger acolytes had trouble taking the order

seriously. Made fun of the bishops and pontiffs with their time-steeped rituals. They had to go.

The ones that remained were prepared to obey the priests in all things, no matter how sacred or sick. The Bishop was surrounded by the best brown nosers in the see. They moved along the aisles of the church, ensured that each member of the congregation was observing the holy rituals. Anyone with a short attention span got poked with a stick.

Wash one paw slowly, then the other. Ears out wide in prayer. Kittens were scolded by their mothers if they didn't keep their tails still. They were so bored, and *Moggy & Mog* was on TV.

Sabbath School was dull – a lot of tall tales about Bastet creating the world with an accidental wink of her sleepy eye. The stars were the glints in her pupil as she looked down on Bast from the heavens. One day the cats would build their towers high enough to reach her, and there would be a reckoning for this would make her angry. She would sweep away civilisation with some disaster or other (as she was wont to do every few centuries) and the construction of the city would recommence from scratch. That's all for this morning little Johnny, thanks for coming and don't have nightmares on your way out.

After the ceremony, Otto was honoured enough to be allowed an audience with the learned Bishop. His vestry was a walnut-soaked harbour for cushions and soft drapes. Otto made himself comfortable, breathed in the scents of messages sprayed on the walls from visiting celebrities. *Thanks for the hospitality Bish, have a fine time all the time, Yours Swampie McMahon.*

The priest hunched down opposite Otto and got to the point.

'These are harsh times for us, Mr Mayor.'

'I'm crying for you.' Otto lit a stout cigar, breathing the fumes in the Bishop's face.

'The people are – not as generous as they used to be.'

'Tell me about it.'

'They can't afford to be. Your levies and duties have crippled them. They are hungry and tired. They need our succour. But it's going to cost them. Our entrance fees will continue to rise, for we know that our flock will pay whatever we demand in order to avoid the risk of brimstone and damnation.'

'Who reaps the profits, Father?'

'You can. I understand Brother Kafel explained our arrangement with your mother. We're willing to offer you exactly the same deal, with allowances made for inflation of course… on the quiet. The public need never know.'

'You're willing to feed me a slice of your angel cake?'

'If you must put it in culinary terms, yes. That's right.'

'I'm not scared of you and I'm certainly not scared of some fictional female deity. We only have one life to lead, that's it, finito. We don't get eight reruns. No second chances. You can take your offer and stick it in your almighty hallowed litter tray.'

As Otto stood up, a look of pity clouded the Bishop's face.

'Bless you anyway, Mr Mayor. I'll pass your answer on to my superiors. Have a good day.'

20

Half a dozen cats led by a tall, silent wraith of a tom, waited at the end of the corridor. They wore red robes with hems that brushed the floor, long sleeves that covered their paws, hoods that shielded their faces. They looked like demons, spike-topped goblins, circling him. They were the most forbidding security guards he had ever seen. He felt cold in their ugly presence.

There was a glint of white under their long sleeves and their teeth looked impossibly sharp. Tiger ducked into an office, hunched as short as he could behind a bureau. Black eyes swivelled in his direction. He'd been rumbled.

The tall guard approached, paws together, sleeves joining so that the arms looked like one flowing silken tube. He said nothing. The silence shook Tiger far more than any mewled threat. The detective stepped into the open, chin up, defiant.

'You can't kill me. I'm cute.'

The guard did not reply. Slowly, he opened his arms and the sleeves fell open. Revealed a set of glittering claws as long as bread knives. Ten daggers clattering together as the guard opened and closed his paws in a languorous stretching motion.

Tiger started to back away. The other guards shucked their robes, displaying their own cruel talons. They moved in and out of vision like dancing tongues of bright red flame. Extended their arms to block Tiger's exit. There was only one way out and he didn't want to end up on those claws, long enough to skewer a mule.

'He's right.' The guards turned in unison to find Bug dressed in an orange trouser suit, a cheeky grin on her face. 'He's cute as a button and twice as dangerous.'

Tiger piled past the guards, scattering them like fleas off a dead dog's back. He raced for the exit, dragging Bug with him. In the old days he would have stopped and fought the guards along-side his partner. Now he was struggling simply to survive.

JULIUS KYLE

Sal liked the tree on the corner of Miro Street. He liked to think of it as his tree. He didn't dare tell his best friend Warren. The tree was supposed to be a communal totem, a natural monument to the longevity of his gang. The tree knew who it belonged to, and so did Sal. It would be their secret. He liked keeping secrets.

'You ever seed a dog?' Warren asked, scratching his left buttock thoughtfully.

'What do they look like?' asked Sal with a half-cocked smile.

'Like hideous. Bestial. Worse than your mum.' Warren leaned against the tree trunk. Sal suppressed a pang of annoyance.

'That's bestial. Why do you ask?'

'Because I'd like to feed you to one.'

'Why?'

'I remember the time I fought one once.' Sal didn't need to ask who won. 'Had him begging for mercy. Big giant blood-hound he was. Thought he could chase me. Me! He didn't know that fightin' is my middle name.'

'I don't have a middle name.'

'You don't have much brains neither, do you? If you don't keep your mouth shut, you'll get me in bother with the boss.'

'What have you done to upset the boss?' Sal looked up and down the street, checking for Wildcats.

'Done some business behind his back. You imbecile. Yapping away about my sudden unexplained windfall –'

'I thought it was nice. Thought you'd want to share.'

'If you'd kept yer eyes open you would have seen I was up to something anyway. What do you think was in those little brown bags I was passing round?'

Sal wrinkled his nose thoughtfully.

'I figured on aniseed balls.'

'You're in now whether you want to be or not.'

'I don't mind.'

'Not a word of this when Samson's around, and look out for snoopers.'

'You gonna take over?'

'We are. The lot of us. It's time for a little equality round here.'

'If you say so.' Sal's tail quivered involuntarily.

'You can keep this secret, can't you?'

Sal gave a vigorous nod. 'I like secrets.' He stared at his

tree, a thought dimly forming in his sloped head. 'You wouldn't really feed me to a dog, would you?'

'Nah.' Warren gave his friend a rare grin. 'Never did like dogs. They smell bad. Funny. Like they're sweating all the time, getting hot, running around too much. Maybe it's their diet. Yeah, I hear their breath's so bad you can't get within five feet of 'em without chokin', or throwing up or something. Nearly got locked up in pokey with one once. Yeah, same cell and all. Ugly critter he was, name of Biff or Jeff or something doggish. Mutt spent most of his time with his paws around the bars, pads like chipolatas. When he said hello it was more like a growl, or a bark. Didn't seem pleased to see me. Hated cats, just because it was cats what judged him guilty and locked him up. Can you imagine, a jury of twelve cats good and true with a dog in the dock? Hardly gonna let him off with a caution, are they? So, suffice it to say he wasn't pleased at the prospect of sharin' his cell with me. It looked like I'd pulled the wrong number out of the box. Last minute, the guards changed their minds, not that they had a wit between them. Couldn't be arsed to clear up my blood and guts, like as not.'

'What were you in for?'

'Indecent exposure. On the run from a jealous girlfriend – I had the misfortune of bumping into some coppers.'

'Nobody's perfect.'

Warren produced a cigarette and struck a longlife match on the bark of the tree.

'Hey, Warren?' said Sal, jumping between his friend and the totem. 'This is my tree.'

'Whatever, Sal. Whatever you say.'

Julius had been tucked away in his pokey study for weeks, trying not to think about Morris, Moira or King. A rough draft of his new novel was complete, thanks to the notes he had dredged up from his time as a best-selling author: *The Kitty Killer Cult*, a proposed thriller that had never taken shape because of his fall from popular grace. The public had lost their interest in heroes, concerned with real issues like interracial strife and economic hardship. Perhaps it was time for heroes to resurface, a necessary good. Julius needed one.

He sat on the warm black rug, hindlegs spread, forelegs lolling, licking his downy stomach until it was clean. It helped him concentrate. It was an operation that he repeated several times a day, when he could find the time. It relaxed him and gave his creative juices a chance to flow.

A tap at the window startled him. It was his first visitor since Pa's B & E. Moira had come to pay him a call, still dressed in stark black.

She greeted him with a smile, letting herself in and helping herself to a salmon sandwich.

'I need your help.'

'Isn't Pa your designated guardian angel, sweetheart?'

'You know how hard he is to contact. Roaming around like a stray all over the city. I need you, darling. Now.'

'How can I help?' Julius shrugged. She'd taken the last of the salmon. His fridge still stank of rancid milk.

'Do you read your rag?'

'The *Post*? No. I haven't been in touch with them since –'

'Since the funeral. Yes. If you'd bothered to pick up a paper, you'd know what happened to Tufano a while back. Seems he had a run in with a pack of rats.'

'I can't tackle the Clutes, Moira. I don't want to end up like my friend Mick. This has got nothing to do with me.'

'Things're going to get worse. Spread. Disrupt your cosy little world.' Moira picked up the rough draft, digging her claws into the paper. 'All these words won't mean grit.'

'Okay, okay. I said I'd do what I could to help you. What do you want from me?'

'A little company.' Moira shivered. 'This place is draughty. Did anyone ever tell you that?'

'You're right,' admitted Julius, 'I can never seem to get warm. You need a hot water bottle?'

'I need you.'

'So what's stopping you?'

'It doesn't seem quite right here.' Moira took Julius' paw in hers.

'You want to go somewhere less private?'

'The moon's out tonight.'

Stars twinkled through the ugly fug that smothered Bast every dusk. Ecological concerns had lost out to the cats' pursuit of leisure; despite their innate link with nature, they were more interested in getting plenty of naps than saving the planet from pollution.

Moira described Tufano's death in tabloid-tight detail. 'Apparently he looked even uglier without his face.'

'You've got a morbid sense of humour, you know that?'

'I know it. I like talking about things like that. Helps me. I don't wanna sweep it under the carpet.'

'Of course not.' Julius' head shook in rhythm with his tail.

'I feel like I'm surrounded by it.'

'Not yet.' Moira looked at Julius quizzically.

'I've got the perfect catharsis for you.'

Cat morgues consist of a series of tree trunks propped against each other to form an enormous tepee structure. Inside, long rows of slabs hold the bodies of felled cats for a period of up to two weeks. Scents at the foot of each slab note the personal details of the corpse, plus any other useful particulars – time and manner of death (if known), the attendant in charge, where the body was found and the date of delivery. It didn't take long for Julius and Moira to find Tufano's rotting skeleton.

'Cold in here, isn't it?' Moira kept an eye out for the attendant.

'That's because it's a morgue. I'm always amazed how they keep it cool in here.'

'I'm surprised they can read these scents. Some of these bodies reek.'

'I don't hear anyone else complaining. Look at the way these bones are snapped in half.'

'Rats,' she shuddered. 'Nasty.'

'No chance. It would take something way bigger than a rat – or a cat – to break bones in two.' Julius examined Tufano's corpse, the claws still sharp and shiny, with traces of blood on them.

'Probably slit himself open trying to get them off him. Even Tufano would panic at a time like that.'

'What's this?' Moira plucked a scarlet strand from one of Tufano's remaining pads.

'Fibre. Like cat hair, but too thick...' There were a couple more of the coarse strands stuck to one shin.

'From the factory. Julius?'

'Yes?' He turned, moonlight reflected in his eyes. Moira gave him a tender kiss and the cats clasped each other by the paws.

'I'm... scared,' said Moira, looking for an excuse to pull Julius closer. A noise from the far side of the morgue made her hiccup in fright. 'Quick!' she whispered, pulling him onto a free slab, draping a white sheet over their shivering forms. Someone was coming. They caught a glimpse of two green eyes before the sheet covered them completely.

'This is starting to get cosy.' Moira clamped a paw over Julius' lips, wary of the cat so close to them. Hopefully the smell of death would mask their own scents.

'I've never had a one night stand before.'

'I find that hard to believe.' Julius didn't dare to move.

'No, honestly. I've never had a one night stand.'

'Maybe you'll want to see me again.'

'No, Julius. This is it.'

Their noses were close. They could feel each other's fur warming them, a smooth nestling. Their whiskers quivered, entwined, sending shivers along the thirsty vines of their nervous systems. Their eyes were closed, sensing each other, probing. Julius cradled Moira in his arms, licking her under the chin. They rubbed against each other harder, tighter, panting. Tried to stay quiet, not to move too much – this excited them further. Julius began milk treading, kneading his paws against his mate as if she was his mother. His mouth was happy-slack. Moira returned Julius' caresses and for twenty minutes, he was in love.

21

THE ALICAT GYM HAD been set up to keep aggressive Doghouse residents off the streets. Bridget had fixed the place up with high-tech sports apparatus, opened it up and welcomed everyone in. An expensive publicity stunt, it had bought her a few votes come election time, but the gym had fallen into neglect and the apparatus was quickly hocked by enterprising thieves.

The Wildcats had presently moved in, got rid of any earnest athletes, and used it as a meeting place. Anyone who wore the right colours and talked the right talk could work out, make some deals and catch up on local gossip.

Buzz was, Missy had taken Tufano's place as leader of the Clutes. The boys were in awe of her, fantasised about meeting her and setting her ideologies straight. It would never happen, of course. She'd dice them before they could open their mouths. Only Samson was a match for her, and he was getting old. It was time for a new generation to take over – if it wasn't wiped out in the next gang war.

Even though the Wildcats were united by their creed, they were divided by their favourite sport. Canvas climbing was dominated by two major teams, the Razors and the Braves. Warren and Sal favoured the former; most of the Wildcats preferred the latter. This slight difference of opinion had segregated them, colours within colours like a refracted rainbow.

By the time Warren arrived at the grey slab structure, the sun was at its zenith and male cats posed outside, hanging out, adopting their coolest manner – trying to attract a mate. His gang buddies waited inside (where no non-Wildcat dared to tread). Lean signs and symbols had been carefully shaved into their fur. Words of alienation and hate were tattooed on the soft pink insides of their ears and the pads of their forepaws. He felt a sense of importance as he greeted them. He belonged, and he felt safe – life was a precarious thing to hold onto and it took courage to wear gang garb.

Everyone had their own little area of the gym – the boys needed their personal space. If someone entered your area, accidentally or otherwise, he became a natural sparring partner. Warren made sure that he always won a bout. He could see a potential prize-fight coming as soon as he reached the far wall. It held a high stretch of canvas, blue, hanging taut from the ceiling. In front of it stood Malvo, a Brave supporter, thick-whiskered and broad to suit. He needed no prompting, challenged his rival on the spot.

'Been hearing sorry stories about you, Warren. Going your own way. Trying to rip Samson off.'

'No way am I messing with the boss,' said Warren, glad that his brown paper bag was stashed tight in his pocket.

'I know what you got going on behind our chief bastard's back.' Malvo snarled. Warren couldn't have read his body language easier if the signs had been set up in six foot neon.

Malvo looked him up and down, loyal, indignant. He didn't need to say much. The two cats insulted each other through a series of complex blinks and winks, prowled round each other, constantly circling as if they were hungry. Their hearts beat fast, heads filled with the memories of past battles – old wounds opened up again. They fought the urge to let their instincts take over.

'Care to test the size of your balls?' asked Malvo.

'I didn't come here for a hissing contest.' Warren shrugged, but he was ready for anything.

'You gonna race me up there, or are you too sissy?' Malvo pointed at the canvas.

Boxing mitts crowded in the corner, curled with sweat in a mound of bruised purple. In the early days of boxing, mitts had been tethered with long laces. The athletes – and the audience come to that – had been so distracted by the dangling togs that many matches had stumbled to a halt. The laces had been replaced by elastic, and boxing had been replaced by canvas climbing. These days boxing was frowned upon as a barbaric activity. It had gone underground, a passion amongst gangs, prevalent in the Doghouse.

Windows set high above remained eternally closed, grimed with soot. The Wildcats didn't want any ventilation. They wanted to smell their own odours; these were the kind of males who'd leave their faeces in a prominent place, a sign of dominant defiance.

The canvas swung against the wall with a satisfied hum. The blue was reflected on the uneven floor, like a rippling pond. The hardwood floor was slippery, you could hear the scud and scrape of hindclaws and pads. There were no soft landings here – this was a place for tough guys, the land of playing rough; sparrers didn't expect an eiderdown crashmat when they were knocked on their arse. You wanted to hurt your opponent – that was the whole point, whatever your game of choice. Warren's was canvas climbing, and he accepted Mal's challenge with a cheeky grin.

He leaped for the canvas, yanking himself upwards, claws digging into the soft material, carrying his weight until he could scrabble with his hindpaws. Malvo was a breath behind him, stretching long limbs out to gain purchase on the canvas. As he levelled with Warren he swung at him, batting at his opponent with a curled paw. Other cats on the ground cheered them on, placing wagers on their favourite climber.

Warren's tail twitched, keeping him vertical; the canvas was ragged and torn from past contests, and to put his weight on the wrong part would mean a long fall. Mal took another swing at him, and he slipped downwards a span. His opponent was above him now, almost at the top. Warren hoisted himself up, emitting a deep yowl. Both cats reached the top of the canvas together – they still had to descend. Last one down's a damp rat. Their job wasn't made easy by the funsters below, who were now clutching the bottom of the canvas and swinging it forwards and backwards, trying to dislodge the players. All part of the game.

Retracting their claws, the two cats started to slide down, spurs springing back out as required to slow their fall. But Malvo misjudged his descent, and on the ground Sal gave the canvas one last shove. The Brave supporter fell, somersaulting in the air to land on his feet. He ended up in a crumpled heap on the relatively safe cushioning of Sal's head.

Warren had won – not quite square, but as fair as things

got in the gym. He savoured the feel of the material under his claws. The sport provided some good exercise. Dispose of that gut. Warren had beaten them all, hanging high above his brothers, his drool splashing their hot brows. He allowed himself a victorious meow.

Far below, Sal lay on his back gasping heavily. The fall had winded him, and it took a while for his breath to regain its natural cadence. Malvo shook his head, his legs bandied by the drop, disappointed with Sal.

'Laddie's on the nip,' he explained to his brothers. 'Moves like a crawling Clute. You don't wanna touch that nip. One taste o' that and it's got you hooked like a dog on a hydrant; hooked for all your nine lives. It's ugly, I've seen guys addicted to that stuff, eyes pokin' out, bowl size.'

Warren had reached the floor, sensed that someone was approaching the building. He ignored his opponent and padded over to the entrance as his boss came in. The other Wildcats turned to greet Samson. He seemed hesitant, as if he had something difficult to tell them.

'You know when you introduce some friends, and you're not in a welcoming mood, and it's not who you might expect? Well, I feel like in a difficult position. Keep your lips shut, your claws sheathed.' Samson ushered in the newcomers. 'These are our allies. Greet them as your kin, they may be in a position to save your lives one day.'

Some cats wanted to leave in disgust. Only Samson's clout stopped them. A lot of them had never seen creatures like this before, not in the flesh. They were fascinated, curious, repelled by the odour.

Warren reached over to touch one, show his pals he wasn't

afraid. The hair felt coarse and stiff. His new friend snuffed back at him, making him recoil. Malvo laughed and Samson wrapped his arms round the allies' shoulders, hunching them up into a semicircle.

'It'll be cool, guys. It's gonna take a while –'

'Too soon,' said one of the newcomers. 'Too early.'

'They've gotta be told. My gang has gotta know what's going on. Now's the time.'

'So what is going on?' asked Warren, recovering his pride.

'There are a lot of people sympathetic to us in this city, boys. We're going to expand – the Clutes won't know what hit 'em. Pretty soon they'll be a dead memory, and we'll be on top. Ain't that right fellas?' The allies grunted, pulling away from Samson. He respectfully put some distance between himself and the creatures. Warren suppressed a shudder.

'We don't need them,' he declared, and for once Malvo agreed with him.

'They'll make us more powerful,' Samson explained, 'so long as we don't let this divide us. You're pretty nifty with that canvas aren't you, Warren?' Malvo nodded ruefully. Samson looked at the creature nearest to him. 'Fancy taking a crack with a new opponent?'

'Sure. I'll beat anyone.'

'Then go!' Warren took heed and raced for the canvas, ready to launch himself upwards and sink his claws into the material again. Before his haunches could tense up, the creature was on him, ripping his beautiful tail away with one swipe of its jaws.

Warren collapsed in a scream of pain. The other cats

were too sensible to help him up. Instead they watched his attacker trot over to the canvas, sniff at it in disdain, then return to its brethren.

Warren was left to lick his wounds, while Samson's boys grouped together for a peace pipe meeting. The Wildcats wanted to know what had happened to Tufano. Samson wanted to allay their fears.

'This is a good thing. It couldn't have come at a better time, while the Clutes are so weak. We've cut off food supplies, they're tired, lost their leader. We've got them over a futting big barrel. And with our friends here –'

'We'll whack the lot of them.' Malvo supplied an evil grin, parodied by the newcomers.

'Whaddabout this dude who's been snooping round?' asked Sal, desperate to get in on the act. He held Warren's tail in his eager paws.

'Which dude would this be?' Samson looked at Sal, as if he were a flea that was daring to look at its dinner.

'The scribbler. Writer. Works for the papers. He been asking questions, talking to the neighbours.'

'Squish him. To be on the safe side. Gotta be small fry. Now the big demolition jobs – they go to these fellas. They're my best boys.'

Warren and Sal looked at each other, sullen. Sal passed the tail back to its spiteful owner. They were no longer the boss' main operators; he'd obviously made a mistaken judgement. Something would have to be done about that.

22

CAMILLA WAS LOOKING FORWARD to seeing her lover. She had some jobs to do first, arrangements to make, medicine to buy. The barren North Country had not been kind to her; she'd developed the sniffles and her legs ached. The cold still sat in her bones, refusing to budge. She sat as close as she could to the radiator that lined one side of the train.

She'd got her story. That was the important thing – performed the task she'd been bound to complete.

Her carriage was a spotless gleaming silver. Passengers demanded cleanliness; the trains were scrubbed from ceiling to floor after each journey with long sponge tongues, moistened with cleaning fluids containing the unique scent of the rail company. Within seconds of the train filling up, it was covered in hair and fluff.

Every seat was backed with a mirror; if travellers got tired of watching their reflections in the window, they could amuse themselves with their looking glass images. The rail company liked to keep them happy; a trolley was pushed along the aisle from passenger to passenger, stocked up by kitchen staff, keeping hunger on hold until they reached their destination. The catering carriage was the longest on the train – twice as long as the others on heavy trips.

Camilla felt fat. She'd been stuffing her face the whole

journey. Perhaps she'd get stuck on her way out, a stuffed curio for ticket collectors to inspect. Her meal tariff would be higher than her travel expenses. She suspected that the rail company made their profits on the tariffs, and that was why food prices were vastly inflated on the train. She had never been more thankful for a bloated expense account.

Camilla walked slowly out of the station, not because she had time to kill, but because she wanted everyone to catch sight of her and admire her beautiful body. She strutted, carrying herself with the grace of a model and the charm of a panther. And yes, she did turn heads and make the males stop and stare. She smiled demurely, counting up the gawps in her head. She hoped to beat her usual target that day, fourteen drools, twenty pairs of popping eyes and two cats walking into lampposts. What was a city with a large male population for, if not to admire her?

After an exhibitionist trip to a nearby drug store it was a short walk to the *Scratching Post* offices, where she had agreed to meet her companion. She wondered what Julius had been up to – mail to the North Country was infrequent to the point of being nonexistent. They'd tried to keep in touch, failed miserably, and the weeks had spun by as they worked.

Her lover was waiting for her on the bridge outside the newspaper headquarters. He leaned against a railing, a pointy-toothed yawn escaping his lips. He seemed to take up half the path.

'Good to see you back, m'dear,' he said, giving her a tight embrace. She endured the wrap of fur and fat that engulfed her, threatening to smother her.

'That's nice, Morris darling,' she choked. 'How are the minions?'

'As restless as ever. As long as we get a paper out every day, that's the main thing.' He began to groom her fur with his monstrous tongue, and her tail automatically sprang erect. 'Did you pass on my little invite to our friends in the North?' Morris asked between rasps.

'I did. Quite a while ago, in fact. I'm surprised they haven't been in touch.'

'What do you mean?'

'They must be here already. They were trouble, Morris. Real animals.' She could feel saliva dribbling down her coat. 'They should be tearing up the town by now.'

'Did they hurt you?' Morris gave his star reporter a frown.

'Don't tell me you'd care if they had?' Camilla stared down at the water, in a hurry under the bridge. She wondered what poor faithful Julius would think if he knew that she was sleeping with his editor. (Write about it, probably.) It had given her career a considerable boost.

'I'm a busy tom, Camilla. But I always make time to care about you.' Morris hawked a furball over the side of the bridge. Camilla swallowed hard, and the tiny bell necklaced at her throat rang. He noticed it for the first time. 'I suppose you're going to see that whippersnapper Kyle,' he added in a churlish drawl.

'He does not snap whippers,' Camilla was indignant. 'I've never seen him snap a whipper in his life. He gets some good scoops for you doesn't he?'

'Not any more. He's gone. Out of here months ago. He's

off writing his great novel.' Morris stuck his nose in the air, dancing in a discreet circle.

'We'll see about that.'

23

Tiger Straight slumped at the dining table, too exhausted to shovel food in his mouth. Straight's faithful companion, Bug, nudged a bowl of meat nearer to him. Straight arched back in his seat; the smell of the food seemed to offend him.

'Lost your appetite, Tiger?' asked Bug, hair shrouding her rounded face. 'Heroes've got to eat too, you know.'

'I'm no hero.'

'Oh yeah, sure. Like all cats spend their mornings rescuing a maiden in distress from four ne'er-do-wells.'

'I don't wanna talk about it.'

'You got three of 'em with one punch! It was incredible... damnedest thing I ever saw.'

'Enough!' Straight slammed the food across the table, bolting from his chair. A tear dribbled down his left cheek. 'I didn't mean to hurt them.'

'But they deserved it!'

Straight was already heading for his study.

'I don't want to be disturbed.'

Speechless, Bug watched as Straight made a dramatic exit. Bug shook her head; maybe Straight was disturbed, or getting too old for the crime fighting business. He certainly needed to brush

up on his social skills. Bug began to clear up
the spilled food.

'Good to see you back, m'dear,' he said, giving
her a tight embrace. She endured the wrap of fur
and fat that engulfed her, threatening to smother her.

JULIUS KYLE

Julius tidied his place up, cleaned his clothes, groomed his
fur again – was there any evidence to give away his indiscre-
tion? There was no lipstick on his collar, no new scent on his
tainted paws.

Guilt was an emotion that cats didn't experience often,
but Julius had felt so much over the preceding months, for
Mick, King and now Camilla. Instead of feeling pleased with
himself for the one night stand, he was depressed. Moira had
not been in touch with him since their tryst together, and
that had saved him from embarrassment. Camilla loved him,
she'd missed him, and that made him angry. Angry that he
couldn't love her back, he'd lost the passion for her that he'd
felt in their first weeks together. Angry with himself for being
so weak, and scared that some small detail would expose his
infidelity. He cared a great deal for Camilla, and he'd pined
for her. Another weakness. She was trapping him, changing him
into a moral, fragile thing. Who'd ever heard of a journalist
with scruples?

Camilla made her presence known with a flustered flourish,
dumping a heap of luggage on the floor. She tried on her
damsel in distress look – it didn't fit. Julius was busy working
on a proof copy of his novel.

'When's it due?'

'Beg pardon?' Julius felt awkward in her presence.

'The book. I want to read it.'

'Rush release. As soon as they can, 'to capitalise on intense media interest,' as Boston put it.'

Julius wasn't sure if it was Camilla's long absence or the bang with Moira, but it had done wonders for his libido. He couldn't keep his paws off his partner, and with the book revisions out of the way he was free to chase her round the house. If she got sick of it, she'd head into the office for a breather. Camilla didn't give him butterflies in the stomach like Moira did, but he put that down to Camilla's cucumber-cool façade. She only let it slip when she was in the right mood. He made sure she was in that mood as often as possible.

The book was nothing short of iconic, and the old logo and picture on the front (Tiger Straight chained and locked in a flooded cellar by a bad guy) made Julius feel nostalgic. His head filled with images of books rushed from the shelves, stacked in windows, promoted with enormous cardboard standee displays, tills ringing a rapid fire melody –

Unfortunately, a celeb book (Swampie McMahon's autobiography) came out the same week. Although Swampie had retired from wrestling, he was still loved by schoolmaids and grannies everywhere. Wrestling had recently undergone a revival. It was more vicious, there were fewer rules, more pomp and finery – loud music soundtracked the fights; when wrestlers got into the rhythm of the piece, lashing their tails to the beat or downing an opponent as the tune ended, they received extra cheers from the audience and extra cash from the sponsors. Swampie was master of the choreographed kill.

He was also an accomplished raconteur, and had become

after-dinner speechwriter for a generation of fellow wrestlers – the writing had naturally developed into a book of memoirs. Or so the official story went. Julius was sure it was ghost written, he recognised the prose style. It read like one of his contemporaries fallen on high times.

The autobiography had the press on the ropes and the sensation-hungry public in a heavy headlock. A daily mention in the *Post* helped. Despite his cratered face and hunched shoulders, Swampie had become a universal pin up – there was hope for all the ugly wannabes out there – and used his new daytime TV chat show as a vehicle to plug the book.

More popular than mouse pie, his face leered from every bookstand in every department store throughout the city, as well as newsagents, supermarkets, tobacconists, libraries and church halls. Hoardings bore down, watching citizens wending their antlike way along the streets; ads on the radio, in the papers hailed the book's virtues with a shopping list of raving comments. Bold. Big. Brash. Cool. Odd. Wit. Great. Best. Read. Buy. Now!

Julius' novel looked small and grey beside Swampie's mighty tome. After an initial curiosity, interest in the continued adventures of Tiger Straight seemed to wane. But Julius had more important matters on his mind than publicising a book, and before long so did the public.

In the city's local television studio, long brown corridors were walled with soft fabrics well known to viewers of live broadcasts throughout the decades. They were illuminated by reflective circles of glass overhead; there were no windows – day and night did not rule here.

The place was a maze. There had been accounts of parties of schoolchildren getting lost in the lower bowels of the building. These levels were cluttered with heavy, old fashioned equipment that every other production company envied because they didn't quite know what it did; keen cubs shivered in portacabins adjoining the studio, exploited by their employers, glad to have a foothold in the broadcast industry. They pored monastically over strapped-up towers of dog-eared tapes and leaderless film cans. The outer fascia of the studio centre held a wall-length bank of video screens, filled with the furry friend-of-a-nation face of Swampie McMahon in his latest incarnation: daytime talkshow host. The cats who worked here were full of themselves. They were an elite. Everyone looked up to them, they were providing a national service and they were the best at it in the world. By Bastet it made them precious.

The heaviest activity came from Studio Alpha, a buzzing hive of luvvies and light lunchers who were busy filming Swampie's live show. On a satin blue set with cushions for seats, he was interviewing Bridget and Professor Blane, a Burmese longhair, in a regular book review slot. Bridget found television a useful tool in her ongoing campaign of self-promotion; the Professor had a creed to preach. He embraced any opportunity to share his longhair view with the rest of the nation.

Swampie had developed a smooth series of mannerisms since starting his new career. Before dropping names he would pause, scratch his nose, take a breath and then launch into a famous nomenclature, naturally followed by an embarrassing anecdote.

Mirrors were used to refract images from one camera to different monitors, giving multiple angles. Technicians toggled switches to adjust the angles. Back in the early days of programme making the mirrors had been moved using a complicated pulley system, involving various tendrils of string. The crew had been unable to resist sneaking off with the dangling lengths (to wrap round their boxing gloves or as a plaything for the kids), so the strings had been cut and automation had swiftly followed.

Swampie kicked off the slot by giving the viewers at home a brief précis of the day's subject. It was a tale of romance and revenge, featured the return of crime fighter Tiger Straight, and was written by the journalist, Julius Kyle. With a volley of his wrestler's charm, Swampie introduced Bridget and Professor Minglan Blane, Anthropological Studies, Burmese Hall of Scientific Research.

'The animosity that raddles our species,' began the Professor, brandishing Julius' book to illustrate his points, 'breed against breed, cousin against cousin is an expression of one's hatred of the self. What this book so adequately expresses (in simple terms, of course) is that the Other, the enemy of which every animal is wary, exists within ourselves as well as beyond our molly-coddling environs. We must fix ourselves if we are to fix the world and make it safe for our progeny. *The Kitty Killer Cult* supports my own belief that we should one day be able to live in harmony with other species, offering them succour even as we learn from their alternate approaches to life. The way they cope with the pith of progress.'

'Nothing less than a disgrace,' was Bridget's opinion of

the book. 'The sort of narrow minded, anti-establishment liberal claptrap that leads to decadence and corruption. Now, I don't hold with the kind of sensationalist violence this author's previous books revel in, but at least they had simple, solid villains to teach youngsters patriotism. We all need someone to hate. It brings the group together.'

'This is the first time cats have been presented as bad guys,' Swampie pointed out. 'Is that your problem?'

'Don't know, I haven't read the book. But I've heard enough about it to be sure that it shouldn't be in the stores, within easy reach of tots.'

'You're saying you'd prefer impressionable kittens to grow up hating dogs and wolves, rather than learning that cats are also capable of being a threat to them?' Swampie was sure that he had her in a hypothetical half nelson.

'Yes. I'm also saying the book shouldn't be around for kittens to pick up anywhere.'

'So adults will lose out as well?' Down on the mat. She'd be out in ten.

'There are plenty of adult cats out there just as susceptible as their children, with lower intelligence than you or I.' Bridget's claws had popped out, and were busy raking the red cushion she sat on. 'Someone has to make decisions for them, for the greater good, and it may as well be the cognoscenti.'

'What about creative expression?' asked the Professor, losing his cool.

'The day I start calling trash like this 'creative' is the day when my tail drops off.' Bridget threw her copy of the book onto the floor in front of her. It lay forlorn, with Julius' face scrutinising her from the back cover.

Swampie tried to diffuse the thickening atmosphere:

'I remember dining in a fine restaurant, the Grand Canary, when I last met...' (Pause, scratch nose, deep breath) '...Julius Kyle. He was having a little trouble with a rabbit.' The audience laughed. 'His tablemate didn't seem much happier to be there with him. I was wondering which one would scarper first.'

'I can see where this dude's coming from,' said the Professor, feeling a little more relaxed now that Bridget had said her piece. 'I mean, what Mr Kyle's doing is he's looking at the conflict between ourselves, the way that we fight each other like cats and... well, you know. If we can look at that, try and control our conflicts, then perhaps we could learn to live together, learn to integrate. Breeds would tolerate each other, species would tolerate each other. Could you imagine what we could achieve if we all worked together?'

'Well, that shows us how fanciful this book must be.' Bridget folded her hefty arms. 'It's full of impractical ideas, it shows that this writer has his head in the clouds, doesn't know what to believe. He doesn't understand the principles that hold this society together. You need conflict, we need people to pick on, we need a species to fear. Don't need to mention the name of that species, do I? And then we all pull together against the common foe! No disrespect to the Professor here, but look at the longhairs. They want a relaxed environment where anyone can wander in and out whenever they please no matter what they are. There are some aggressive types up in the North, I can tell you. I've been up there, it wasn't pretty, it wasn't pretty at all. I wouldn't want to go back. That's for sure.

'The Professor may want universal harmony. What he really needs is a bit of sorting out. He needs to put his own house in order. When he's satisfied, and stops squandering research funds on these crazy ideas, I'm sure he'll come to understand how impractical coexistence would be. There would be fur flying everywhere. There'd be lots of death and horrible things like that.'

'I'm all for being practical, I don't live in some theoretical fancyland where I think that dreams can come true. I do know that it is not a silly desire to want to improve things. Books that make us look at our society, show us what's wrong with it and make us think can't be a bad thing.' Professor Blane sat back on his cushion with a smug twitch of his whiskers. End of slot. But it was Bridget who had dominated the proceedings, and she was the one that the audience would remember.

24

The latest Tiger Straight novel continues Lauriston Books' run of tawdry, ill-conceived, overly commercial, high concept low brow books. It's the most recent knot in a string of bad moves from publishing editor Boston Cook, who believes that he can continue to print drivel without going bankrupt.

Cook is the only cat in current literary circles who contends that allowing old hacks to attempt novels, reviving well-worn cliché characters and using celebrity names to sell ghost written books can be a viable publishing proposition. The celeb volumes may have led to moderate sales (the public has been desperate to wrestle with Swampie McMahon's new self-portrait) but no critical approval (particularly from me.) Lauriston's run of cookery tomes such as Fun With Basmati Mice keep the publishers going, and Boston has thus far managed to hang onto his job. Even these old favourites seem to be running out of steam – how many ways are there to prepare rats, cheese, chicken, beef and fish?

The Kitty Killer Cult's publishers are doing nothing short of ripping off the kittens who must be this book's target audience.

REVIEW SECTION
THE PERUSER

Most paths circumvented the river – many cats couldn't bear to look at water, never mind cross it. The undrinkable mire didn't provide much of a view anyway – brown as coffee and five times as bad for you. The odd tourist came for a butcher's, to discern whether it was as bad as the guides promised. They came away with minds assured and pegs on their noses.

Julius was feeling brave that day so he skirted the water slowly. He took in the sight of the towering office blocks behind him, the dockland cranes, and the slums on the opposite side of the bank. He didn't want to be too early for his mystery meeting. He'd been brought up to be punctual, whatever the situation.

This particular mystery had started with a phone call, a kind of bark at the other end of the line, followed by a late-night time and a secluded place and the sombre click of a disconnected line. Julius was sure he'd spoken to Pa, gruff and to-the-point. The first mystery lay in Pa's reason for wanting to meet him. The second was Julius' desire to turn up. Although his reporter days were over, he wanted to know more about Pa, what made him tick. For some reason, he'd developed respect for the old hound.

Respect for a dog! Julius surprised himself. He'd never thought of it before. He didn't see Pa as a mutt but as someone he'd gone through a lot of grit with. He was a bigot, but as long as there were worse bigots Julius could live with it.

Thin, delicate cranes arched overhead. They used a complex set of weights and pulleys. Built on the cat model, they had four stilt legs and a tail for balance. Their stretched-out necks jutted across the moon-salted water, fetching raw materials from passing boats. Beyond the docks, factories belched their smoke signals, producing goods for export from the city.

'You know where they take that stuff?' asked Pa, rising from the shadow of a shelled warehouse.

'The factory,' Julius blinked, 'one of the factories.'

''Sright. Ugly places.'

'Didn't they use your kind in there for a while?' Julius remembered subbing a piece on the factories; something about harsh conditions.

'They dropped em long ago. Before I got here, before King was born at least. Dogs work cheap, sure, give a dog a bone and he won't howl, but the blue-collar cats didn't like it. Bosses said it was causing unrest.'

'I never heard about that.'

'If you had, you wouldn't have listened. Anything to do with us, the public shuts their ears off. So much for acute hearing. The dogs got kicked out. Not laid off, mind you; one day they was working hard as you please, next day the gates were locked and they weren't allowed in. No pink slips, no leaving jamboree and definitely no gold carriage clocks. The dogs had no food and nowhere to go. Cats'd domesticated them if you like, they could hardly fend for themselves. That's how the ghetto was born. Buncha sad-asses with cardboard homes and cardboard hopes.'

'You had some news for me.'

'I'm not sure how to break it to ya. Maybe you should take a load off.' Julius sat down on a hitching bollard, looking down into the river. It sparkled with twilight mischief.

'You know how... sometimes a cat keeps a secret. The public has a right to know, but some cats think too much knowledge would cause a fuss. There're certain chunks of information that they keep to themselves.'

'What're you getting at, Pa?'

'These nuggets, if made known, could save a few lives. But the panic that would ensue could cause more suffering. So they let my son die.'

'Who let him die?'

Pa lost his cool. His muzzle wrinkled back in a snarl, he grabbed Julius and held him bodily off the dock. Julius looked down to see his hind paws dangle over the water.

'Your bosses!' Pa barked. 'Your bloody paper, your fat son-of-a-monkey editor, your sanctimonious –' As Pa ranted he shook Julius violently. The cat's jacket came apart at the seams; he was crying, Please don't drop me Pa!

Pa looked up as he heard the name, looked into Julius' eyes but saw his son's, dead, the light escaped from them forever.

'Pa, please don't do this to me.'

The dog set Julius gently on the dock, patted him down, subdued a shudder. Julius felt a wave of pity.

'I lost a good friend too.'

'Mick was in danger because of what he knew. He didn't want you to be in trouble as well. Then Morris gives your partner a good talking to just before he takes his dip.'

'Mick killed himself...'

'Because the cat he trusted most in the world, Morris, was up to no good in a serious way. He couldn't face the betrayal.'

'Why didn't he tell me? This is crazy! Why should Morris cover all this up, put me on the assignment?'

'He doesn't hold much store in your journalistic skills, from what I hear. Thought you were too lazy or dumb or arty-farty to discover the truth.'

'I am. You've done it all. How did you..?'

'Infiltration. Espionage. A little common-or-garden-as-you-please eavesdropping. For some reason the *Post* wants this conspiracy kept quiet. Maybe they got a vested interest in seeing the gangs knock each other off. I never did understand politics. But my kid –'

'I'm sorry I got him involved.'

'Ah, don't beat yourself up about it. Cubs that age, they either join a gang or run away to play soldiers. There's no future for them. It was idealistic of me to suppose otherwise. You gotta get this scoop to the readers, ed or no ed.'

'Wait a minute! How many people have died so this scoop won't get read?'

'Couldn't tell ya. One way to find out how hot this thing is...'

'What's that?'

'Print it.'

25

Tiger jumped at the chance to watch Hairy's back, sure that the Kitty Killer Cult had Bug. She hadn't been in touch since he'd spurned her cooking, and he didn't consider her the sulking type. He agreed to trail the actor at a discreet distance, following him into the Beggars' Temple.

Hairy gave the temple guard two voles, an offering to the spirits of long-gone beggars. The guard asked the same of Tiger, who produced a juicy hare. It had been a wedding gift, but the guard insisted on taking it. Hairy had already flounced up a flight of stone steps. The guard put the hare in his mouth, clamped down his molars and smiled.

Hairy had vanished by the time Tiger got inside. A tall cat stooped under the canted ceiling. He showed Tiger a veiled entranceway. The detective doubled up to descend into a tunnel; it was poorly lit. Ancient tools and weapons shone above his head. They had been bronzed to the tunnel roof.

He reached an antechamber, tiled brown. On the tiles were obscure scent-messages and hieroglyphs. He looked at the symbols and attempted to translate them. For the first time –

He understood.

JULIUS KYLE

In a city as teeming as Bast, it was hard to find a place in the open where you could be alone. You had to climb out of the centre, up the Western slopes of Lauriston and into a lush wooded area for some peace. Julius visited the woods when he needed to focus, work on an article, block out the dreary intercourse of daily life.

He brushed through the trees looking for his favourite spot, his mind toiling over Pa's words. He'd never stuck his neck out in his life. He'd chased a good story, risked a poison pen letter or two from critical readers – that was the extent of his audacity. He was as steeped in his ways as a stick in a toffee apple. He couldn't suddenly transform into a champion of the common cat, wake up in the morning with a suit of shining armour waiting in his wardrobe.

There was a breach in the trees where he could see across the city. The view accentuated the steep hills and dips on which Bast was built. Five spires probed the clouds, two angular, one domed, two of mixed breeds. A clustered maze of brown houses rose and fell in domino layers, the poorer areas down by the river, the centre of the city as far from its stink as possible. The wealthier you were the higher you climbed, scrabbling up towards the Mayor's office, which overlooked the plebs.

The centre was flanked by tan office blocks, long sun-tinted windows and vaulted roofs. Other red brick office towers lurked in the background, enslaving half the city's workers and hoisting corporate flags. They waved at the volcanic region to the north; long extinct behemoth mountains, curling like a half-submerged sea serpent. Mist rose and dissipated quickly in the city, the air as way-up thin as the citizens were mean.

Julius knew what went on in the city. Thought he did. He was aware of the evil, the praetorian injustice, the imbalance of it all. No one cat could shift the scales, purify the corrupt and rescue the world from itself. To consider such a path would be hypocritical. There was something else at stake, however. A cracking, racing, ball-breaking story. He had a yarn to spin, one that the tabloid sniffing public was entitled to hear. There was no way he could keep it to himself.

The hat still fit. Although the trenchcoat was a little tight at the tummy, he managed to wrap it round his middle-aged body. He'd been given the outfit by his book publishers a long time back, for a publicity stunt, pretending to foil a robbery at some small-fried sea food merchant's. Now he looked the part again, assuming the mantle of Tiger Straight, the paperback PI, the stealthy detective, a lonely urban hero dancing to the beat of a different bummer. It gave him the conviction he needed to go and ask for his old job back.

As far as Julius could recall, the definition of a news editor was a ruddy, cynical, unapproachable cat whom everyone had to approach. Morris revelled in his role, ogring into the office every morning, sending copy boys out to fetch him snacks at frequent intervals, and pacing around the basement presses when the mood took him. Julius happened to meet him there, sent down by the Queen to have a heart-to-heart.

The presses were cold and silent; Julius could hear the gush of the river nearby. In a corner of the basement a group of proofsniffers checked over the day's copy. Old and jaded by years of stock horror probes, they didn't look up as Julius bounded in. He cleared his throat to catch Morris' attention. The editor didn't turn round.

'This is what reminds me I'm alive, J. Smell that? All those different story scents, lingering in the air?' *Yesterday's news*, thought Julius. 'All those yarns waiting to be digested when fresh nozzles are placed on the presses? I find it intoxicating.'

Julius sneezed. All this technology. It was his bread and butter, the paper had paid his heating bill for the past decade or so, but he was old enough to remember the days when cats were more in tune with nature, before some nutter had convinced them that living in a semi-detached bungalow with all mod cons was preferable to sleeping in a bush.

'When we send you out there – and your tram tickets ain't cheap – we want details, reports – not some antiquated moral viewpoint. I asked for dispassionate journalese – none of this waste of war nonsense. A little purple prose, fine – we gotta get the readers hooked. But please, if ya wanna moan or preach you've picked the wrong profession. Get yourself a cassock and get outta my office.'

'Pass the incense burner, vicar.' Morris was the bigger cat in a dominant position, but Julius refused to back down. He kept his belly covered, his hackles raised, teeth bared, eyes wide, ears splayed listening for security guards.

'I told Mick he should look out for himself,' Morris gloated. 'Compromise. Listen to the good advice I was giving him and take it to heart.'

'What advice was that?'

'Keep quiet or your mama will suffer a nasty turn. It's her poor ticker, oh dear, it hasn't been so strong since papa lost his head in the Last War. They sent it back to her in a box, those dog bastards. She didn't know what it was until she opened it up, then – what a surprise that must have been. It wasn't even her birthday.'

'Blackmail.'

'No. I just wondered out loud how Mick would feel if he got a package one day. Tied up with a bow, a little fluff and blood on the edges.'

'He snapped.'

'He got scared! He had responsibilities, to me, to the paper... to you, damnit! He chose to ignore those responsibilities. Fixed it so he'd never have to make a decision again. He gave up. Decided he didn't want to live any more.'

'Because of you!' Julius grabbed Morris' forelimb, forcing the fat cat to look him in the face.

'No court in the land would convince me. My conscience, such as it is, is clear. Yours should be too. You were out of the running at the time. Dumped on a barge like a sack of dirty litter. You should watch what you drink.'

'You wanted to keep me out of the way. Spiked my drink, had some pals of yours chuck me on that barge.'

Morris scowled, a dark stare penetrating the brim of his hat. The editor was released, and Julius took a step backwards.

'Get out of my sight.'

Julius lost his temper, flung himself at the editor, pulled back a paw to strike him in the face. At this angle, if he twisted his claws, he could rip Morris' eyes out. Instead he walked off, turning for a glance at the surprised editor. Julius disappeared into the darkness. 'We won't be seeing each other again,' Morris called after him, rattled but loud. 'Security will see to that.'

Julius ignored him, pleased to escape the must of the presses. This was no way for a hero to act.

26

It may be difficult to believe in our contemporary societal climate, but an experiment was once tried in which dogs worked alongside cats in factories on the North Bank. The project was called to a halt several years ago, due to accidents caused by the dogs' laziness and poor attitude.

Because of their low intelligence, they fail to comprehend the importance of hygiene and constant tongue-scrubbing. On the rare occasions when they do wash, they home in on particularly unpleasant parts of the body. The way they greet each other is similarly indecent.

Sports consist of pointless running around and bare biting contests - these involve two or more competitors who proceed to bite each other until 'one don't like it no more and admits it.'

Most of their vocabulary consists of barks and growls, due to their underdeveloped vocal chords. Their written language (such as it is) includes many phonetic spellings - for example, HOWS (HOUSE), KAT, BYT, CHAYS and TAYL. They can't stand to be around cats - they want to chase us, but they also find our superior intellects threatening.

To sum up, dogs are stupid; a dog is so ignorant

as to consider the moon to be a ball. It feels
an inordinate desire to chase it, snatch it
between its teeth. Some cat factions suggest that
they are worth preserving, that some of their
number should survive. The longhaired cats (a
minority themselves in significant cities) are
advocates of this. Perhaps breeding them in iso-
lated areas would be possible, but the longhairs
desire total integration. The two races are so
different that cats and dogs will never unite.
Dogs are too ill tempered and troublesome, and
the worst offenders of the species are the Weiler
and Doberman breeds. In the hostile Northern
areas where dogs have built their own cities,
these breeds are barely tolerated, calling themselves the Bad Dogs.

ANTHROPOLOGICAL RESEARCH PAPER
PROFESSOR JO SANDS

Camilla was waiting for Julius when he returned, still dressed
in his trenchcoat and hat. She wasn't happy. She seemed
uneasy, as if something bad had happened to her that she didn't
want to talk about. 'How are you going to pay the rent? Get
back to the *Post* this instant. Ask for your job back.'

'I've got too much on my mind.' Julius suppressed a
laugh. 'I'm worried about Morris' politics, for once. I'm
worried that he'll brainwash me with his unethical crap.'

'Don't worry about that. These things have a way of
working themselves out.'

'Don't give me that homespun tosh. I'm glad it's on my
mind. I'm glad it's giving me grey fur. If nobody worried about

'these things',' he said in a sarcastic tone, 'then we'd still be stuck in the Pride Age. I thought you'd be more practical.'

'I was just…'

'Do you like me? Do you really like me? Or do you just feel sorry for me?'

'Don't be silly. You're strong.' There was a pregnant pause. Her eyes narrowed, dry throat choking on fat words. Despite her anger, she loved Julius more than ever. She was quieter, less confident than usual. It looked like she'd been through terrible times up North – she'd grown older, looked tired for the first time since they'd met. She didn't usually need much sleep. She was stretching a lot, her tail wagging – it all made Julius feel uneasy himself.

'You're just saying that,' he moped, the weight of the world on his sloping shoulders. A thought struck him. 'Did you spike me drink?'

'What?'

'The night before Mick… You mixed me a cocktail before I went out. What was in it?'

'Milk and stuff. Go to Morris. Talk to him once more.'

'It's too late now. He'll be long gone, the paper'll be closed up for the night.'

'Please go. For me.'

Dusk had draped its sooted tentacles over Bast Tower by the time Julius returned. The front entrance was uninvitingly dim, so he entered warily.

As he headed down the corridor that led to Morris' room, he noticed that the reporters' offices were closed and the presses underground were silent. He'd never known the place so empty, so ghostly.

He wasn't alone. The shadow of a large cat glimmered at a glass panel, waiting for him, draping him in shade as he called for his editor. Pulling the panel open, Julius was greeted by Warren, looking smug with pieces of meat between his teeth.

'I'm looking for Morris,' Julius gulped, 'my editor. I want a raise.'

'You ain't getting no raise.' Warren tried to bar the writer's exit but he edged back into the corridor. 'You're getting lowered. Three feet under.'

'I don't get you.' Julius risked a glance down the corridor. No reinforcements.

'I mean underground. Buried. Like in a grave.'

'Oh.' Looking down as if to ponder his fate, Julius waited for Warren to follow his gaze then pushed him off-balance, racing for the exit. He burst out of the building, sucking fresh air into his lungs in frenzied breaths, trying to work out why Warren was at the *Post*. For all he knew, the Wildcat couldn't read. There had to be something damned important in Morris' office, unless… he'd been expected. He closed his eyes to thank Bastet for his lucky escape; when he opened them again he was nose to nose with Sal.

'One for the pot.' Warren grinned, appearing behind him, none the worse for his sprint.

'Pleasure to meet you again, Mr Kyle,' said Sal. Julius could smell nip, the same odour he'd detected the last time he'd met this junkie. He tried to control his breathing, act calm.

'Whasamatter? Rat got your tongue?'

'This guy here ain't no talker,' Warren explained to his friend, 'he writes stuff down, that's what he's good at.'

'Fellas, it's great to see you but this isn't exactly –'

'It ain't great to see you.' Warren was at his flank now, Sal helping with the old one-two pincer movement.

'We don't like you.'

'And cats we don't like –'

'– we lose. In the river.' Warren prodded Julius in the back with a claw.

'What's going on, boys? Don't you like my book or something?' He unbuttoned his trenchcoat, ready to run if the chance arose. Camilla had sent him here, set him up. The Wildcats intended to silence him for good. Whatever Camilla had going on with Morris, it was nothing pretty.

'Doesn't matter what we like or don't like. The boss wants you aced.'

'Yeah.' Sal giggled. 'You've written your last cliché, you nib sucker.'

The Wildcats dragged Julius to the docks, stopped under a crane. It was quite a drop to the water.

'Over there, lead sniffer.' Sal motioned towards the water. Julius complied.

'Co-operative, ain't he?' Warren smiled. 'For a dead cat.' Sal held Julius tight as Warren raised a paw to slash his throat. There was a flurry of mottled hair. Something heavy dropped onto Warren and Sal from the crane. Julius heard screams, saw large grinding teeth, slavering jaws, darkness. He plummeted into the river, swimming away from the horror. Behind him, the water began to turn red.

27

IF THE PAPERS WOULDN'T print his story, Julius would take his information straight to the top. Even though he didn't have all his facts straight, he had enough suspicions. He'd seen enough blood to justify a visit to the Head Honcho.

Outside the Mayor's office, a side alley had been blocked off. A prominent amber sign on a tall wooden pole provided the explanation: Danger, Cats At Work! Julius couldn't see anything dangerous – half-naked pipes were dressed with a garland of neglected tools. Copper snaked from the cracked street with the determination of a tree root. Although a few zealous labourers had attacked the road, work seemed to have slowed to a nail's pace since. Narrow trenches spanned the street. Automated shovels and road drills lay around, growing cobwebs.

A straw poll had once been taken by the *Post*: eight out of ten citizens who expressed a preference agreed that if the Council had put as much energy into maintenance as it did into inventing such labour-saving devices, the city would have been a well-oiled utopia.

Instead, the road to that utopia was still full of potholes, lazily repaired by workers with plumber's smiles and their tails tucked in their belts. They would puff themselves up when females passed by – when they weren't dozing in their portacabins. They certainly made the most of their three-hour tea breaks. Few cats felt the call to manual labour a particularly enticing one. Those that could stomach hard work insisted on a generous pay packet, plenty of food and naps to recover from the strain of getting their fur dirty. Budget cuts meant that they could be home by four. Today they had left soon after they'd arrived, because something wasn't right. They felt uneasy. They'd gone and called in sick.

The steps that challenged the town hall were steep and cheerful, flanked by whiskering red flags and twin statues of legendary two-legged beasts. The mythological creatures, furless and ugly, scowled down at Julius as he shouted through the front entrance. I'm here! Come to share some secrets! No answer.

Inside, the stairwell was silent as well. Julius could hear the distant hum of traffic outside, the chuckle of a flambeau at the top of the flight. He called out, wary now. The Chambers were never left unguarded. It was against the law.

The first room he found was small, tidy and poorly lit. An unassuming sign on the desk told him that this was Tarquin's office; the aide's chair sat empty. Yet the writer sensed a presence, something in the shadows.

He sniffed around the room, went over to the desk, leaning on the polished wood. A sheaf of papers were spiked on the out tray – court orders, memos, budget breakdowns, take out menus – nothing exciting. Satisfied that he was alone, he checked the desk drawers: they contained pencils, erasers, a filofax and a communiqué containing an agreement with the dogs that ruled the North.

Something brushed past the window, knocking an ornament from the sill. Julius ran over to it, but the clumsy something had gone. He looked out of the window idly, expecting to see the Chamber guards.

He'd seen the leopards in action, expelling reporters from their master's den. Felt their rough paws on his jacket collar, seen a camera smash in slow-mo on the pavement. He was ready for them. He wasn't ready for the high-pitched scream that echoed from a side alley. He raced out of the office and down the steps to find the source of the cry.

Tarquin ran three feet before he reached the end of the alley. It was still blocked. Those lazy wasters! He'd take great pleasure in giving them the sack, if he could force his way past the dogs. He glanced down, saw that his waistcoat was torn. It would cost a bomb to repair, his tailor was out of town – thump! The dogs were on him, butting him in the temple, unbalancing him. He stumbled against the masonry. There were only three of them. Carefully manicured claws sprang from his forepaws, buffed and blunted from years of accountancy.

He bared his teeth and the hairs on his back sprang up. Do your worst. I'm ready for the lot of you. One of the dogs gripped his neck with greasy pads. Tarquin's eyes watered, he choked, a set of fangs drew a chunk from his ankle. He'd never brawled in his life, didn't know where to begin. All heroic dreams of champion boxing and bare-clawed fighting were shattered as he was spun from one attacker to another. He clutched a paw tight to the tear in his waistcoat, eyes streaming with cold salt tears.

A grey fist slammed into the Doberman's back, causing him to yelp. Tarquin's ears swivelled and he tried to flatten himself against the Cats At Work sign.

Two snarling Weilers twisted their fat heads round, not-necks wrinkling, spittle sparking onto Julius. He jammed his paws into their faces, released razor claws into their eyes, then pulled them out with a brutal pop. The dogs hardly felt the pain, stupid berserk. They could still sniff out a foe at fifty paces, and charged for Julius without missing a beat. He ducked, twisting his body lengthways so that the Weilers flew over him, colliding with each other.

The Doberman had uprooted the works sign, swung it at Julius and caught him on the chin. With the force of the prang Julius was flung into the waiting jaws of the blind Weilers; his claws sprang out again, driven with all his strength into one dog's heart. Allowing his instinct to guide him, he twisted the claws round, ribboning the dog's ticker. By now Tarquin was up and away, barging past the barking Doberman, heading for the steps. The work sign came after him, thrown like a javelin straight at his legs. It caught him in the thighs, tripped him so he fell flat on his nose with a groan.

Julius' eyes were red as his claws. His head hurt, he wanted out, the dogs were stopping him. Thoughts grated at his skull, of civilisation, good breeding, cultured social order. He knew which knife and fork to use at a dinner party. He also knew how to grind his teeth from side to side as he sank his jaws in the second Weiler's throat, going straight for the jugular – he who hesitates is lunch with the fish knife laid furthest to the left, my dear fellow. He knew how to savour the warm taste of blood on his gums, the rich, tender flavour of murder.

The Weiler dropped away, limp as wet lettuce. Tarquin had wrapped his arms round his belly, eyes closed, whimpering like a bairn. A drop of spittle nudged his chest and the Doberman growfed in triumph. Tarquin felt a gust of displaced air on his face and opened his eyes to see the dog flat on its back, Julius breaking the road sign on its wrist.

Tarquin joined in, kicking at the dog's head, until he narrowly missed losing his pads in the dog's fangs. Then he backed off, left Julius to deal with the rough stuff, returned to the piecemeal safety of the Office steps.

The Doberman forgot about Tarquin, snatched half of the sign between its teeth, spat it at Julius, made him duck, giving the dog time to get up and relaunch at the cat.

What does it take to wear out this yob? Instead of renewing his offensive, Julius allowed himself to fall backwards. He scrabbled for the sign, grasping at thin air – the dog had seen its two dead comrades, its anger multiplied, a roar emanating from its guts. It leaped at Julius, mouth wide open, lips curled to show foaming gums. Julius felt the dog fall heavily on top of him, teeth around his neck. Death didn't arrive. The dog had landed on the sharp end of the sign, driving it clean through its groin. The pain had been so great and sudden that the dog had slipped into oblivion. It would bleed to death in minutes.

Julius released his grip on the sign, pushing the deadweight Doberman onto its back. He grimaced at the mortal wound he'd incidentally inflicted. Very nasty.

Who was holding the dogs' leash? They were under someone's control, some force desperate to create havoc in a city where the most unwanted creatures were the hounds that lay before him.

Tarquin was peeking down the alleyway, cautious, breath slight. Julius stumbled over to the bookish official, blood caking his chin.

'The guards're gone,' panted Tarquin, 'the leopards. They've done a bunk.'

'Paid off.' Tarquin found this hard to believe. The leopards were jobsworths, always on call to protect the Mayor and his cohorts. The big cats had been bred to guard since the Pride Age; duty intertwined with nature. He couldn't find them.

'Where's the Mayor?' asked Tarquin, interrupting Julius' thoughts.

'I hope he's upstairs. Someone was up there with me.' The two cats rushed back into the Chambers, searching corridors and offices until they came to Otto's lair. His huge body lay face down on a fawn rug. It had been a gift from a foreign dignitary.

'I believe you've had the pleasure?' asked Otto as Julius helped him up. The lion certainly had presence. Despite his wounded paw, rumpled composure, mane clotted with gore, Julius felt inferior.

'That's right, we've met.' He strained under the Mayor's weight.

'Some rally or other?' Otto grunted. Full strength had yet to return to his limbs. He sank dizzily onto his throne.

'Somebody's funeral. Not so long ago. My name's Kyle.'

'Fortunate for me you chanced along.' The Mayor offered a cigar to Julius, who declined. He lit one for himself and sucked on it heavily, waiting for the office to stop its catherine wheel whirl.

'There's been an attempt on my life!' said Tarquin, breathing heavily for maximum effect.

'Who'd want to kill you?' snarled the Mayor. 'You're not worth it.'

'This guy saved me.' The aide patted Julius on the shoulder.

'He wasted his time.' Otto smiled to show he didn't really mean it, ordered Tarquin out of the room. Julius lowered his voice.

'I wanted to talk to you about –'

'Unfortunate that we didn't see the attackers, isn't it, Mr Kyle? There's no way I could possibly identify them. They were too swift, too wily.'

Julius couldn't believe what he was hearing.

'Your aide will spill the beans. The bodies of your wily fellows are down the street. You can't keep this one quiet, Your Honour.'

'My aide will do as he's told!' Otto wasted his cigar in an ashtray. 'The bodies will be cleared away and no one will hear of this. Can you imagine the panic that would ensue if the restless public heard about this? Bastet knows what unholy creatures roam the city at night, let alone our – Northern cousins.'

'Someone wants you dead.'

'They were looking for this!' Tarquin entered the room holding a scroll aloft. He stretched it across the Mayor's desk, flattening it down. 'While I'm here, I would like to tender my resignation,' he declared as Otto read the piece of paper. It offered the dogs in the North a deal: a quarter of the city in return for an eternal truce. Blood dripped onto the parchment from the hole in Otto's paw.

'Drawn up on behalf of some friends of mine,' Tarquin explained. 'They know you'll sign anything put in front of you, never read it. Those dogs downstairs were here to finalise some dots and dashes, check out the fine print.'

'Funny way of doing it,' mumbled Julius. Tarquin nodded sadly.

'Is this why the accounts were so late?' Otto asked, slowly shaking his mane.

'I was kind of busy with this. Wasn't going to tell you, of

course. By the time you had found out about the deal, it would've been too late. You would have had to go with it, sell it to the cits as one of your forward-thinking ideals.'

'Until today.' The Mayor lit another cigar.

'I don't know what happened. I'm sorry you got hurt, sir. Glad to see you're still alive... Never trust a dog.'

Tarquin backed out with one last, deferential bow. Too weak to give chase, Otto slumped back in his chair, rolling his eyes at Julius.

'Everyone wants to be a boss.' His big nose twitched, inhaling the treasured scent of his cigar.

'You're going to disregard all this, aren't you?

'Be assured I'll do something about it, Mr Kyle. In my good time.'

'There's gotta be more dogs out there. How many more innocents have to die before you act?' Otto ignored him. Nice going, J. Convert the lion with clichés. 'I can see I'm wasting my time here.'

28

A small, crumpled body lay in the last pool of light. Its limbs were outstretched like a bather doing the backstroke. Tiger knelt down beside the stiff, his brow furrowed, his mind puzzled. Who would want to kill Bug? Knock her down, razor her throat, rip off her orange-red mask? It had been tossed aside, screwed up, its two antennae limp and ragged. That didn't seem right.

Tiger looked at her dead eyes. It was Natasha, the secretary with pretensions towards being a hero-ine. He'd been too blind to see it, protect her before she got herself killed. Some detective.

Her tiny paw gripped a piece of cloth, green checked and grubby. He picked it up, recognising it immediately.

'Bless you, Bug.' An invaluable asset till the end. With the help of her pathetic scrap of evi-dence, he'd be able to catch a killer. It would be the most difficult bust he'd ever make.

JULIUS KYLE

Bridget wasn't expecting company when her lover barged in. In fact, she was getting ready to go out. Her fur was wound in rollers and she held heating tongs in her paw. Tarquin slumped on the floor beside her, nosing at her, burying his face against her until the heat got too much for him. He pulled away, cleaning his claws with nervous precision.

He waited for Bridget to ask him what the matter was. She was too busy with her beauty treatment.

'Where are we going?' Tarquin caught the acrid smell of rollered hair.

'Just the one of us, darling.' Bridget was getting herself all primped up for something.

'Where you headed?'

'I'm taking my grandchildren on a little trip. Somewhere secure and secluded.'

'Aren't you worried that you'll lose some popularity points,' Tarquin asked sarcastically, 'with your face out of sight for five minutes?'

'I'm taking my annual rest with the cubs I adore so much. I think they deserve me for a while, don't you?'

No one deserves you, my dear, thought Tarquin. 'Is there anyone round here who doesn't see those little ones as political thumbscrews?' he asked ruefully. 'They're thinking, feeling cats, Bridget.'

'They're stupid. So are you if you think I care for your opinion. You should approve of me taking them away from here. A war brewing, priests rabble-rousing, restless long-hairs desperate for equality of some kind or another – you should know, your breed are the worst trouble-makers.'

'No need to bring that up,' Tarquin sulked.

'My dear young cub, you have no idea who you're bugging, do you? You've only seen one side of me, my little Tarquin. You've seen the loving, romantic side. Don't you understand what I control? What I live through you could never experience. And if you think that sitting by my side on the odd illicit occasion will allow you to achieve some level of strength... You're not riding on my political coat tails, my dear fellow. Oh no. Wrong breed, wrong time, wrong female. I've seen enough of you now. I think it's time you were toddling back to your little desk, don't you?' Bridget began to lick between the folds of her well-groomed fur, wetting down the coat in places, adding swirled patterns.

Tarquin tried to think of what to say. He'd been too trusting. That didn't seem to matter now. What mattered was the fact that he'd jeopardised his job, his future, the good name of his race for some misshapen love affair. What if her husband found out? If she spilled her beans, Tarquin would be dead. Even though he was feeling sorry for himself, he enjoyed being alive. Since his battle with the dogs he appreciated every breath he sucked into his lungs, the euphoria of fresh air. He felt sorry for Bridget.

He'd always believed that the fun they'd had during their trysts would keep him happy forever, the memories bringing great riches; but nothing was worth this rejection. The shame, the disappointment. The depression that was sure to follow.

He'd wondered how long it would take Bridget to get bored with him, as she grew bored with everything else in her life. He'd expected her to take a while longer, a period of grace once she'd used him. He had been intelligent enough to see this coming. So now here she was, erasing him from her life. He could handle that and he had something to throw back in her face.

'You cause trouble for me, I'll tell the world about all this.' Husband or no husband.

'You do that, and your miserable life won't be worth a grain of litter!' Bridget threatened.

'I don't like this. It's too hard. I have responsibilities, Milady. To the Mayor, the populace. If I let either of them down – well, that'll be it. No second chances. I represent my own breed, you know. If I fail them it'll reflect badly on them all. They won't feel so good about themselves. Most of them spend their lives clearing garbage or tipping their caps to hotel guests. They have nothing. That's why they look up to me. They see – potential in me. A potential for their cubs to grow up with a chance in life.'

'There's no caste system in this city. My administration saw to that! You're not going to be treated differently just because of a few markings on your back. How you consider yourselves is a different matter. If you have no respect for yourselves, that's no fault of mine or anyone else.'

'We've been treated as cattle all our lives.' Tarquin shed a tear. 'Beasts of burden, nothing better.'

'You've acted like cattle! Never stood up for yourselves, always waited for someone else to do it for you.'

'Well, I'm standing up for myself now. I'm leaving.' He had to go. He'd seen enough of her.

'Good.'

'What do you mean, 'good'?' Tarquin frowned.

'It suits us all. Me, you and my son. If you quit now you'll do us all a favour.'

'I knew this would never work.'

'That's enough back talk from you. I was giving wee fellows like you fat lips while I was still learning to hunt. We knew there was a risk involved. Dogs are forgetful, bean-brained animals. That doesn't mean we shouldn't see the deal through. Everything's under control.'

Exasperated, he showed her his waistcoat. She wasn't impressed.

'The Bad Dogs are uncontrollable! They're too ugly to consider, they have a death wish, and their language is appalling. They should all be wiped off the face of the land. Instantly.'

'Splendid,' Bridget smirked, 'I'm glad you're finally seeing things my way.'

'But the treaty –' She'd ordered the attack. 'They tried to kill me. Eat me.'

'You got in the way. Otto was the target.' Her own son! He should have realised. He'd given his heart to a cruel, loveless, splendid creature. He understood why she was a perfect politician – something he'd never be. He cared.

'His death would get me the sympathy vote,' Bridget explained. 'I could live out my last spiteful years in the role I was born to – ruling this province – until my progeny can take my place.' She patted her swollen stomach. 'This time, I'll make sure he turns out right.'

'What good is a province in tatters, with killers on the streets and people living in fear?'

'It would make them easy to manipulate. Malleable. My kind of cats.'

'Do you care about anyone, Milady?'

'Sure I do. I care about myself. Everything – everyone else is mere entertainment to me.'

'I didn't think this would last forever, but...'

'I'm bored with you, Sinner,' Bridget yelled. 'Get out.'

Julius washed himself carefully, gagging at the taste of blood and drool, recoating himself with the scent of his own saliva. His mind raced with the consequences of what he'd seen that day. A bundle of newspapers lay in the centre of his lounge, all containing damning reviews of his novel. Camilla was working on an article for Morris; after a few cooed words of sympathy, she'd left him to tend to his bruises. Yet now and again she'd look over at him with a loving shine in her eyes.

'Will you take a look?' he asked after a while. She of all people would be able to appreciate his book. One last constructive criticism before he ditched his pens and paper forever.

'I'm busy.'

'I need an impartial appraisal of my work.'

'You won't get it from me – I've read your reviews.'

'So?' Julius gazed down at the newspaper pile.

'No one wants to read your stinking book. I wouldn't buy it for my granny.' Camilla picked up one of the papers. 'Naïve, simplistic. Amazing that it's taken years for author to take such a backward step.'

'Do you seriously think I should take notice..?'

'Or this one. Pretentious… unsophisticated sentence construction.' Camilla picked up another review. 'Cliché ridden – why publish something we've all read before..? Unmemorable… my two-week-old cub has a better grasp of language… such an easy read it can be digested in a five minute tea break.'

'I thought that was what they wanted.' Julius looked crestfallen.

'Face it. Any delusions you had of being a great writer are – well, that's all they are. Delusions. Why did you do it?

Why are you always so damned unhappy? Why can't you be content with what you've got?'

'Writing's all I can do, Camilla. Without that... there's no point to me being here.'

'What about me? I used to be the point. What you lived for. Now you can't wait to see the back of me.' Camilla threw the paper onto the table and got on with her work.

'Is it safe yet?' asked Julius, inspecting his clean pads.

'I suppose so.' Camilla stopped writing. 'Is what safe?'

'Your story must be all done and dusted by now. Surely you won't be giving anything away.'

'You want me to tell you what I was working on up North?'

'You know me, I'm no leaker. You were gone a long time. If you love me, you'll tell me what you were doing.'

Blackmail. Cats could be solitary beings. Camilla pursed her lips, curled up beside her beau.

'This stays in the house. I don't want you telling any of your little Doghouse buddies, or writing a book about it, or screaming it from a rooftop. This is between you, me and Morris.' Julius offered her a vigorous nod.

'There is no story,' she explained ruefully. 'He sent me up there to contact some dogs. He's working with Bridget, the ex-Mayoress. They want to restore some nationalist pride to this grey nation of ours. The politics don't interest me. I did it to make some moolah, appease my editor and have some time to myself. I could tell you were getting sick of me. I thought a breather would be best for both of us.'

'There'll be another attempt on Otto's life.' Julius jumped up, snatching his overcoat from its hook. 'He should be warned.'

The hunters kept their eyes peeled for the slightest motion, waiting for a papaya blade to budge or a leaf to flutter. Their blood was sky-high up, revelling in the anticipation of a kill. Only the Mayor remained calm, imperious. Any excitement he suffered was bottled beneath the surface. He would not allow his emotions to show in front of his courtiers.

The cats parted, spreading out to form a silent web round the overgrown copse, sniffing at the ugly, rounded leaves of the bushes. They were inedible. The critters that inhabited the copse used them for shelter when the hunters came – they were a delicacy fit for a Mayor.

Woodrow spotted one, slowed his breathing, looking to his left without moving his head. He got Otto's attention with a tap on the shoulder; a flash of silver hair behind a frond had alerted him to his prey. Woodrow began to sidle towards the animal, chest heaving, trying to still his excitement. The frond waggled – the prey was on the move.

Woodrow sprang, body twisting in the air, landing claws outstretched in a patch of frosted earth. A bushmouse broke cover, making for the sanctuary of the trees. It ran straight into Otto, who waited mouth wide open to snare the rodent between his teeth. It squealed as he clamped down on its neck, savouring the flavour of blood and bone.

Woodrow looked up from his frosty patch, sneering at the Mayor. That popinjay would go hungry if his employees didn't drive the prey to him. Otto never got his paws dirty, always got the politician's share of the mice on a hunt: the most succulent catch, the fattest and strongest morsels. By the time the children were pandered to as well, there was little left over for Woodrow and his colleagues. The pay was good though, and he'd found his picture in the paper a couple of times. The press loved these woodland exploits and damning him for squandering public funds. They adored him, although the hacks were sick of writing about him. The Mayor was news.

The first interruption to the hunt came when Mowbray, Otto's eldest, started rolling on the ground in agony. A swift investigation led to the discovery of some poison fronds. Mowbray had been chewing on them, dumb with hunger, green stains on his chin.

Instead of comforting his heir, Otto chastised his aide.

'Why weren't you watching him? I'll have your balls for brunch.' With an acquiescent bow Woodrow ordered a stretcher for the cub, who was duly rushed to hospital.

Otto's younger son Milo was playful, curious, no help at all – too concerned with his own little world where he ruled everything, from friendships to physics. He was alert and quick-witted. He would make a fine lion by the time he reached maturity, Otto decided proudly. Milo seemed oblivious to his brother's suffering.

Coronetted with cigar smoke, Otto picked at his teeth, licking excess curds of blood from his hairy paws. He shook his mane, enjoying the sensation of the frost tumbling away from his coat. There was nothing he loved better than the hunt, a simple, natural pleasure – a chance to show off, strut his regal stuff, prove how much bigger and better he was than the measly cats he ruled. He could display poise, assurance, quick-wittedness, a damned well refined attitude while his lackeys ran in circles round him trying to catch their prey. Granted, much of the running around was for him but he was the calming influence, the one in control, the ringmaster of this mouse-hunt and that puffed him with conceit.

There's one! Right there, minding its own beeswax, snuffling at the muddy ground as if it's heaven scent. Otto stepped sideways towards it, finishing his cigar, lips bubbling with scarlet lust, anticipating the succulent little morsel. His desire was crushed like the bracken that sundered beneath Julius' hindpaws. An interloper. A saboteur! The mouse made a dash for its life, bursting into a pouch of plant stems, taking one last backward glance to scoff at the hunter.

'What in gyrating thunder do you think you're doing here?' bellowed Otto, squaring up to Julius.

'Asking you to leave the city, sir. Lie low for a while at least. There will be more attempts on your life, more Bad Dogs. Why risk the lives of this lot?' Julius looked up at Otto's courtiers, who were told to back off by the Mayor.

'I'll tell you why,' said the lion once everyone was out of earshot. 'This play-acting, this foraging is for show. The real hunt begins when we join battle with the dogs. You'll be pleased to know I'm sending an expeditionary force North to sack their city. Payback for the recent attacks. That'll teach them to double-deal behind my back.'

'Won't that make things worse?'

'Some lives will be lost.' His voice dropped to a whisper. 'When I think of the wonders it will do for my next election campaign, I quiver... conflict is a splendid rug under which to sweep one's indiscretions.'

'If your citizens don't stand together, realise what's going on, this could be the beginning of a new dark age.'

'Good!' Otto smiled as he donned his top hat. 'I own the

power company. And I've got plenty of controlling interests in the heating industry too. What's the matter, little one? Afraid of the dark?'

'I'm afraid of cats. I know what they're capable of.'

Compared to me they're nothing, Mr Kyle. Lions have ruled Bast since... well, as long as I can recall, and the history books along with me. There is no competition. No one to rival me. I'm all the citizens have. Without me there'd be no city. I even understand there's a new faith establishing itself amongst the proles. A new religion. Me!'

'If the public knew about this...' Julius snarled.

'They'd give me a round of applause!' Otto enjoyed winding the writer up. 'Probably offer to help me too. My kids will be joining me as soon as they're on solids. I'll teach them the fun of the chase and they'll love it. My people are in awe of me. They watch our family from afar and envy us. By Bastet they love us.'

'Not for long.'

'Nothing you scribble can dent their affection for us.' Otto cleared his throat with contempt. 'We're immortal because of them. We make the rules and they obey us and thank me for it. That's politics in action, my friend.'

'We've found a horde of 'em, sir,' Woodrow mewed in excited tones. 'Cowering in their burrow. Flushed 'em out. They're all yours.'

'Excuse me.' Otto followed his lackey and Julius saw the other side of his character – a ferocious, bellowing, primal warlord, jaws open wide like a scoop, diving for the rodents that fled for cover, swallowing them with one snap. He turned round, a content look on his face. There was no way

Julius could argue with this beast. He left the scene of the crime, passing civil servants with sacks full of live booty. He had an old friend to visit.

29

Tiger's wife was waiting for him when he got home. She was wearing a green checked dress, slightly torn at the hem.

'I wondered how long it would take you,' she said as he unsheathed his claws.

'You made me so happy.'

'I don't want to stop. Think about tomorrow, Tiger. Can you live without me to wash and cook and clean for you? Keep the kids happy? Care for you all when someone falls ill? Do you love me?'

'Yes. Doesn't mean I'm not going to kill you.'

'Go on then. She deserved to die. She wanted you too much and you didn't ever realise it. She was never going to be happy.'

'Why did you take off her mask?'

'I did it before she died. I wasn't there to kill Bug. I'm not one of those damned arch-villains you're always chasing after. I wanted to kill Natasha. She was the one who deserved it. Your mud-slinging love slut, not your crime fighting companion.'

She unbuttoned her blouse, exposing her soft-furred throat. A deadly claw sprang from his pads, and he touched the point against her skin.

The slightest jab and justice would be done. She didn't dare swallow, ready for him. She stared into his eyes, silently imploring. She wanted him to get it over with.

Life would not be over for her for another decade, which she spent in a municipal jail after being frog-marched to the local cops by her husband. His evidence put her in the slammer for good. Despite the strict penal system, she made the best of her last years. Studied, wove baskets, sang in the choir. She didn't talk much. She lived in the past, tucked up warm with her family. She seemed almost oblivious to her incarceration, did as she was told, served her sentence. By the time she was due for parole, she fell ill. Passed away in her sleep. Tiger still mourns.

JULIUS KYLE

Once a dog makes a home for himself, he finds it difficult to move. A flea may itch and bite your back, but you get used to its presence and miss it when it's gone. The factory bosses had helped their workers to settle down on the bank of the River Hune, a stud-collar community of dogs eager to please. A town had built up along the bank, with stores, a square that served as a meeting area, taverns and troughs. Now all the inns were gone and the stores had nothing to sell. A ditched shoal of dogs scraped an existence from the wares washed up on their shore.

The lanes were strewn with iron, sewage, food wrappers and other trash. Tatty curtains hung limp in dirty windows. Puppies ran round the slum chasing each other's tails. Neighbours greeted each other, offering stupid smiles, barking the time of day. Big-nosed friends sniffed and licked each other, or drooled on the pavement. They ignored the cat who trudged through their world, looking worried. Julius squinted as he checked the side streets, his nose wrinkling at the smell of excreta. Channels had been dug in the earth to form gutters either side of the streets, but there was little rain this time of year to wash away waste. He tugged his hat down tight over his brow, brought the collar of his coat up – if the dogs saw him, smelled his concern, they might chew him to morsels in minutes. He'd been stupid to enter the slum. He had to warn Pa, talk to him, let him know what could happen. Convince him to leave, take the pups and oldies with him. There was no time to think twice.

The dogs had worked hard to construct their huts and shacks, using driftwood and rusted crane parts from the river, towboat hulks, corrugated glass panels. The flotsam was held together with mud and nine-inch nails, threatening to collapse at any moment. The hovel interiors were warm, spacious, stinky-dirty, with family mementoes splashed on the walls in affectionate urine murals.

It didn't take long to find the right place. Moira had described it to Julius once or twice, and the sign nailed to the front was a dead give-away. PA'S HOWS. BEWAIR OF THE DOG. Swallowing hard, Julius took a look inside. There was only one room, and a distinct lack of toilet facilities. Furniture was limited to a couple of pallets and a driftwood stool. An old brown dog sat on its haunches on the stool, beady eyes fixed on the cat.

'Can't you read, pussycat? Says beware of me.' The dog opened its mouth wide, drool falling from jagged teeth. Instead of biting Julius' ears off, the dog was yawning. He offered the writer a seat on one of the pallets.

'Don't mind the fleas and they won't mind you. Pa'll be

along soon. He's putting me up here till my place is fixed. There was a flood.'

'Unlucky.'

'Pa does a lotta good things for folks round here. He said you might be turning up. He teaches at the local – well, you wouldn't call it a school. Not by your standards. He supervises the pups sometimes, that's what I mean. My name's Leaky.'

'Why they call you that?'

Leaky didn't answer. Instead, he lifted his hindpaw and scratched behind his ear. Julius looked aside in dismay.

'I ain't gonna roll over or play dead for you, if that's what you're anticipatin'. I don't know much about much. I can sniff and piss with the best of 'em. I ain't proud. I'll beg or fetch if my life depends on it. Over the years I've tried to keep a childish sense of wonder about me, but I keep my nose out of mischief. If I get in neck deep, it's by accident. I don't ask for trouble and it don't often require me. How much you know about Pa?'

'Not much.' Julius shrugged.

'I'll tell you something about him. He makes a difference. For instance, there's two gristly dogs live near here, Ritchie and Bruno.'

'I don't have time for a story.'

'You got time for this. Some kind of feud from generations back set them against each other. Plenty friends to keep 'em apart; leave them alone together and ooh! They'd get to fightin' as ugly as their faces. Last winter got so cold, the fellows became miserable. Once they got gnawing at each other, didn't matter that they was in a pile of company. Didn't take much to get 'em started. I recollect Bruno was at it first:

'You smell something?' he says, pointing his nose in Ritchie's direction.

'Nope.' Ritchie shook his tangled mane. 'Lessen it's you.'

'You been rollin' about in your own bottom sauce agin?' Bruno asked in an innocent tone of voice.

'I don't dump in the street, Fleaboy.' That was it. The two pugs ran out of insults and into each other, a full-on ram that stunned Bruno for a second. He came to with Ritchie's teeth besetting his leg, chewing and dribbling on it like the dog hadn't eaten for a month.

'The only dude would dare come between these two in such a rage was Pa. He ain't nobody's true Pa, far as I know; that's what we call him anyways. He's taken on the mantle of town counsellor since puppydom, though why he hasn't moved on I couldn't say. He was as big as the two pugs put together, so with a smack on Ritchie's snout he pulled them apart, asking Bruno why he'd become dish of the day.

'His daddy stole a bone off my daddy,' Ritchie ventured.

'So you thought you'd get a replacement off your buddy's leg?' Pa checked out the chomp marks on Bruno. His fur was matted with blood and saliva. 'I seem to recall it was your granddaddies that started this tussle. Furthermore, Bruno, your daddy dropped his teeth when you were still a pup. The only thing he can do to a bone now is suck it.'

'Suck this!' cried Ritchie, swipin' at Pa with a grizzled paw. Pa dodged sideways and sank his teeth into the dog's ear, ripping it clean off. Ritchie began to cry as Pa spat the ear into the gutter. Bruno picked it up, dusted it off and helped his old rival to the clinic.

'I hear the offending appendage was sewn back on, but

it kind of flopped to one side, curled over on itself. It never worked again. Neither did Ritchie and Bruno fight. I guess they were sick of knocking chunks out of each other. Pa continues to keep the peace wherever he can. He's the best adjudicator a slum like ours could ask for.'

Leaky started to lick his nether regions. 'Must you do that?' Julius didn't mind what creatures did when they were alone and in private; this was different.

'Aw, you're jealous. Too upper-crust to relax in company. You think us dogs are dull because of the simple lives we lead. I'll tell you why we're better than you. We don't need all this comfort, these luxurious trappings that tie you down. We're free agents, independent, we can go where we like with nothing to slow us. Why should we cook our food? Our bellies are warm enough. When we swallow the food, it'll soon be heated up. We don't need any fancy electric light – we can smell just as well in the dark. As for taking a bath, we have long tongues to wash ourselves. And the outfits you wear! What's the point? We have coats of hair to make us look fine. You're a race of mollycoddled, technocratic tight-arses. You used to be one with the environment; now you can't sit down without a cushion.' Leaky's tail was wagging all over the place. 'I'm itchy. I need a wash.'

A tiny something bit Julius. He rubbed his shoulder in irritation, turning his head in time to catch Pa as the elderly dog entered the room.

Pa couldn't contain his concern. 'What you doing in my house? You've got some gall coming here. Don't expect us to smuggle you back out again. The scum round here's likely to rip our lungs out.'

Leaky shook his head, signalling Pa to take it easy on the feline.

'I gotta go relieve myself again,' he explained as he left his seat, 'that's how I got my name. It weren't no river what flooded my shack. See you later.'

'I came to tell you – I've taken your advice,' said Julius as Pa shook snow from his coat. 'Spread the news however I can. Not everyone's going to be happy about it; more to the point, not everyone's going to be pleased with dogs in general. You should be thinking of leaving. For a while, at least.'

'You're expecting me to haul everyone out of here?' Julius had been thinking of Pa's individual safety, but the pooch had a point. Everyone in the slum would be in danger. 'We're used to victimisation, sonny. Water off a dog's back. We'll deal with whatever grit bricks are thrown at us.'

'You could be facing something worse than victimisation. You might have to bite back.'

'Hey, I'm the one who convinced you to do all this reporting, cat. Worry about yourself, and – and Moira. My world, my home, my memories are here – I can't let them grow cold. If I have to fight for this hole, I will.'

'Promise me this at least.' Julius looked up at Pa imploringly. 'You won't cross the river, not till things have settled down.'

'Hoo boy. If I was a character in one of your books, and I promised not to do a thing like that – what do you think would happen?' Julius bowed his head. The character would doubtless cross the river before things settled down. Pa laughed. 'Good job this ain't one of yer books. You got my word. I'll be here looking after my own.'

Julius hopped a sand ferry back across the river, thinking

about Moira and her adoptive parent. He'd never realised a dog could be noble. He knew cats could be wrong.

The sun seemed to set early that night. It lingered on the horizon for a few moments, waiting for its cue. It looked squat and ripe like a crushed, bleeding fruit before striking beyond the mountain range and leaving the cats in darkness.

Light burst awake from windows. They shed little light on the courtyard or the surrounding landscape. The citizens huddled under bedclothes, warmed themselves with boiled milk, or made love by firelight. Something was wrong and they knew it. Cats had been disappearing throughout the city, and the authorities were unable to tell them why. A day of judgement had arrived, and they were determined to shrug it off and go about their normal business until the last moment possible.

Slowly, the lights died and the citizens slept. Only one light remained, deep in the heart of the city where the Mayor sat with a despised rival. Neither of them could sleep, and there was much to be discussed.

The dark volcanic hills that bordered the city acted as a natural defensive wall. There were a sure number of valleys and passes invaders could use to cross the terrain; the cats were masters of ambush, raids and guerrilla tactics.

This time they were on the offensive, marching through the hills rapidly, purposefully. They did not rest until they reached the plains beyond, a vast battleground of pock-marked craters and cracked dry earth.

Cold trees with grey cauliflower stems dotted the land-scape. Clumps of branch peeked over the broad horizon.

Mist transformed distant hills into desolate islands, as black as the clouds that shadowed them. The plains would dip and yield, crosspatched with hedgerow and lake, delineating hard-won territories.

A sea of mongrel cats made up Otto's expeditionary force – hundreds of Persians, Siamese, bobtails, berserkers painted blue. The cats wore little or no armour – breastplates if anything – preferring to rely on speed rather than heavyweight protection. Some carried spears and staves; the army bigwigs had also developed a small projectile weapon (based on a riot police model) that fired acid pellets. These were only made available to officers. Most of the soldiers would make do with tooth and claw, and they were ready to sic the first canine they clapped eyes on.

Pub brawlers had hurriedly knocked themselves into shape: warmongers with yellow bellies itching for a fright, helpful in a paw to paw skirmish, clerical workers desperate for a change of pace from their rutted lives, husbands ready to defend their families in a haze of glory, fathers with ploughed brows, heads crowded with the memories of ancient combat.

Their hindpaws were matted from the powdered ground, eyes darkened by grains of dust; bones aching from the cold. The winds never stopped their heavy song, invisible choirs entreating the army to go home.

Hardship did not come naturally to these animals, yet the damp and grit made firelight camps appealing, and the closeness of their comrades warm. If they started getting homesick, missing the sweet sight of their mates, the General would kick them into shape.

The soldiers had been dragging their flimsy tents on a series of armoured carts. They set them up on an arid plain, a hundred rows of a hundred cloth boxes. No cat shared with a fellow troop; even in this wild, alien environment they needed their territorial space. Only during a heavy briefing or in the brimstone of battle would they tuck close together, guarding brother souls.

The canvas lushed up the plain, livening it with wood-land green. The troops scurried about, bellies yawning, keeping their stopgap homes in order, straight and narrow, ready for instant inspection. A path had been left alongside the tents for the General to wend; lookouts were posted at vantage points, stooped low, eyes keen, ready for a sneaky attack. Billy cans bubbled along with a big pot of stewed cod in an open-air kitchen.

Smoke and steam billowed into the sky, posting the army's presence. It was more important to fill the soldiers' stomachs than to retain the element of surprise.

During the forthcoming campaign, they'd live on tinned fish, smoked fish, a great deal of salted fish, dried fish, battered fish. Of course the common troops, the grunts, grumbled about the menu; they demanded more fish. They were not afraid to challenge their superiors, though they placed their trust in them. They understood that discipline could win a war.

Above all warriors, the grunts trusted the General. None of them knew the cat's surname or what he did between wars. Their fathers had told tales about him; he seemed immortal. And when his troops believed in him he could win a battle. In fact, common propaganda had it that he hadn't lost a war yet.

When the General arrived to inspect them, the troops were impressed. This was the hardest son-of-a-queen ever born, at least that's what they'd been led to think. He had a lot to live up to, and he didn't disappoint.

'This may surprise you, kits and kitlens.' The General wheeled round, kicking up a cloud of dust. 'I'm not a warmonger. I don't enjoy the sight of blood and I don't believe in unnecessary carnage. Not in keeping with my perceived image, I understand, but discreet withdrawal never did me no harm. So I'm not looking forward to going out on that battlefield, I'm not relishing the prospect – with Bastet's blessing there'll be no need to unsheathe our claws. Yet we must face the possibility, however small or unlikely or ill considered it may be, that we'll be fighting for our lives by dawn. I want you to be ready for that bugle call, in a killin' frame of mind.

'My mother – bless her departed soul – taught me good. She told me about our land's precious resources, how a fear of the unlike was irrational and unworthy of a cat. How peaceful coexistence with all species was necessary to the survival of our race and our ethics.' The General's nose twitched.

'She was bitten. By an Alsatian. It held her throat in its jaws and shook her like a rag doll, till she was murdered. When I see one I'll tear him apart strip by strip! I'll cut his nose and rip into his balls! Maim! Destroy them all, every last stinking, killing, worthless one of them! Are ya with me?'

The soldiers cheered, whipped into a frenzy by their foaming leader. Blood dribbled from the corner of his mouth; he'd bitten his tongue in anger.

'No prisoners!' By the time the General was finished with his men, none of them were able to sleep. They wanted to fight. Find a dog and roast it for their supper. The General liked it that way; it kept the troops alert.

Not far North an army of dogs massed, teeth gnashing, hackles raised. They champed at the bit, ready to charge. They nipped each other on the bum, tails wagging in anticipation. Although the dogs were regarded as lazy and stupid by the cats, their pack mentality was strong enough to crush any resistance. They were hungry and cat soup was said to be a delicacy. A mouthful of moggy was all they wanted, war the only word on their breath. They wore leather caps to protect their heads though their own mothers would not have cared if they lost their scalps.

These animals were the lowest of the low, the stupidest, larger louts, bulldog breeds, serial warriors, the dirtiest of dogs. They never bothered to wash; their stink attracted flies and other insects to feed on while they waited for fresh orders. As yet they were sworn to defend their Northern territory. Once the enemy arrived, they would have the correct excuse to march on Bast. They would be unstoppable. They'd chase the cats into their tasty little city and gobble them all up.

30

AMBIENT MUSIC WAFTED FROM the radio station, and the cats who heard it nodded in appreciative agreement. This was the time of day when everyone could tune into the Central Channel, which was usually snarled up with the kind of fast driving beats (designed to match bright flashing video clips) that could only appeal to youngsters. But this gentle soul music signalled the on-air arrival of the laid back DJ Scratch. His booth was large – he needed space to stretch and prance about between talkie bits.

'Here we are again with a host of platters, mind your ears don't shatter. This is DJ Scratch giving you that itch that makes you want to hop. Males and females, bopping till the light of day... I know the whole city's listening in, 'cos this is the station to tune to, I'm the DJ with the tunes to move to. We have a selection of ooh... for you jungle cats out there here's a little bit of music to give you an idea of what the scene's all about at the moment.'

Scratch was lanky, well groomed, with no waist going to waste. He was so thin it didn't look like he had a middle. He had legs so long he could reach from one end of the booth to the other, roller-skating between three turntables, discs spinning at the same time like potter's pancakes, his whiskers twitching to the beat, bopping his head, eyes darting across a flickering console, checking that the dials were reaching the right levels so that the sounds he adored so much were going all across the city.

He had to be one of the most popular DJs in this part of town, so popular that the radio station had given him an en suite bathroom complete with bowl of sand and chain-pull flush. This DJ was so hot that his booth held state-of-the-art equipment, colour coded so that he could quickly match records to the right days, the right moods, changes in climate, keeping everybody happy because everybody was listening in, and he gave them what they wanted, doping the masses with groovy beats. He tried to appeal to every different kind of cat, but knew that all they really wanted was cool music.

'Now, kits and kitlens, time for your favourite and mine. A non-tinny tune from Suspicious Package, I can't recall the title, I've played it so many times my brain's mashed and the label's worn clean off.'

Scratch placed a claw on the vinyl grooves to form a needle, mixing the tunes as he went along. Most cats could talk the legs off a table, so they all thought they could do a DJ's job. Yet Scratch was respected as one of the best, a true individual.

Anyone who knew him was a fortunate soul. Julius happened to be so fortunate.

'How's it going?' Julius meowed as he entered the roomy booth. Scratch hushed him, pointing at a red light on the wall. Once it had blinked off, the DJ bumped foreheads affectionately with his old friend. It had been a while.

Julius had interviewed him a long time back. Scratch had insisted that he was a creative artist, with no time for being sociable; Julius had suggested that a DJ was nothing more than a record spinner. There was no need to be pretentious about it. The two cats had grown to respect each other, and Julius dug his taste in music.

```
Wanna kill
Eat everything in sight
Fed up
I need one last bite
```

'I need a favour.' Julius was answered with a nod. Blaring from the DJ's headphones, squirming to get out, Suspicious Package were still crooning.

```
I'm nothing much
No one to touch
I'm nothing much
Need you to clutch
```

'You lookin' fat, Mr K. You bin holed away with that book of yours too long. Neglected your acquaintances, like me. I looked at your book.' Scratch held his nose and pinched his face into a grimace.

'Quit it, Scratch. I need your help.'

'Anything for you, Daddio.'

In a hurry, Scratch shoved his headphones back on, flipped a switch and addressed the city:

'An old friend's with us today, super scribbler Julius Kyle. He's had the balls to raise Tiger Straight from the dead. Wanna tell us about it, J?'

'No.' Julius shook his head. 'This is urgent. I've got something –'

'Chill out, partner. You're gonna pop an artery. Be calm.'

Julius grabbed Scratch's mike and the DJ backed off in as casual a manner as possible. 'It's all yours.'

'This society was built on truth. Forged in good will. Polished with honesty. Most cats understand that they have to co-operate, make do together to keep this city ticking. A few think they know better. They're superior, they're more intelligent, they'll show us how it's done. Not in a blatant fashion. They're subtle. Insidious. They think they're doing what's best for the city. They're wrong. Who'm I to judge? I'm a nobody, a writer of nothing that anyone wishes to read, a talentless creator. Nevertheless, I know these superior few are stuck on the wrong track – I've seen so many cats die because of them. A reporter, a small cub, Wildcats and Clutes. They died needlessly. The few didn't care. Casualties in their grand scheme to cut a deal with dogs.

'Good dogs, their ambassadors, the Joe J. Public of the canine communities up North, and even in this city – they have some principles. They don't know anything about this. But there are also Bad Dogs. Foul, demonic, ugly and incorrigible.

'These are criminals outside your homes, carving up our cosy lives, eating anything in their path. These hounds are killers. If we cut a pact with killers – if one is made outwith public knowledge or assent – we'll go to the dogs.

'Your children, your parents, your world will be threatened. The dogs should be stopped. Morris Erson, editor of the *Post*, should be stopped. He's behind this, the Mayor knows about it and he's not prepared to do anything about it in a hurry. I'm going to lobby the City Chambers. I hope you'll join me.'

For a cityful of animals whose watchword was apathy, the cats' reaction to the broadcast was totally unexpected.

They didn't lobby the Chambers. They ransacked it, ripping up the furniture (including Otto's satin throne) with angry talons; they chewed at the wallpaper, smashed pictures and mirrors, spat on paperwork and nicked all the red tape. By the time midnight came, the building was an uninhabitable wreck. The Mayor was nowhere to be found.

That's because he was with his mother in a palatial safe house. He'd aimed to give her a long-in-coming dress down. As usual, she wasn't particularly pleased to see him.

'I suppose Tarquin snivelled the whole story to you?'

'He didn't have to. I'm the Mayor. I have authority here. You lost it long ago, mother, and it's too late to drag yourself back from your has-been Valhalla.'

Quite a mouthful. Bridget looked hurt.

'You know that's not true. The multitude look up to me. I guide them.'

'I love you, in a twisted kind of way. I learned everything from you. You raised me to be ruthless and merciful by turns, keep the dullards around me on their toes. But when you programmed me, made me the power grubbing machine that I am... you didn't leave room for yourself. No failsafe forcing me to respect you.

'I love you for the way you wrap Dad round your little pads, the way you can bite a bird in half with one chomp, the way you can reverse an opinion poll with a flip of your eyelashes. Never give up. Always scheming and using and hating. If you'd left me to fend for myself as a cub – the thought never crossed your mind, did it? – who knows how

I would have turned out? A Tarquin or a tiger. Do you care about me at all?'

'This deal with the Bad Dogs –'

'I'll talk to you about a deal, mother. I spent the afternoon talking to Brother Kafel, the Archbishop's accomplice. I've agreed to give the Church some serious support.'

'How can you benefit from that?' Bridget was horrified.

'Easily. They've agreed to one or two terms of mine in return for some political speeches on their behalf.'

'What terms?'

'They'll no longer continue to support your moral campaign. They'll denounce any moves you make to oust me as Mayor. I always knew the Church was strong, that many people believed in the throttlehold it has over our culture. I didn't know that they despised dogs as much as I do – and they don't find your double-dealing too healthy, either. I've seen the light, and I'm on the payroll.'

'They'll swallow you up like they've devoured everyone else in this city, with ritual and ridicule.' Bridget looked tired. 'You haven't stalled me by much, my son. You've made things bad for yourself and made a pact with priests. I hope you'll live to regret it. You can close down the MMA. I won't be so easy to shut up. A new organisation will pop up in its place, and if I disappear you'll pay, blessing or no blessing.'

Roy Fury, chief reporter on the *Post*, knew who the dog lovers were. Certain misguided, left wing cross breeds had campaigned equal rights for mutts since he'd moved to the North Bank. He knew their names and where they lived. He'd been bottling it up, waiting for the chance to set them right. So he got a few friends together, mostly tabbies with big teeth and heavy appetites for booze. It was about time they used those teeth for something other than opening bottles, used them on the longhairs who'd been begging for trouble since their march down Main Street with sedated dogs at their heels. That had freaked Roy out. He didn't want to see that sort of thing in his city.

It didn't take long for his posse to reach the block where the pinkos lived. They grabbed whatever they could find – bricks, pieces of wood, empty milk bottles. Only a fool would throw a full one through someone's window. That woke the longhairs up. They were scared to rush out, stayed barricaded in their bright-painted flats. The posse (increasing in size, joined by curious onlookers) lobbed more missiles at the flats, stones and collars and discarded fag ends, pipes and trash and abusive comments, until they smoked some of those dog lovers out. Then they pounced, ripping them to shreds. They beat the shreds to a pulp, ventured into the flats for second helpings.

Roy forgot how to think straight. He was enjoying himself too much, and he wasn't going to rest until every longhair on the North Bank had got a good kicking. That would teach them.

Cities don't explode like matchheads or firecrackers. In some parts of Bast the inhabitants slept tight. They made the most of the fragile peace a cushion, pillow or warm cubbyhole could give, in blithe unconsciousness of the riots that hooped their homes. The danger, the threat of attack was exciting and unsettling. Dogs with their chiselled teeth and anvil paws; the domesticated cats wouldn't stand a chance with their soft bellies and tolerant natures. Such an attack had not happened for centuries. The possibility was enough to make everyone feel uneasy.

What mattered so much to Roy meant little to most cats; he had found a core that needed to let off steam, and that core had grown into a mass of fervent compatriots, their sights lined up for easy fodder. Tell us where to point our claws, and we'll do the stabbing. With pleasure. They need the exercise, haven't had any in sooo long. This was what they had been built for, not office work, not trendy café bars, trips to the pictures. Why sit still when there was adventure to be had? Aren't you curious about the sound a longhair makes when they're struck, the squeal of a punctured back? Roy's lot wanted to know, and they had the whole night to find out, a night alight with burning dwellings and gleaming talons.

The Bad Dogs were sick of waiting. One of their number nibbled at his hind leg, a fugged odour filling the warehouse.

They had work to do, mayhem to spread, harbingers for the hound army to come. The Wildcats had been daft enough to hide them up until now, they'd played along with the gang's plans. There would be no need for that any more. The dogs would continue to eat their way through the city's population. Their mission had always been intended as a one-way visit, a kamikaze holiday to mogland. When they were caught, strung up, more fear and panic would spread amongst the enemy. Perfect. The cats wouldn't stand a chance when the canine troops arrived, and the intelligence the Bad Dogs sent back to their leaders would be of great help.

As soon as the Wildcat chief arrived, he'd be meat. One less cat to worry about in the cold war they were determined to heat up. They'd seen Samson in action; he deserved no less than death.

Samson did arrive eventually, bringing help with him. The floor shook, the dogs falling against each other, leaning on walls. It got darker. Dirt fell from the ceiling and blinded them. They stumbled towards the exit but found it blocked off – wood panels slid into place and girders held it fast.

The Wildcats responsible for this were already busying themselves with another job. They were dragging a stilted wooden structure towards the warehouse. A large wrecking ball dangled from its neck. It had been built as a labour saving machine that did the work of fifteen cats; under the gang's control, it was a weapon of cold steel evil.

Earth fled in all directions under the marsh-brown wheels of the tower, landing in clods against the white ware-house. Samson brought up the rear, bossing his gang around. He wore a khaki cap and yellow raincoat, flapping at his sides as if trying to escape.

Samson had gladly got rid of Warren and Sal – they'd been getting too cheeky. The inconsequential writer had been a perfect excuse to get them off guard, out in the open. Now that writer had blown the whistle on the dogs – it was time to spring his trap and wipe out any trace of his involve-ment with them. The chaos spread by the broadcast meant he could start to widen his empire. The whole city was weak and defenceless, thanks to a few ugly pugs. By the time the mob recovered from the night of long claws, the Wildcats would rule half the riverbank. Graffiti would be scrawled on all the walls, gang members would squat in the finest houses, no one would dare set foot in Samson's territory for fear of losing all nine lives in rapid succession. He'd never been happier.

Full of cheer and charm, he'd suggested one last meeting to the Bad Dogs.

'Don't want no more meetings,' the leader had replied, 'want to bite someone.' After reassurance from Samson, they had agreed to get together in the warehouse.

Now he had them trapped, all evidence ready to be crushed in an enormous sarcophagus. After the riots, Samson wanted no evidence that would connect him with the dogs. He wanted no dogs at all. They were too unruly, almost uncontrollable. A liability.

The wrecking ball rammed the warehouse with a quaking thump. The ball crumpled with the force of the strike, but it had served its function. The building began to crumble, imploding in a shower of plaster and brick dust.

The dogs never realised what was happening to them. All they knew was that they were in deep trouble. Blocks of stone and bone white plaster fell on their hides, the Bad Dogs unleashing howls they hadn't spoken since childhood. The place was angry with them, grinding them in its awful teeth until they were entombed. Heavy weights crushed their chests or choked their broad throats as they whined for mercy that never came. Their appeals were drowned by the monstrous noise of Samson's wrecking tower.

Gravity did the rest. Roof tiles splintered the rafters and the dogs were speared by falling masonry.

Samson happened to be in a thoroughly ruthless mood

that day. He ordered his gang to drag the tower backwards, then swung the ball again. It scooped up piles of brick with its pendulum attack, ensuring that the dogs were dead and buried. Descending from the battered vehicle, he nosed through the rubble, checking for signs of life.

One dog had clawed for escape, one paw and a crumpled snout jutting out. Samson scraped at the nose – nothing stirred. He ordered his lackeys to cover the mutt with large blocks of stone.

'Enjoy that?'

The Wildcats agreed with glee.

'Then let's finish the rest of em. We'll terminate every hound in that fleabit shantytown across the river. And we'll be heroes.'

A rhythmic noise like a pneumatic drill, charging up, boring deeper. Pounding at Julius' skull. The sound was accompanied by the ting of smashing glass, the bark of splintering wood – and a chorus of cat calls, unhappy mews, a cry to anyone close enough to respond.

This was no drill. Pounding steps echoed round ravined city streets, deafening, threatening to engulf Julius' senses and eat his mind. He clutched his ears and backed into an alley for fear of being trampled.

Here they come... bursting everything in their path like a tsunami searching for a dam – C'mon, take your best shot, try and stop us! Filled with the power of panic, the crowd felt – if they were capable of feeling – invulnerable. Immortal. Their deeds, mindless, childish actions formed in the heat of the moment, would live forever, long after the crowd had dispersed. They intended to play this game of follow my leader to its bitter, stupid end. Julius realised how cruel his fellow cats could be, and that scared him more than a dog ever could.

Snaring a rodent or hunting a hare was very different from waging war against a species that was larger and deadlier than yours – a species that outnumbered the cats by ten to one. Julius was aware of the consequences and so was Otto. The Mayor had his own agenda, thinking of himself instead of his people. Julius wanted to bury his head in a sand box and wait for the furore to end. He couldn't do that. If he was the only citizen who wanted Bast to survive, then he would have to be the one who did something about it.

Wanted the city to survive? This sweaty, ancient, tick-ridden home of his? There was nothing else. Nowhere else to go. Like Pa, Julius knew his place and had to keep it.

He would find the mob, show them how he felt – somehow.

The longhairs were on the defensive. Blocking up their homes with upturned teeth and tabletops, arching their backs, making themselves look as big bastard as possible. It didn't help. They were outnumbered – the whole city seemed to be against them, and any amount of rhetoric about minorities and equality could not save them from the mob.

They prayed for the dawn, for the fires to burn themselves out. Hopefully as the sun came up the citizens would come to their senses, go home, get ready for work.

Julius could hear the ringing of a tiny bell. He noticed that he had an ulcer, probed it with his tongue, feeling a metallic tang. Stress. Or too much salt. He picked an old cat up off the street, dusting down his fur. The elderly gent began washing himself instinctively. His eyes were wild with fear, pupils dancing to a salsa beat. Julius clutched his shoulders, keeping him upright.

'There! Over there!' Twenty toms rushed his way, led by a drink-crazed Roy. Julius stepped in front of the old gent, ready to defend him, but was snatched back into the shadows.

'What's going on?' he asked. Camilla clapped a paw over his mouth, dragging him into an alcove without a word. The bell round her neck still tried to give her away. Clem, her photographer, accompanied her.

The toms were murdering the gent right in front of him; he was powerless to stop them. Once they were sure the gent was well mauled the toms drifted off, yewling and screaming.

'What are you doing here?' Julius' whispers echoed down the street.

'Looking for the big story. You coulda got yourself killed, helping that old boy.' She sounded genuinely concerned. She also wore her 'dedicated reporter' face, eyes cold, lips tight.

'Who was he?'

'You didn't recognise him?' Clem was busy taking shots of the dead cat.

'Should I have?'

'Professor Minglan Blane, Anthropological Studies, Burmese Hall of Scientific Research. He was well known a while back... had the audacity to suggest cats and dogs descended from the same species. Not exactly Mr Popular.'

'This hysteria –'

'Your fault. Roy lost it when he heard the broadcast. I tried to follow him – seems he has some like-minded pals.'

If I started this, I'd better stop it.

'Are you going to be all right?' Julius asked tenderly.

'Sure. Fine.' Camilla let a smile escape. 'I've got Clem here to keep an eye on me. He's good at that.'

'I've got to get after them,' said Julius, drawing a deep breath.

'I know.'

'We'll catch up with you later,' said Clem, pulling a new roll of film from his dungarees. 'Got to get the bigger picture first, ken what I mean?' Julius was off, following the distant sound of shouts and wails. Camilla was safe for the moment, and he didn't want to drag her into more trouble. She could do that herself.

A pocket of fire met Samson's grain silo in the Doghouse, allowing his vat's worth of pet rats to escape. Driven from their home and alarmed by the fire, the rats began to swarm. At first they were wary of resistance. When no cats beat them back or threatened to gobble them up, they began to curry into houses and nibble at grandmothers.

The cats who'd stayed home, avoiding the mob histrionics, found themselves fending off a new attack – tiny, furry, repulsive, germ-ridden, everywhere.

They repelled the rats with saucepan lids, hoover handles, sink plungers – whatever they could find. They had never realised how wide, how mean, how guileful the creatures were. Now the cats and rats fought for their lives and something more – possession of Bast.

The mob would return home to find their larders raided and their old folk eaten. Julius tumbled into a flat, Roy's boys barging after him. A psychedelic face had been painted on the ceiling in vomit-inducing yellows and greens. A Justice For Dogs poster lolled on one wall. By the window, staying low, moonlight brushing the tips of her ears, hunched a young female. Beside her cowered Camilla, shaking with fear. She'd found her big story.

Julius bent down to help the young female up. She pushed him away, surprisingly strong. Before he could recover his balance Roy was on top of her, clawing at her dress, punching and kicking her. Julius tried to help, but he didn't fancy the same treatment. He shoved his way over to Camilla.

He'd heard the cries as he passed the block of flats on the West side of the city. Roy and some of his best friends had broken away from the rest of the mob to deal with one last longhair. 'We've got to help her.' Julius stared at Camilla's zombie eyes. 'Snap out of it!'

Camilla got to her feet, shaking her head to clear her mind. Slowly, murkily, as if she was surfacing from a deep pool, she began to hear Julius' voice, pick out intelligible words.

'We've got to do something!' Julius fended off a fat tom, protecting his girlfriend. Trying to keep her on her feet.

'You're right.' Camilla headed for the little female, battered and purpling, still under attack. By now she'd bunched into a concertina shape and was offering her belly in submission – a perfect target for Camilla's taloned hindpaws as she kicked her. Julius tried to stop her as she attacked the female with vigour; Roy growled at him, making him jump back. Julius grabbed Roy's length of pipe and started to lay about him, swiping his way to the window. He brought the pipe down on Roy's head, stunning him unconscious.

The female gathered her ebbing strength to fight back against Camilla, rending her belly open with a gnarled claw. Camilla slumped to the floor, both sets of eyelids fluttering closed. The female bolted for the exit in a flurry of black fur. Roy was close behind her, heading out of the flat and down the street. Making sure that Camilla was as comfortable as possible, Julius followed the mob at a discreet distance.

The City Infirmary had admitted too many patients. It was not equipped to handle a great emergency – most cats coped for themselves after an injury. This was different, and the staff were having to rearrange the wards to manage the extra admissions.

The rooms and corridors were littered with the bodies of half-dead cats, their fur splayed, curled into tight balls, legs tucked under their bodies. They were too sick or wounded to care where they were.

A female with bleeding pads was visited by her mate. She leaned forward in her wheelchair to hug him. On a nearby gurney was a cat with a cardiac tamponade. Fluid had gathered round the heart, squeezing it so it couldn't pump. A cardiothoracic surgeon put in a drain and sewed up the ventricle, tidying up with a make-do sailor's knot.

At the admissions desk, a Triage Nurse filtered out the most serious cases, the ones who were serious but could wait, and the ones who could wait all night. The desk was littered with chains, sticks and knuckle-dusters from incoming gang members. The Clutes and Wildcats were using the riot as an excuse to settle old feuds. A shivering cub with damped-down hair said his name was Oliver Sudden. The nurse noted this with stoic acceptance.

Patients were relieved from their suffering with anaesthetic injections in their hunkers or the flabby part of their necks. Nasal prongs fed them oxygen. The nurses tried to observe universal precautions – sanitary conditions, aprons and mitts to prevent spread of feline diseases. In this chaos it was easy to forget protocol. Bed baths consisted of a quick lick from the nurses, and supplies of sand pans for beds had run dry.

A few feeding bowls lay around, empty. Cold cats were wrapped in electric blankets, anal thermometers reading their core temperature.

Nip addicts, usually sectioned off in a secure wing, roamed freely until they were caught and expelled by Hospital Security. It was the only way to make room for the influx of citizens caught in skirmish or flame; burnt cats were treated with flamazine, their ears crispy and their whiskers frizzled.

Doctors rushed about in their fine white coats. They were learned enough to sense how ill each patient was, dealing with priority cases. Their hearing was sufficient to detect a heartbeat simply by placing an ear to the casualty's chest, but in this sea of drooping whiskers, wet noses, matted fur, dirty eyes, and plaintive mews the doctors were overwhelmed. Many of the cats were left to be cared for by the friends or relatives who had brought them in.

Nurses stood back as newcomers were rushed in, strapped down for blood transfusions. A doctor snatched up a bag of plasma, explaining to his patient how to insert a saline drip, left to sew up a claw slash.

Dark clouds shuffled over Captain Feargal Cutter's head in a lazy daisychain swirl. They followed him wherever he trod, he was sure. More effective than any siren or light, a dark aura was enough to stop many sidewinders from going astray.

He'd felt so proud when he'd first donned the uniform. Punters didn't see him, they saw the badge. Something to hide behind and something to use to get his own way, a better way. He'd felt so strong until the trouble started. Plenty fear, no respect. Pushed about by his superiors, ignored on the streets, the cat under the hat going unnoticed. Unloved.

Dreaming of promotion, working his way through all that public service muck, he'd planned to make a name for Feargal Cutter as a caring, tolerant Captain. No abuse, no patronising attitudes towards the lower ranks. By the time he'd reached the apex of his career, he'd ceased to care about civilians or underlings. All that concerned him was his salary, because that sexy old wage packet paid for his food. Those square meals had always been the core of his bulked being.

Prowlers. That was what they were called these days. Prowlers, almost as amoral as the cutthroats they apprehended. It was a question of statistics. If the police had attempted to arrest every cat who got in a scrap, they'd be working twenty four hour shifts nine days a week and the whole city'd be against them. No line had been drawn between acceptable and illegal behaviour. The prowlers made an on-the-spot decision, issuing a fine, tearing an ear, or finishing off a lawbreaker's worthless life. The worst penalty a prowler could impose was to have an offender's claws removed. This was the greatest ignominy, for without its claws a cat is not a true cat.

Some coppers collected the claws they removed. The Captain had a beltful round his ample waist. The claws would clink against his radio and cuffs from time to time; thieves might be warned of his approach, but they also knew he was a tough hombre.

Tough or not, tonight the police had been overwhelmed by the rioters, thanks to Julius Kyle and his grit-stirring newsflash. Well, forget 'em. Captain Cutter wanted to survive the night with his tail intact, and he didn't want to waste his cops in some firebomb. He was prepared to enter the City Infirmary on an emergency call, bringing with him a number of reinforcements. He located a band of squabbling Clutes and Wildcats, led by Wes and Malvo respectively. He was not prepared to get his paws dirty; better to stand back and look threatening. He had trained his squaddies to knit their brows in a menacing frown – very important in the battle against villains.

Moira placed salves on Camilla's wounds, licking her bruises tenderly. A bowl of water lay beside her – she was curled up on two sheets, spread smooth on the floor. She'd been washed in on a wave of hysterical wildcats. She had been too weak to talk yet still worried about her appearance. As was custom in the Infirmary, a nametag had been clipped to her tail. When a patient's name was called they were supposed to wave it in the air, attract attention. Right now, Camilla had lost too much blood to raise a whimper. With a heart rate of 240 and resps of 38, she needed constant care.

Along the corridor, the gang youths hurled abuse at their doctors, refusing a tranq shot or a bandage. Dressings were for wimps, so the medics had to settle for staunching any excessive bleeding and placing splints on broken legs.

Soft fur bedding reminded the patients of their mothers, an attempt to relax them. Monitors purred and sang a lullaby sine wave stanza, adding a green hint to the dim hospital lights.

Moira had come into the hospital earlier that evening. She'd found a Burmese longhair lying in the street, left for dead. Dragging him all the way to the medical establishment, she'd been dismayed to find that the staff refused to help her charge. There weren't enough beds, or staff – only shorthairs would be admitted. Half the nurses had left to join Roy's mob anyway, so she'd determined to care for the Burmese herself.

As the beds had filled up and wounded were brought in to lie in the corridors, she'd helped where she could, offering water or medicine to the patients whenever she could find a fresh supply.

One of the wounded was Camilla, playing the difficult patient, dismissive of Moira's low breeding. Are you sure your paws are clean? You have disinfected that, haven't you? I need more drugs.

Moira was calm and efficient, making Camilla as comfortable as possible. She was in a bad way, coughing up blood from internal injuries – Moira knew she didn't have long left. However she had other cats to tend to, so she settled for checking on Camilla as often as she could.

Across the way Wes and Malvo faced each other, circling, their tails beating time to a silent aria. The cops hovered around the two gangs, a peacekeeping force with little strength. Their ears burned at the insults hurled across the corridor.

'Don't mess with us, litter runt,' Malvo hissed.

'Least I had a family,' Wes giggled. 'Didn't your momma abandon you first time she saw your pug face? Didn't they try to drown you as a kitten? What's your gang called? The Nappy Crappers? The Mumma Lovers? The Ass Wipers?'

'No. The Butt Kickers. And you're the butts.'

'Oh, the Butt Kissers. Well, here's ours but you'll have to beg us, baby.'

'You're gonna be the one begging, Clute. When you're trying to drag our hooks out your messed-up nose.'

'Pardon me? Sorry, I'm finding it hard to understand you, you seem to be filling my ears with crap. Better start smooching, Ass Kissers... You gonna stand there and pout, or are you set to rumble?'

The preliminaries were done with. Malvo didn't kiss his rival's backside; he bit it instead, sinking his teeth into the bony rump. Wes let out a howl, tried to twist round and swipe him. A gurney came sailing towards the two youths, knocking them flying, Wes losing half his precious tail.

Missy, appearing at the end of the corridor, backed Wes up.

'What's she doing here?' cried Malvo, his face hot, saliva bubbling on his lower lip. 'You're gonna end just like yer lover.'

Missy's body shook. Tufano. She still wanted him. He was too worthy to be considered by a Wildcat. She did what her dead mate would never have done, and lost her temper. Ignoring the row of police officers, she sprang at Malvo, sinking her claws into his groin. Caught by surprise, he lifted up his head to yowl and this allowed her to sink her teeth into his neck. Within seconds he was on the floor, and war had erupted in the hospital corridor.

Wes waded into the fray, batting Wildcats from his path to protect Missy's flank. Together they were unstoppable.

Nurse Kay herded more patients away from the scuffle. The police would deal with the troublemakers – she had a lot of respect for the mogs in blue. She didn't want to see anyone get hurt, but her main priority was the safety of the patients, innocent cats who'd got caught up in the riot. She was there to serve and protect them, not the members of some scruffy cult. She was worried about her litter, tucked up in a nest not so far away, hoped they were all right. She'd been home on leave with them, raising them, trying to be a good mother when she'd been called in on this emergency.

Every responsible nurse on the hospital register was struggling to deal with the riot, failing miserably. They did not have the facilities to cope with chaos. She tried to hold curious onlookers back from the fight, corralling them along the far side of the corridor. There was too much of a show going on. Everyone wanted to watch as the police got in the way of the two gangs. The cops came off worst. Cutter shook his head, still refusing to get involved. Plenty more officers where those had come from. The Wildcats would soon tire themselves out, they'd be fed up with this fight, go somewhere else and that was his main priority – to see them out of the hospital, out of the district, away from these injured cats.

'Take some more water,' Moira offered Camilla a saucer when she started to pant. 'Help cool you down.'

'What do you know? You haven't even seen what it's like out there.' Camilla's eyes grew wide. 'Is there a 'phone?'

'What do you need that for?' Moira smiled. Camilla was growing delirious.

'My story. I'm a reporter. I have to 'phone in my story to the *Post*.'

'There is no *Post* any more,' Moira said gently. 'It's been razed to the ground. Everyone who was working there at the time... No more reporters, no more editor, no more newspaper. Nothing but ink and ashes.'

'All my notes!' Camilla tried to sit up, grew weaker instead. 'My mate could have been – he worked there...'

'So did mine. I mean, this tom I was with. Don't know what happened to him. I hope he's all right.'

Camilla choked and spluttered. 'They're all out there. Trying to save their homes, or hunting down stray dogs.'

'Oh, Julius wouldn't do that. I don't think he's got it in him. That killer instinct. Even if he did have nothing against dogs.'

'Stupid.' Camilla shook her head slowly. 'Julius has a problem with any creature that doesn't come from his part of town. I should know. He's been living with me for years.

The old buzzard thought he was being clever. Hurting me. And I was doing the same, two-timing him.'

'He doesn't know?'

'Right under his big grey nose. His editor, of all people! The late Morris Erson. We got so cold. Julius and Camilla. Toast of the city. Hotshot newsgatherers with hearts of snow and ice. Scruples tossed aside with a careless gesture.'

'He's not like that,' said Moira under her breath.

'I wanted him to remember me like I used to be, when we found each other. I hope he doesn't see me like this.'

'You look radiant,' Moira assured her. A patient groaned for assistance from a nearby bay.

'I've never felt so old,' said Camilla, her eye puffed up. Moira felt a sudden urge to embrace her, hold her tight. She could feel Camilla's heart beating faster, erratic, struggling to recall its rhythm. It gave up. Slowed to a stop. Graceful as always, Camilla relaxed in Moira's arms and was gone.

The Captain stood his ground and waited patiently for the little ones to run out of steam. The youths dirtied the white hospital walls, fur and blood matted along its patterned corridors, cats thrown about, smacking into wheelchairs and dripstands, annoying the more well-to-do cats in the wards close by with their screams of pain and frustration. No time for taunts now, they were out of breath, fighting for their lives against bigger cats.

Police officers foolish enough to get in the way were scratched or bitten, disappearing under an animal mound, resurfacing in pieces. Make no prisoners, that was Missy's motto. If they tried to run for cover it was quite justifiable to kill them while trying to escape. One less Wildcat on the market, polluting the atmosphere with their presence. One more little territory for the Clutes to consume. Sometimes they kept souvenirs to confirm their kill. Usually they left that to the police.

The Clutes didn't have to contend only with Wildcats and cops. The skirmish offered the perfect opportunity for old scores to be righted within each gang, cats stabbing each other in the back to climb a link in the food chain. As latest leader, Missy was the most eligible target.

She's a female, I can do better than her! Why should she be leading the race? Spiro, a crafty little tom with ideas above his station, wanted the top job. His ass switched from side as he coiled up his body, muscles tightening, crawling towards his leader.

Needs taking down a boot or two, I'll sort her out, there she is, she doesn't see me, too busy grappling with some other fat runt. I can sneak up behind her. Yeah. She won't hear me. I'll finish her for good and all. Thinks she can be boss. Edging my paw closer to the back of her neck... One claw in the right place, she'll never know what tricked her. Me, I'll have my reputation, I'll be the worm that destroyed that witch, me I'm going to get –

Without caring to turn and look Spiro in the eye, Missy flipped a leg in his direction and he fell backwards.

I needed that paw! Bleeding all over the place. This is no good at all. What's my dad going to say when I come home with a paw missing? He's gonna kill me! Worse than that, he's gonna chop off the other one. I'm going to be the laughing stock of the gang. Mr One Paw. Shouldn't have got out of my box this morning.

Spiro began to feel faint as he lost more blood, unable to dodge the attacks that came at him from all directions. The Wildcats smelt blood and so did the cops, sinking their claws into his stump. He began to crawl towards a nurse; she moved away, busy with real patients. She'd be back to mop up any survivors once the fur had flown. Spiro collapsed unconscious.

Missy had already forgotten his treachery. She was too busy grappling with Malvo, trying to match his strength and avoid his talons. She pushed the tailless monster down the corridor, and he spun into the outstretched paw of Captain Cutter. He'd grown impatient with his waiting game, stamped on Malvo's head instead. Gave Missy a courteous nod and ordered the rest of his officers to attack. Alarm bells rang as they joined the fight, their heads battered against the antiseptic walls. Patients picked themselves up from their beds and fled if they were able.

With Malvo down the Wildcats scattered, leaving their wounded for the medics to deal with. Some would be turfed out to join the low-priority patients on the steps outside. The youths continued to squabble, and the victorious Clutes spat at the Wildcats as they left the hospital and made for the river. A relieved police squad went back out on patrol, waiting for the next emergency.

'I've been looking for you everywhere!' Julius rubbed his forehead against Moira's.

'Your mate's dead.'

Julius tried not to weep, a cry welling up in his smoke-dry throat. 'I'm sorry.' He looked down at Camilla's body. The bell at her throat would never ring again. She looked as beautiful as ever. 'I'm sorry I lied to you, that all this happened... everything –'

Camilla had changed since her travels in the North, he thought. She'd always been haughty, self-immersed, critical of his down-home common ways. She'd respected his feelings, until her return. Could a couple grow so far apart in so short a time? Were a few months all it took – had their relationship been that fragile?

Julius dragged Moira towards the nearest exit.

'You're coming with me.'

'I've got wounded to tend to. Plus you're not my favourite tom right now.'

'In a few minutes, there won't be any more wounded. They'll be corpses, and you'll join them if you don't move now!'

'Where are we going?' sighed Moira, her mind made up.

'Somewhere dangerous. I don't wanna take my eyes off you. If I lose you...' *Like I've already lost Camilla* '...I can't. If you stay with me, I can make sure nothing happens to you.'

'You need someone to take care of you,' Moira nodded as they left the hospital.

Outside, police dragged away a miserly collection of offenders, slowing down the stretchers. Half-naked kittens wandered past. A distorted noise and light attracted Julius and Moira's attention. They began to follow the source, weaving along roads, through alleyways towards the river.

31

Mountain goats don't scare us
Mutts better beware us
We got plenty of guts
Behave, or lose your nuts

THE SMELL OF FUR CD
SUSPICIOUS PACKAGE

THERE WAS NOTHING LEFT to break. The town hall, the library, every house in Julius' street, butcher shops and Bast Tower were all gone. Only the Church was left unscathed, for fear of retribution from above. Beware of the god.

The mob's energetic trail of mayhem led inexorably over the bridge behind the *Post*, along the riverbank, towards the sleepy slum where dogs lived. The destructive impulse had consumed their minds. They did not know why they'd burned books and smashed down murals; it had happened, and it made them feel good. Their work was not over. The dogs had to be extinguished.

Nearing the slum, Roy was joined by Samson and band of Wildcats. The mob continued their advance, members of the gang joining their trail. Samson stopped Roy, recognising him as one of the ringleaders.

'What are you doing?' Samson snarled.

'Killing dogs.' Roy's response was greeted with cheers from the cats around him.

'This was supposed to be my city. It's in pieces.' The mob's fanaticism troubled him.

'The pieces can be picked up again. Join us, Wildcat. Help me finish this.'

'Do I have a choice?'

'You want to be a hero, don't you?' Roy was already catching up with the others. Samson reluctantly followed him.

Moira and Julius had been following the dancing lights for some time. They'd followed them as they passed the hospital, through skinny streets, across a bridge where the river was at its most narrow, along a muddy bank before they realised where the lights were headed.

They edged closer until the bright blur of movement became a recognisable group of animals, a crazed procession strutting along the sloped river bank. No words were exchanged; the large group of cats were set on something. They had a mission. The mob was in a hurry to get to the shantytown.

'The dogs are in trouble.' Julius looked at Moira steadily.

'They can deal with anything.'

'I'm not sure. I think they'll win the war – if war's where we're headed. Good luck to them. We cats have been complacent long enough. This battle – they're going to suffer. Pa could suffer.'

'We've got to get ahead of them,' Moira whispered in reply, 'warn my dad, get past these wasters.'

The cats blocked the entire path – to get round them unseen would be difficult. Moira and Julius had to try. They crouched low, began to skirt the cats. Good hearing and eye-sight meant nothing to the mob in their singular frame of mind. The burning torches hid the sound of rustling bushes as the couple pushed through gorse and thorn. They kept down, glad of the dark, steering shy of the flame's glow, ducking whenever Samson or Roy turned in their direction.

Samson was not as single-minded as the rest of the mob. He was working out a new strategy, an attempt to salvage a victory from Roy's mess. His thoughts were interrupted by a reflection in the darkness – the glint of Moira's eyes, watching him from the undergrowth. He ordered two toms to seek her out; they returned with two captives, snatched by the scruff of their necks.

'Bring 'em over. What're youse playing at?'

'The dogs.' Moira stared at Samson defiantly. 'We wanted to warn the dogs…'

'What are you going to do with them?' asked Julius. He already half-knew the answer.

'Fry them.' Samson looked back at his mob. 'You with us or against us?'

'It can't happen.' Julius tried to break free.

'It will. They're scum, vermin, they deserve to be cooked alive.' As the mob lurched forwards again, Moira and Julius were dragged kicking towards the shantytown.

The mud streets of the ghetto were cracked with cold. Ice puddles reflected the lanterns that gave the quarter its mea-gre light. Cardboard wind tunnels shot blasts of sleet from the river. The residents stayed in the prefabricated huts that had become so precious to them, under blankets in the streets, or in corrugated lean-tos.

As the cats approached some of the dogs fled, but hundreds remained: the old, infirm, dumb pups and expectant mothers. Those too stubborn, ill or insane to leave. In an instant, it was too late.

The streets got brighter, warmer. Sleet was joined by graining clouds of dust. The dogs were woken by a high-pitched chant, a song. The ice puddles caught an extra glint. Torches. Some of the dogs started to panic, milling about in the streets, looking for their loved ones. Others closed their eyes and lay down flat, accepting their fate. The cat's chorus – the angry, teeth-numbing chant – became louder, deafening. There were so many of them, all with a single purpose.

Samson struck the first blow. He grabbed a lantern from its post, swung it over his head and hefted it towards a fragile wood hut. Despite the sleet, the hut caught fire in a second. It began to coarsen and blacken, sparks catching neighbouring homes unaware. Other cats helped the nascent blaze along with more smashed lanterns and flambeaux.

Crackling flames and cats' triumphant cries drowned out a pitiful yelping. The dogs were too weak to put up resistance, caught in the gathering fire. Ice puddles melted and turned to steam. The cats backed off to surround the ghetto, clawing any fleeing hounds to death. The canine quarter lit up like a tinderbox, and Samson made sure it was shut up tight.

Pa could hear a crackling sound, a roar like a charging bull elephant. Someone had left their oven on – he could smell the burning meat. Peeking out his back window, Pa decided that he was still asleep. He was an unwilling bystander in a vivid nightmare.

My neighbour is a candle, wax flesh dripping from her body. A yelping, burbling candle.

Shaking his head to clear the dread, Pa bounded through the house, dodging drifting tinder, smashing through the front wall. Pa turned back to see his house explode. When the smoke settled there was nothing left but a crumpled shadow.

His friends, his neighbours were howling ghouls or blackened husks, and he was next if he didn't keep his head. He made for Sniffer's Square, the meeting place of his community. He had to organise any survivors.

Dogs were looking round as if they didn't know where they were. The heat and smoke were sufficient to overcome them.

The cats looked for anything flammable, chucking their torches onto roofs, in buildings, through windows, the flames reflected in their angry green eyes as they watched the town burn. These flames were different from the gutting pockets of amber in the city. This was one fat red inferno, angry and unstoppable – only the river dared to lie in its path. As Julius got closer the heat warmed his cheeks. The crowd was dancing at the brim of their prefabricated hell. It was the largest pyre he had ever known.

Julius was ignored as he pulled away from the mob, looking for Moira. He saw her with Roy, being dragged towards a clearing on the outskirts of the town. The cats began to congregate there, still watching their fire. Julius needed a distraction that would help him rescue Moira.

There was no one to organise. The square was almost empty and streaked with smoke. One body lay near the memorial stone that was its centre, overcome with burnt plastic fumes. It belonged to Leaky.

The prevailing winds had fanned the flames into an inferno, and Pa was trapped in the middle. He didn't stop to help his friend, racing into the old stone bathhouse, hot red embers spitting at his fur. He did not stop until he landed in the cold bath, a painful belly flop, sinking into the water until only the top of his head showed. Wood rafters crashed into the pool around him, but he kept his cool. His sanctuary simmered in the heat as he paddled around, dodging the falling roof timbers.

He had to survive. He would not let a cat get the better of him, and he was sure that a cat had started this disaster. No other creature could be so cold or vicious.

The water was getting hotter, bubbling with unbearable venom. Pa leaped from the pool with a yelp, diving through the exit as the place fell apart. He couldn't shake the image of Leaky's smoking form from his head. He hurried back towards the town centre.

Gotta go back. Go back and help him. It's not too far. It's like when you forget yer wallet and you have to go back home to get it. It's gotta be done, won't take long. Just a second and that's all I got.

Reaching Sniffer's Square, he was too late for Leaky. The body was beginning to burn. He checked Leaky's body for vital signs. He was too late. Pa backed off, looking for a way out of the town. He'd seen out the worst of the fire, but most buildings were still crackling away, fed on the fat of their occupants. Whoever had done this would be long gone by now; Pa headed for the river, head swivelling from side to side as he ran, looking for survivors.

There it was, draped over a chest of drawers. Pa sniffed at

his charred window frame, wheezing on the fumes. He stretched an arm through the pockmarked glass, grasping for the dribble of black cloth. It languished out of reach, a breath away. Flames licked his hide, bothering his tail. He forced his way further through the window frame, cracking the rest of the glass into prickling shards.

Got it. As Pa pulled his arm back the frame collapsed in a flurry of charcoal timber. Hot amber splashed his shoulder, roasting the fur on his forearm. Gritting his teeth, he rolled on the baking ground, put out the flames.

There was nothing more he could achieve. His kingdom had become a lump of ash. He had his son's bandanna; there was nothing else to salvage. He ventured towards the river, evading spikes of flame and sizzling dogs.

Some dogs are too big, too tough, too good at what they do – being dogs – to lose a fight. Pa was singed at the corners, worn down by the fire and the loss of life it had caused. When he found Samson standing at the tattered edge of his town, he faced his demon. He was angry, in pain with anger, and his eyes bulged from their sockets. Pa wanted to use everything at his disposal to destroy the maniac but he was weak. Felt sorry for himself. That was all the opening Samson needed.

'Get him.'

Roy looked at the boss, back at the multi-tonned tram of a dog. Could he be gotten? Roy shook his head, seeing the passion in Pa's face... too late. No one else noticed Roy's hesitation; they were too busy pouncing on the dog, ripping at his fur, trying to knock him to the ground. A Wildcat bandanna was wrapped round his foreleg. Once the mob saw this they fell on the creature with renewed vigour.

Samson watched his cronies take on the hound. They'd been raring for this all night. Their other kills had been easy, cold-blooded. This one was putting up a fight.

Three cronies were flung away, tossed salad too close to a whisk. Others joined in, biting at Pa's left cheek with razor teeth. Pa moaned with pain and crashed onto his back. The cats withdrew, allowing their leader to grasp Pa by the neck, squeezing until there was a subtle pop.

'Bye-bye, little doggie.'

Julius saw the dog fall amongst the frazzled bracken and rushed over to help. Samson was bigger and meaner than any archive photo could auger. 'King was right,' said Julius, striding through the undergrowth to face him. 'You are an ugly bugger.'

Dropping Pa hard on his blood-crusted nose, Samson leered up at Julius, round at his apostles. Claws sprang from his callused pads and he showed Julius the back of his paw. As he beckoned, the claws rang together like crystal dirks.

'Come on then. Help your friend up.' Pa was motionless. Julius heard him fight for breath through broken teeth. Julius bent forward, reaching for Pa. The dog was choking, and the writer wished he'd paid more attention in the hospital. He felt helpless, didn't know what to do. He unknotted King's bandanna, placing it against the wounds, trying to staunch the flow of blood. Pa hacked and coughed. Time was running off. Julius wanted to do something, anything. Roy held Moira back; he was laughing uncontrollably.

The apostles unleashed their claws, ready to shish kebab the writer. Instead of hefting Pa onto his feet, Julius sprang at Samson's chest, digging his hind and foreclaws into the boss' torso.

Pa held a side-on, squint-angled view of the combat, he was finding it hard to move at all, tough to breathe. It was as if he was drowning, swimming that great river and losing his way. Maybe it was the dust kicked up by the clamouring animals, but for some reason his vision was obscured. He thought about his adopted children, hoped that Moira was okay, that she hadn't got caught up in all this nightmare, that she wasn't out looking for him.

There she is! In the distance, standing there, why doesn't she do something? She looks horrified. Come on, help Julius, he's losing the fight... what kind of daughter do you call yourself? She's moving away. It's too late, it's all happened so fast, she's trying to move, blocked by some of those toughs. But I don't want to sleep now. I don't think I have the choice. The world looks so much less ugly.

Pa imagined Leaky's smoking corpse, a grin melting from his face, beckoning him to a better place. He felt Moira's paws on his torso, saw only black. Heard some reassuring words. Hoped the bastards would burn in their own flames.

Overbalanced, Samson rolled over and tried to crush Julius with his hefty weight. Fear threatened to overwhelm Julius, Samson was twice as big, louder and stronger. Pa was dying, blood gargling in his windpipe, death rattle erratic. Julius let out a deafening yowl as bloodlust consumed his senses. He pushed Samson backwards, straightening his hindlegs, the bigger cat's eyes wide with surprise. Something seemed to give way in Samson's spine and Julius leaped on top of him, spitting his hatred. Samson lay still, offering his underbelly to his opponent.

Leaving the boss to wallow in the soil, Julius raced over

to Pa, nuzzling his wounds. Moira tugged free of Roy and ran over to attend to the dog. Pa craned his neck up to whisper to Julius: 'Go away. Now.' The last words he'd ever utter – nothing clever, but wise nonetheless. The mob was closing in, ready to tear them apart. Julius and Moira had no option but to heed the dog's advice. They would regret leaving for the rest of their lives. The dog's eyes were quiet before they'd left.

32

Dogs caused a riot last night as they left their shantytown on the South Bank to wreak trouble in the city centre.

The dogs were quickly despatched thanks to the police, headed by Captain Feargal Cutter. Concerned citizens, many of whom were injured, aided the authorities.

The City Infirmary carefully filtered the large influx of casualties without delay. The hospital reported a 'positive success rate' in treating patients.

According to Captain Cutter, a feline minority of longhairs provoked the dogs. 'They were led by the Sinners,' he stated today. 'It's a crime to see such irresponsible behaviour coming from civilised cats. They call themselves pacifists, but they caused a great deal of death and mayhem last night. I hope they'll learn from their ghastly blunder.'

Mayor Otto has made the most of the night's squabble, appealing to each faction in turn. He has made a sincere public apology to the short-hairs, mourned the death of the shanty dogs and wept at the sudden disappearance of his mother and two sons. The Church has rushed to support him, and a fresh election victory looks likely.

POST NEWS REPORT

ROY FURY

Carrots didn't tempt Swampie; his night vision was perfect. Sprouts made him break wind, and cauliflower ruined his breath. For him it was meat or nothing. Anything from a deer to a dog would do, as long as he could sink his pointy teeth into some regular flesh.

He had a lot of eating to do. Swampie had never been the largest wrestler in the ring. When he sat in Morris' chair, one of the few pieces of furniture to escape the fire, he felt tiny. The arms were bent after years of weight from overfed limbs. The frazzled chair still bore food stains and teeth marks.

Not that Swampie wasn't doing a creditable job of filling the editor's chair. After the riot he'd bought up Bast Tower, given Julius' column to Roy Fury and revamped the journal as he rebuilt the offices. Headlines had got more sensational. The articles spread Swampie's dubious word, observed society gossip and plugged the new editor's book. Sometimes, buried in back were a few columns on Samson, who led a dwindling gang called the Wildcats. He rarely made the headlines any more.

Cats being cats, the deaths of hundreds of citizens had been swept under the hearthrug and ignored. Any mention of the riot in polite society was frowned upon as unwholesome. The paper had blamed the wholesale wreckage on a small band of renegade dogs; with an apology from the enemy and no war to fight, the armies had been recalled to deal with the rats, leading the vermin in a swift well-oiled manoeuvre into the river to drown. The taxpayers were pleased to see the military earning its keep and making itself useful for a change. There were rumours of using the army as an emergency rescue service in the future. In the meantime, the soldiers had been detailed to rebuild the city.

The wrestling section had doubled in size. The price of the *Post* had gone up to recoup the cost of reconstruction. Nobody complained, and his skeleton staff respected him for attracting readers through his reputation alone. Morris had had only one distinction – he'd been a complete blaggard. Now the more cats bought the paper, the more the reporters' bylines would be read. Swampie paid well; although his judgement could be erratic at times, he didn't change too much of their copy. He was too busy with his TV show, not to mention the new cookbook he was writing.

As a cub Swampie had dreamed of fame, sneaking into the Capital Ring to watch his heroes wrestle. Fighting Joe Jones, Sam 'Big Legs' Nader, Mr Grit – they'd lived a life of disgusting amenity. It was something Swampie had striven for and eventually gained. Now he had too much responsibility.

Roy Fury, who had replaced Julius as senior reporter, was causing trouble. Roy was one of the paper's better surviving writers but he wrote prejudiced articles, annoyed his colleagues with tasteless gags and ran off at the mouth. Swampie envied Julius, wherever he was – leading a quiet life with caring friends.

Water lapped at the riverbank like milk splashed into a saucer. Curled up in the silt, recuperating from a dunk in the junk, lay a ball of fluff. The fluff had wandered round the docks for weeks, stumbling in an amnesiac daze. It had always returned to the bank. It could keep watch there, look out for the dogs that had savagely attacked it.

The fluff shivered. The dunk had actually done it a lot of good, given its body the breathing space to detoxify its system; it had not had the strength to find a fresh supply of nip.

After a painful period of cold turkey, the fluff could even remember its own name.

Sal continued to hallucinate from time to time. Right now he could see a small creature with a bandolier, watching him with intent yellow eyes, nose and tail twitching, preening its whiskers.

'Lucky you didn't drown there, pussy cat,' said the diminutive creature, pulling its paws from the silt with each step. The sucking noise rang in Sal's ears. 'Currents can pull you right down, you can't swim back up again.'

Sal looked down his nose at the wee figure. He needed his nip. 'Some dog tried to eat me.'

'Oh yeah.'

'I swam away. I think it got my buddy. I miss him.'

'Now you know what it's like. You're another stop on the food train, that's all.'

Sal began to uncoil himself. He licked his lips, feeling hungry. 'You're clever. For a mouse.'

'A mouse. A futting mouse! Hey, fellas. He thinks we're mice!' The creature's pals came to laugh at Sal – twenty or thirty of them all, each wearing a bodkin, gauntlets or suits of armour, with beady eyes and sawtooth gapes. Their leader wiggled his bottom in Sal's face. 'Look at this tail, amigo. Does this look mousy to you?'

'We're much better looking,' piped up one of his cohorts.

'Don't cats chase rats?' asked Sal innocently, his stomach rumbling. The pack leader nibbled at his leg as if deep in thought.

'Nah. Not what I heard.' The pack joined in, thinking about it then shaking their heads.

'Whatever. Where are we?' He felt lost without Warren.

'South Bank. Near the Doghouse. Not through choice, eh?'

'No, not through choice.' Sal wiped water from his head with a matted paw. 'Don't all those teeth get in the way when you talk?'

'About as much as your brain gets in the way of you thinking,' one of the rats cackled.

'What happened here?' asked Sal, drying off in the winter sun. The rats explained that they were from a silo not far away. Some cat had shoved them in a pit a while ago. During the cat riot, they had climbed up some fallen timber, crossed the bridge, run amok... until they'd been chased into the river.

'We're busy, er, regrouping. As you can see.' All Sal could see was a group of the rats engaged in amorous activities. The leader assured him that they were following their natural instincts.

'Watcha gonna do?'

'Get in training. We got an army to fight. Hence the get-up.'

Sal wandered off to find Samson.

'Watch yerself,' the rat called after him, adjusting his bandolier.

'You too.'

Tarquin sat bolt upright, two thin slices of cucumber sliding from his eyes. His ten minute nap was over, and he would be in dark trouble if he got back late. Sidling from the broom cupboard where he took his breaks, he checked that no one had seen him and swiftly returned to his desk. He wiped cucumber juice from his fur, munching on his greens with a nervous chattering motion. Now that replacement guards had arrived to maintain security in the Chambers, everyone was obedient.

Tarquin knew what trouble was. He'd met enough of it after going behind the Mayor's mane. Otto had found him, reinstated him then demoted him. Now Tarquin had to face the animosity of his colleagues, the snide comments of his boss and the threatening presence of the leopard guards, sworn to keep a close eye on him. He was the cat who'd invited dogs into the city. He'd fooled the Mayor and betrayed Bast. He was the lowest form of feline, and so he'd been given the lowly position of junior accountant. No more privileges, long luncheons, expensive waistcoats or trips to the grooming parlour. Nothing distinguished him from thousands of other cats toiling in the bowels of the city's corporate sector. He hated it.

His eyes hurt. The pain travelled up to his temples and round to the back of his head. His sight was not as strong as it had been. Sometimes his ledgers seemed fuzzy, out of focus. Still he pored over the Mayor's accounts, meticulous with each sum, preparing them for Otto's approval. The lion checked everything.

Woodrow was the new aide apparent. He'd explained to Tarquin that the reinstatement had been a political decision. Otto had wanted to bite the traitor's head off, but he'd been kept alive to calm the Sinners. He'd always been the token Abyssinian, there for show, appeasing his troublesome breed. Now his rank suited his background. Tarquin hadn't argued with his sudden superior; he'd agreed and bowed his head as low as he could.

He still loved Bridget. When he closed his eyes he could see her, the lines and warts gone. He remembered the good things, the gossamer fur, the cushion talk. That lovely lioness had groomed him, cared for him when he had one of his migraines. He would win her back if he ever found her.

Sometimes the accounts didn't add up. He duly covered up the errors, changed twos to look like eights, rearranged columns to hide any overspending. One day, when the heat was off and the leopards let down their guards, the books would be posted to Swampie McMahon. All the minute discrepancies would be carefully indicated for the *Post* to pick out. Until then, Tarquin worked industriously, wondering what kind of spectacles would suit his face.

33

Soon after the case of the Kitty Killer Cult, Tiger retired to look after his kids. He took small divorce or surveillance cases to supplement his welfare cheque, but stakeouts are tough with a pack of squealing kids in tow.

He loved to watch them grow, let them fend for themselves - yet he was always there for them. He'd amuse them with bedtime stories of old cases, battles with villains like The Goat or the serial kitten drowner. Adventures with Bug, solving mysteries, getting into scrapes.

Rain battered at the windows, begging to come into the house and smother him with damp drops. The panes rattled now and then, craving attention. No Bug to share a meal, no wife to hold him close. His children were his sole joy. Soon they'd be old enough to help with chores, if they didn't bugger off first in a quest for independence.

The house was colder without Kerry. She'd kept him warm, held him close, her hot breath on his neck and lips. The bed was half full, the teapot half-empty. Nobody nagged him or wasted his time conjuring foolish chores to keep him busy. His spare time was flat and there was too much milk

in the fridge. It went off but Tiger still drank
it. His tastebuds were numb and his stomach an
unquenchable well.

Occasionally he'd hear a police whistle or a shop
alarm, grab his coat and hat. He didn't leave the
house. He was getting too old, and worried that
he'd get himself killed. He had aches and buzzing
in his ears, felt slower, clumsier. Who would be
around to welcome the cubs if he got his fool head
knocked off? It was wiser to stay in. Read about
crime in the papers. Give the authorities a few
tips over the 'phone. That was all he needed to
keep content for now.

As the rain withdrew its siege, Tiger drifted off
to sleep. He dreamt of past glories on an under-
world battlefield, his sidekick Bug looking up
to him, waiting for him to save the day.

JULIUS KYLE

Bast had changed irrevocably. Its inhabitants would try to
forget what they'd done, the evil they'd unleashed. The city
would remember, though, with ashen bowels, torn windows,
chipped rooftops and charred schoolyards. The filth could
be cleaned up, the ruins rebuilt. There were holes in the fabric
of the metropolis that would never be mended. Residents
would see the new constructs that replaced the wreckage,
reminders of the time that they smashed their world to frag-
ments. Children would smell the riot in their history books,
shaking their worried little heads, wondering why adults
never learned from their errors. Life went on, yet it would
never be the same again.

Julius had been living with Moira a few weeks before he

dared to tackle any ironing. Back in his previous life he'd paid a laundry to do his dirty work for him, returning it clean and pressed. Now he had no money, and managed to burn black creases in his shirts instead.

Moira blamed him for the deaths of Pa and King. He didn't think she'd ever forgive him. She tolerated him, and he was grateful for that. He worked hard and tried to stay out of danger, an impossibility in the Doghouse.

Now that his house was a lost ruin, Julius had no choice but to hole up with his considerate partner. She helped him settle into his new lifestyle as a Doghouse resident. Moira explained the rules to him, when and where it was safe to travel. She made him comfortable at home, and in return he helped to fix up the house. DIY had never been his forte but the house desperately needed a tart-up. Moira was far more proficient with a hammer than he was. She was too lazy.

Julius was a new cat, freelance yet determinedly monogamous. He had become more self-reliant, took what work he could get writing articles and stories for various rags. There was no more pressure from the daily grind, but plenty from living on next to nothing, fighting poverty rows with his neighbours. Everyday life was a tough mix of hunger, conflict, stress and mourning. After the dogs' shantytown, it didn't seem so bad. Julius had to content himself with his unsteady existence; thanks to his radio station antics, he was an exile from his old territory anyway. Felis non grata.

Julius didn't sniff *The Scratching Post* anymore. He was busy adjusting, trying to be optimistic, spending as much time as possible with his mate. Striving to understand her. He was determined not to end up like his friend Mick, and with her help... Moira was always there for him, but the spark of light that had brought them together had dimmed.

Stepping out for some fresh air, Julius wondered how he'd cope with his new life. He'd always been an outside kind of cat. As he left the house, he gave one of his neighbours a nod and a courteous blink, got no reply. He'd win them over eventually.

He walked along a wall, purring softly to himself. The sun had appeared from behind thick cloud, warming his back; he removed his jacket and slung it over his left shoulder.

A young white cub with a perfectly round nose blocked his path. Trouble already. The cub was going to pick a fight, prove itself. Julius wasn't in the mood for wetnursing. He flexed his claws carefully.

'When's the next one coming out, mister?' The cub wore a black scarf, identical to the one that lay folded neatly in Moira's bedroom. Before Julius could answer the youth dashed off, leaving him speechless.

Someone likes the book! A sleeper? Julius thought little of the encounter for the rest of the evening, but next morning he was up at dawn, compiling notes on a new book: *Tiger Straight in the Domain of the Dogs*. He was sure it would be a best seller.

Some other books published by **LUATH** PRESS

COMING SOON

The Kitty Killer Cult

Nick Smith

ISBN 1 84282 039 7 UK £9.99 US $16.95 PBK

Clapped-out cat detective Tiger Straight investigates a series of nasty murders on his home turf of Nub City. He falls in love with Kerry, a fatal femme who works as a make-up artist on a TV show. Rival investigator Cole Tiddle and Inspector Bix Mortis follow up reports of a Kitty Killer Cult.

Tiger's partner, Bug, suspects that the Auld Enemy are at work – but dogs aren't to blame for the murders. Creatures far more insidious, far more unlikely are responsible. They won't stop until every last cat in the city is dead. Only Tiger can save his friends, but what will he have to sacrifice along the way?

'The animosity that raddles our species,' began the Professor, brandishing Julius' book to illustrate his points, 'breed against breed, cousin against cousin is an expression of one's hatred of the self. What this book so adequately expresses (in simple terms, of course) is that the Other, the enemy of which every animal is wary, exists within ourselves as well as beyond our molly-coddling environs. We must fix ourselves if we are to fix the world and make it safe for our progeny. The Kitty Killer Cult *supports my own belief that we should one day be able to live in harmony with other species, offering them succour even as we learn from their alternate approaches to life. The way they cope with the pith of progress.'*

'Nothing less than a disgrace,' was Bridget's opinion of the book. 'The sort of narrow minded, anti-establishment liberal claptrap that leads to decadence and corruption. Now, I don't hold with the kind of sensationalist violence this author's previous books revel in, but at least they had simple, solid villains to teach youngsters patriotism. We all need someone to hate. It brings the group together.'

From *Milk Treading* p147-8.

Read *The Kitty Killer Cult* and decide for yourself whether Julius Kyle's comeback novel cuts the mustard.

FICTION

The Road Dance
John MacKay
ISBN 1 84282 024 9 PB £9.99

The Strange Case of RL Stevenson
Richard Woodhead
ISBN 0 946487 86 3 HB £16.99

But n Ben A-Go-Go
Matthew Fitt
ISBN 1 84282 014 1 PB £6.99
ISBN 0 946487 82 0 HB £10.99

The Bannockburn Years
William Scott
ISBN 0 946487 34 0 PB £7.95

The Great Melnikov
Hugh MacLachlan
ISBN 0 946487 42 1 PB £7.95

The Fundamentals of New Caledonia
David Nicol
ISBN 0 946487 93 6 HB £16.99

POETRY

Sex, Death and Football
Alistair Findlay
ISBN 1 48282 022 2 PB £6.99

Bad Ass Raindrop
Kokumo Rocks
ISBN 1 84282 018 4 PB £6.99

Caledonian Cramboclink: verse, broadsheets and in conversation
William Neill
ISBN 0 946487 53 7 PB £8.99

Men and Beasts: wild men & tame animals
Val Gillies & Rebecca Marr
ISBN 0 946487 92 8 PB £15.00

The Luath Burns Companion
John Cairney
ISBN 1 84282 000 1 PB £10.00

Scots Poems to be read aloud
introduced Stuart McHardy
ISBN 0 946487 81 2 PB £5.00

Poems to be read aloud
introduced by Tom Atkinson
ISBN 0 946487 00 6 PB £5.00

Picking Brambles and Other Poems
Des Dillon
ISBN 1 84282 021 4 PB £6.99

Kate o Shanter's Tale and Other Poems
Matthew Fitt
ISBN 1 84282 028 1 PB £6.99

THE QUEST FOR

The Quest for the Celtic Key
Karen Ralls-MacLeod and
Ian Robertson
ISBN 0 946487 73 1 HB £18.99

The Quest for Arthur
Stuart McHardy
ISBN 1 842820 12 5 HB £16.99

The Quest for the Nine Maidens
Stuart McHardy
ISBN 0 946487 66 9 HB £16.99

ON THE TRAIL OF

On the Trail of William Wallace
David R Ross
ISBN 0 946487 47 2 PB £7.99

On the Trail of Robert the Bruce
David R Ross
ISBN 0 946487 52 9 PB £7.99

On the Trail of Mary Queen of Scots
J Keith Cheetham
ISBN 0 946487 50 2 PB £7.99

On the Trail of Bonnie Prince Charlie
David R Ross
ISBN 0 946487 68 5 PB £7.99

On the Trail of Robert Burns
John Cairney
ISBN 0 946487 51 0 PB £7.99

On the Trail of John Muir
Cherry Good
ISBN 0 946487 62 6 PB £7.99

On the Trail of Queen Victoria in the Highlands
Ian R Mitchell
ISBN 0 946487 79 0 PB £7.99

On the Trail of Robert Service
G Wallace Lockhart
ISBN 0 946487 24 3 PB £7.99

On the Trail of the Pilgrim Fathers
J Keith Cheetham
ISBN 0 946487 83 9 PB £7.99

On the Trail of John Wesley
J Keith Cheetham
ISBN 1 84282 023 0 PB £7.99

GENEALOGY

Scottish Roots: step-by-step guide for ancestor hunters
Alwyn James
ISBN 1 84282 007 9 PB £9.99

WEDDINGS, MUSIC AND DANCE

The Scottish Wedding Book
G Wallace Lockhart
ISBN 1 94282 010 9 PB £12.99

Fiddles and Folk
G Wallace Lockhart
ISBN 0 946487 38 3 PB £7.95

Highland Balls and Village Halls
G Wallace Lockhart
ISBN 0 946487 12 X PB £6.95

FOLKLORE

Scotland: Myth, Legend & Folklore
Stuart McHardy
ISBN 0 946487 69 3 PB £7.99

Luath Storyteller: Highland Myths & Legends
George W Macpherson
ISBN 1 84282 003 6 PB £5.00

Tales of the North Coast
Alan Temperley
ISBN 0 946487 18 9 PB £8.99

Tall Tales from an Island
Peter Macnab
ISBN 0 946487 07 3 PB £8.99

The Supernatural Highlands
Francis Thompson
ISBN 0 946487 31 6 PB £8.99

NATURAL WORLD

The Hydro Boys: pioneers of renewable energy
Emma Wood
ISBN 1 84282 016 8 HB £16.99

Wild Scotland
James McCarthy
ISBN 0 946487 37 5 PB £7.50

Wild Lives: Otters – On the Swirl of the Tide
Bridget MacCaskill
ISBN 0 946487 67 7 PB £9.99

Wild Lives: Foxes – The Blood is Wild
Bridget MacCaskill
ISBN 0 946487 71 5 PB £9.99

Scotland – Land & People: An Inhabited Solitude
James McCarthy
ISBN 0 946487 57 X PB £7.99

The Highland Geology Trail
John L Roberts
ISBN 0 946487 36 7 PB £4.99

'Nothing but Heather!'
Gerry Cambridge
ISBN 0 946487 49 9 PB £15.00

Red Sky at Night
John Barrington
ISBN 0 946487 60 X PB £8.99

Listen to the Trees
Don MacCaskill
ISBN 0 946487 65 0 PB £9.99

POLITICS & CURRENT ISSUES

Scotlands of the Mind
Angus Calder
ISBN 1 84282 008 7 PB £9.99

Trident on Trial: the case for people's disarmament
Angie Zelter
ISBN 1 84282 004 4 PB £9.99

Uncomfortably Numb: A Prison Requiem
Maureen Maguire
ISBN 1 84282 001 X PB £8.99

Scotland: Land & Power – Agenda for Land Reform
Andy Wightman
ISBN 0 946487 70 7 PB £5.00

Old Scotland New Scotland
Jeff Fallow
ISBN 0 946487 40 5 PB £6.99

Some Assembly Required: Scottish Parliament
David Shepherd
ISBN 0 946487 84 7 PB £7.99

Notes from the North
Emma Wood
ISBN 0 946487 46 4 PB £8.99

Luath Press Limited

committed to publishing well written books worth reading

LUATH PRESS takes its name from Robert Burns, whose little collie Luath (*Gael.*, swift or nimble) tripped up Jean Armour at a wedding and gave him the chance to speak to the woman who was to be his wife and the abiding love of his life. Burns called one of *The Twa Dogs* Luath after Cuchullin's hunting dog in *Ossian's Fingal*. Luath Press was established in 1981 in the heart of Burns country, and is now based a few steps up the road from Burns' first lodgings on Edinburgh's Royal Mile.

Luath offers you distinctive writing with a hint of unexpected pleasures.

Most bookshops either carry our books in stock or can order them for you. To order direct from us, please send a £sterling cheque, postal order, international money order or your credit card details (number, address of cardholder and expiry date) to us at the address below. Please add post and packing as follows: UK – £1.00 per delivery address; overseas surface mail – £2.50 per delivery address; overseas airmail – £3.50 for the first book to each delivery address, plus £1.00 for each additional book by airmail to the same address. If your order is a gift, we will happily enclose your card or message at no extra charge.

Luath Press Limited
543/2 Castlehill
The Royal Mile
Edinburgh EH1 2ND
Scotland
Telephone: 0131 225 4326 (24 hours)
Fax: 0131 225 4324
email: gavin.macdougall@luath.co.uk
Website: www.luath.co.uk